Battle's Flood

J. D. Davies is the prolific author of historical naval adventures. He is also one of the foremost authorities on the seventeenth-century navy, which brings a high level of historical detail to his fiction, namely his Matthew Quinton series. He has written widely on the subject, most recently *Kings of the Sea: Charles II, James II and the Royal Navy*, and won the Samuel Pepys Award in 2009 with *Pepys's Navy: Ships, Men and Warfare, 1649-1689*.

Also by J. D. Davies

The Matthew Quinton Journals

Gentleman Captain
The Mountain of Gold
The Blast that Tears the Skies
The Lion of Midnight
The Battle of All The Ages
The Rage of Fortune
Death's Bright Angel
The Devil Upon the Wave
Ensign Royal

Jack Stannard of the Navy Royal

Destiny's Tide
Battle's Flood
Armada's Wake

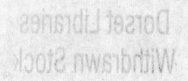

J. D. DAVIES

Battle's Flood

CANELO

First published in the United Kingdom in 2019 by Canelo

This edition published in the United Kingdom in 2021 by

Canelo
Unit 9, 5th Floor
Cargo Works, 1–2 Hatfields
London, SE1 9PG
United Kingdom

Print ISBN 978 1 78863 938 5
Ebook ISBN 978 1 78863 231 7

Look for more great books at www.canelo.co

Printed and bound in Great Britain by Clays Ltd, Elcograf S.p.A.

In memory of Martin Bentley, 1950–2012

Requiescat in pace, *old friend*

If all the miseries and troublesome affairs of this sorrowful voyage should be perfectly and thoroughly written, there should need [to be] a painful [i.e. painstaking] man with his pen, and as great a time as he had that wrote the lives and deaths of the Martyrs. Finis.

Sir John Hawkins (1532–95)

The Spaniards were very close now, but Drake and Hawkins had abandoned them to their fate.

Jack watched the Minion manoeuvre away from the carnage in the anchorage, praying that his Tom was somewhere aboard one of them despite all; praying that, against all the odds, his son was safe.

The few dozen desperate Englishmen left on the deck of the shattered flagship were screaming vainly at the receding ships. A few looked to Jack for leadership, but he had none to give. None of them would see England again, he reckoned. For his part, he would never see another Dunwich dawn, nor the smile on the face of his daughter Meg, nor the grave of—

The first Spanish soldiers emerged onto the upper deck, their morion helmets and sword blades glistening in the brilliant sun.

Jack Stannard muttered the Lord's Prayer and prepared himself for death.

But in his heart, he knew that death was not the worst fate the Spaniards could inflict.

Prologue

The heretic would burn at noon, so Margaret Stannard had time to kill. Her brother had gone off to one of the Westminster alehouses with some of his roaring-boy friends. Her father was in a house on the St James's side of the Sanctuary, where the meeting that had brought him so far from Dunwich was taking place. That left her free to roam where she willed with the short, serious, swarthy youth at her side, whose father was at the same meeting. And where she willed translated into the great abbey, towering over the tallest houses and even over the ramshackle old palace across the way, the seat of England's parliament on those rare occasions when it sat.

There was a steady stream of people in and out of the church's west door: supplicants come to light candles or have Masses said for lost loved ones, cripples come to pray for a cure, and whores come to baptise or bury bastards. And there were more than a few others who had come to witness the execution, but who would spend the time before it began gawping at the countless grand tombs. Regardless of purpose, all who entered the building stopped, genuflected toward the east end, crossed themselves several times, then looked up in awe at the soaring arches and vaults. Many, like Margaret and her escort, smiled at the familiar smell of incense, and at the sound of a chorus of clerks in one of the side chapels singing a new setting of *Exsurge Christe* in Latin, the true tongue of God.

Things were as they should be.

'*Deo gratias*,' said Margaret Stannard of Dunwich, by-named Meg by all who knew her.

'Amen,' said Luis de Andrade.

They attracted many glances as they made their way down the north aisle towards the crossing, for they were an unlikely couple. She towered over the quite evidently foreign youth walking alongside her. Meg's height made her appear older than her nineteen years, while the as-yet beardless Luis, actually a year older than she, seemed little more than eleven or twelve. Meg also dressed better than one of her rank usually did, being attired that day in an expensive yellow kirtle. She walked with the stately grace of a true lady. For a Spaniard, though, Luis dressed carelessly, his shirt creased and his breeches grubby, and he scuttled along half a pace behind Meg. It was probable that at least some of those who cast eyes on them that day in Westminster Abbey assumed they were some well-born lady and her young servant boy.

They made their way to the astonishing Lady Chapel at the far end of the abbey, joined the throng of people at the spectacular tomb of King Harry the Seventh and his queen, and then sank to their knees, crossing themselves contentedly as they did so. Meg took out her rosary, prohibited until recently, and began to utter the *Ave Maria*.

First, she offered up thanks for the restoration of the true faith in this great abbey church, as in all the churches in England, after twenty years of turmoil and heresy. Soon,

3

it was said, monks would return to praise God in this place; in which case, perhaps, they might return to Dunwich too.

Second, she gave thanks for those indubitable proofs of God's providence, the accession to the throne of the high and mighty Lady Mary, by whose grace the errant kingdom of England had been reconciled to the Church of Rome, and her marriage to the noblest prince in Christendom, Philip of Spain, now King of England.

Third, and invoking the specific intercession of Felix, patron saint of Dunwich, she prayed for her father, that God would preserve him upon his voyages and in his many ventures by sea; for her brother, that he might grow a backbone; for the souls of her dead mother and more recently dead grandfather, the last leper of their town; and for Dunwich itself, that what remained of it might be preserved from the further ravages of the unforgiving waves that clawed unremittingly at the base of its cliff.

Fourth, she prayed that the child said by all to be nearly at term in the queen's womb might be born healthy, and a son, an heir to both England and all the realms that King Philip already possessed, and the even greater ones he was soon set to inherit. This was the predominant prayer being uttered by most of those kneeling in prayer in the chapel that day.

Fifth, she prayed that the heretic who was about to die would recant upon the pyre, thereby saving his immortal soul.

Sixth, she prayed that her stepmother might die a painful and prolonged death, preferably very soon, preferably in circumstances that involved flies, rats and large quantities of pus, together with bloody and incessant quickshits. Meg knew this was a distinctly unchristian thought, and a most unworthy one to have in her mind in that most sacred of places, but she could not help herself.

Seventh, she prayed that Luis de Andrade would be a little less stiff, a little less formal, a little less *Spanish*.

She looked up at the face of a carved angel, very far above her, crossed herself, and smiled at it. It was probably a trick of the light, but she could almost have sworn that the angel winked back at her.

Well then, Margaret Stannard, she chided herself, that was hardly something with which to bother God, the Blessed Virgin and the company of the saints. Unlike all her other prayers, this was a matter that she was perfectly capable of resolving herself, here upon earth.

So be it. Master Luis de Andrade was too stiff and formal?

She would soon change that.

—

John Stannard of Dunwich, known to one and all as Jack, loved being aboard ships, and conning them where wind and tide favoured. He loved the feel of a deck beneath his feet, and the sight and sound of sails billowing in a fair breeze. He loved foreign harbours: their smells, their people, their women, and above all their cargoes. But he did not love hearing others talk about ships, harbours and cargoes, especially when they talked endlessly, and when, with only a few exceptions, the talkers were men whose experience of the sea extended no further than being sculled a mile or two up the Thames and then a mile or two back down again in watermen's skiffs.

He was not even sure why he had been asked to this meeting. Almost all of those present were far greater than he and certainly far richer, which meant very much the same thing. He was a mere merchant and shipowner of Dunwich, and if the others in the room had heard of it at all, they would know the place only as an ancient, decayed seaport on the Suffolk coast, now little larger than many a village. Indeed, some in the room would not even know where Suffolk was. These were the Spaniards, a dozen or so of them, now all whispering animatedly in an alcove by the fireplace. With their pointed beards and dark clothing, they resembled an unkindness of ravens. Jack Stannard knew only one of them, the only one who could speak English, Cesar de Andrade by name. He and his brother had come over to England in the old Queen Catherine's time and set themselves up as merchants in Ipswich, where Jack and his father had come to know them well, even to like them. King Harry's rejection of his queen, and the twenty years of madness that followed, drove them from England, but now Cesar was back with his sons. One of them, Pedro, was with him at the meeting: a proud young fellow who was seemingly oblivious of the stares directed at the huge birthmark, very much like a great butterfly, that disfigured almost the entire right side of his face. Another son, presently elsewhere, was of interest to Jack, and, gratifyingly, of even more interest to his forthright daughter Meg.

'S-standing alone, Jack Stannard?' said Will Halliday, returning from the jakes.

'What is this for, Will? Why are we all here?'

Jack's oldest friend smiled. 'P-p-peace and harmony between England and Spain, Jack. Eternal felicity, thanks to the union of our noble q-queen and the mighty King Philip.'

'Hmm. Well, as I see it, there seems to have been precious little felicity in the arguments so far. They want us to sail for Muscovy, and Swedeland. The Levant, if we wish. But not Africa, and certainly not the Americas. Whereas he – who is that old whitebeard with Garrard? The one who spoke with such force earlier, despite his infirmities? One foot in the grave, if ever I saw its like.'

'William Hawkins, of P-Plymouth. A fine s-seaman in his time, so it's said, and a good man. A Member of Parliament, too. He was much in Master Gonson's favour, as he was in the late king's.' Jack nodded. Benjamin Gonson, Will's effective employer, had influence, and was also a good judge of men. A better judge than Henry the Eighth of famous memory, for sure. 'I p-presume the youth with him is his son,' said Will. 'One of his sons, at any rate. They say the k-king has taken quite a shine to that young man.'

The younger Hawkins was dressed soberly but richly, in black, and could easily have been taken for one of the Spaniards. Even from a distance, Jack could make out vivid eyes and an easy manner that made him appear comfortable in the presence of the great men around him.

'Hawkins, then,' said Jack. 'Hawkins the father. He spoke well, I thought. If England and Spain are now one, and to be even more so when the child now in the queen's womb ascends the thrones of both, then why should Englishmen not sail freely to all the King of Spain's lands? Why should we not trade where we please?'

'That, I s-suspect, is what our Spanish friends are m-murmuring about. After all, they hold all the c-cards, my friend. They have the Americas with all their g-gold and silver, they have the armies and navies – ours isn't an equal m-marriage, that's for sure.'

7

Jack nodded, for he had once seen one of Spain's mighty bullion fleets inbound from the Indies off the mouth of the river that led to Seville. England's entire treasury was as a cockboat in the wake of the cargo of just one of those vast galleons. England and Spain were friends for now, but that might not always be the case. Jack had seen at close quarters the vast invasion fleet that France had sent against England ten years before, in the campaign in which the great royal ship *Mary Rose* sank and his friend Thomas Ryman died, but Spain could easily afford a fleet to dwarf it. These discomforting truths were in the back of the mind of every man in the room, from both nations.

Perhaps, though, not in Will Halliday's mind. Instead, Jack's old friend was staring intently at the Spaniards.

'One of them troubles me, Jack. I c-could swear I've seen him b-before, although I know I c-cannot have done.'

'Which one?'

'The one to the left of de Andrade. The one with the double-pointed b-beard.'

'That one? The one who was introduced to us as – what was the name – Pimentel? I took him for an insignificant fellow. He has said nothing.'

'Neither have you, Jack Stannard.'

'Aye, and that's the truth,' sighed Jack. 'I see why you're here, Will. Principal Clerk to the Treasurer of the Council of Marine Causes – you represent Master Benjamin Gonson and the entire Navy Royal of England, my friend, no matter how much you may seek to deny it. Hawkins of Plymouth, there, his son and his like – yes, of course, it's obvious why they're here. Garrard, the Lord Mayor, likewise. My kinsman Barne, too. Merchants. Aldermen. Men of money. So why me?'

Will Halliday placed a hand on his old friend's shoulder. They had been at ease in each other's company since their days in the choir of the short-lived Cardinal College at Ipswich, intended as the sometime Cardinal Wolsey's greatest bequest to his birthplace. From time to time, when Jack was in London and they happened to find themselves in the same alehouse, they would relive those happy childhood days of song, Jack in his mellifluous tenor voice and Will in the confident, lyrical bass that always seemed so at odds with his stammer.

'You answer your own questions, Jack. Your wife is kin to Sir George Barne, sometime Lord Mayor. He in his turn is a p-powerful voice at the shoulder of Garrard, the present incumbent. You're a friend to me, and to Señor de Andrade yonder. You're a Suffolk man, so you represent an interest d-different to Devon and London. You've sailed the northern seas, and the B-Baltic, which no other man here has done. So you fit the b-bill, my friend. The king wants to get a sense of England, of what Englishmen know, of what they aspire to.'

'To see if we aspire to voyaging to his distant lands, you mean? To trading with his colonies? To obtain just a tiny fraction of his great riches? To see if we're likely to make war on him, instead of the French, despite him now being our king?'

'Something very like, I suspect.'

Sir William Garrard, Lord Mayor of London, clapped his hands, a signal for the meeting to reconvene.

'B-but that Spaniard's face still troubles me,' said Will as he took his seat at the long oak table in the middle of the room.

At Garrard's invitation, an obese Londoner whom Jack did not know launched into a tedious discourse on the difficulties caused to the Flanders trades by the ongoing war between the French king and King Philip's father, the Emperor Charles. After a time, Jack felt his eyes glazing over, and he commenced a pleasant daydream of being under easy sail upon an endless ocean…

He was suddenly aware of Will Halliday nudging him and whispering something urgently in his ear. He sat bolt upright, and turned to ask his friend what the matter was.

'I know where I've s-seen his face b-before,' murmured Will. 'On a p-portrait, in the p-palace of G-Greenwich—'

'Well, Master Halliday, Master Stannard?' snapped Sir William Garrard, irritably. 'What is so astonishing as to interrupt the rest of us?'

'B-b-b-beg p-p-pardon, my Lord Mayor,' said Will. 'But I have certain knowledge that Señor P-Pimentel here is not what he seems.'

The Spanish contingent looked at each other, but said nothing. Even though the comment had been translated to him, Pimentel's face was a mask.

'Really, Master Halliday? Pray do enlighten us. If he is not Señor Pimentel, then who is he?'

'Sirs,' said Will, 'he is—'

De Andrade, who was sitting next to the mysterious Pimentel, raised his right hand. 'A harmless ruse, my friends,' he said, smiling broadly. His English was excellent, albeit with incongruous traces of Suffolk inflections. 'Some simple play-acting. It was feared that our discussion might be – what is your word? Yes, constrained, had you known Señor Pimentel's true identity.' Swiftly and quietly, de Andrade spoke in Spanish to Pimentel, who merely nodded. De Andrade looked back at the Englishmen, and raised his voice. 'My English friends, I now name to you Fernando Álvarez de Toledo y Pimentel, the Most High and Most Excellent Duke of Alba.'

Sir George Barne coughed, while Garrard's eyes widened. Jack knew that he himself was blinking furiously, but could do nothing about it. There was a moment or two of silence, then every Englishman in the room rose to his feet and bowed to Spain's – no, all Europe's – most famous soldier, the head of the royal household of Philip, King of England.

The Duke of Alba, too, rose from his place. For several moments, he stood stock still, his eyes falling upon each of the Englishmen in turn, as though he was making a powerful effort to burn every face upon his mind's eye; or, perhaps, to ensure that his features were burned on each of theirs. Jack Stannard recalled Will's words: *The king wants to get a sense of England, of what Englishmen know, of what they aspire to.* The king could not possibly come to such a meeting as this: even if it was not far beneath his dignity, his face was known from every coin, where it was imprinted alongside that of his wife. But he could do the next best thing. He could send his most trusted aide, the victor of Tunis, Perpignan and Mühlberg, the most successful and most feared warrior in the world.

Finally, apparently content that his purpose was complete, the Duke of Alba bowed solemnly in acknowledgement, then nodded, turned on his heel and left the room, de Andrade and the rest of the Spaniards trailing after him.

'Well done, Will,' Jack Stannard murmured to his old friend. 'The cat isn't only among the pigeons; it's well and truly devoured the lot of them.'

–

Meg Stannard and Luis de Andrade left Westminster Abbey by the west door, and made their way round to the right, into St Margaret's churchyard. They had been delayed by the crush to leave the abbey, so the heretic was already at the foot of the pyre. He was a thin man of middle years, his beard long, grey and unkempt. Even from a distance, Meg suspected the presence of a legion of nits.

'Who is he?' asked Luis, in his good English.

'By name, one William Flower,' said Meg. 'Sometime a monk of Ely, they say, but turned heretic, like the foul reprobate Luther. He tried to stab to death the priest here at St Margaret's as he celebrated Easter Mass.'

Luis shook his head. 'Then he amply deserves what is his due.'

Bonner, the Bishop of London, was present, looking splendid in full canonicals, but this was a secular matter under the old parliamentary statute *De heretico comburendo*, so it was a magistrate who signalled to the executioner to begin the business. That dreadful fellow took up a small axe, too small for a beheading, but ideal for the first part of the proceedings. William Flower was pushed to his knees by guards, with his right arm then strapped to a bench. The excited noise from the crowd rose to a new pitch, and Meg and Luis did not hear what the executioner said. Luis was also struggling to see through the throng, but with her greater height, Meg had no difficulty in doing so. Thus she saw the axe fall, severing the hand that had wielded the knife against the priest of St Margaret's. A great gasp went up from the crowd, intermingled with many cheers. To his credit, though, William Flower did not cry out, did not even seem to flinch.

The stump of the heretic's arm was bound so he would not deny God and the law by bleeding to death. Then he was pushed up onto the pyre and chained securely to the stake. Bishop Bonner led the congregation in prayers, but again, only those at the front of the great crowd heard anything. That done, the lighted torches were put to the base of the pyre, and there were cheers as the flames caught.

As smoke billowed about him, and the flames rose towards his feet, Flower seemed to call out at last. Word was passed back from the front of the crowd.

'He be saying, "Oh the son of God, have mercy on me! Oh the son of God, receive my soul!"'

'The insolence of these heretics,' said Luis firmly. '*Madre de dios*, to imagine that Our Lord would listen to the likes of him!'

The flames reached higher, and Flower lifted his bloodied stump with his good arm, as though trying to keep it out of the inferno for as long as possible. The flames were consuming his lower body, although he still made no sound. But a discontented murmuring was beginning at the front of the crowd. Luis craned his neck to see what the matter was, then nodded knowingly.

'I saw this happen once at an auto-da-fé in Sevilla,' he said. 'The fools have used too little wood. The fire will be insufficient to consume him.'

So it seemed. Bonner and the magistrate conferred urgently, and gave a signal to the executioner. He, in turn, stepped forward with two of his guards, and using staves and sticks, they attempted to push Flower further down, into the flames.

'The poor man,' murmured Meg. 'Whatever his sin, none deserves this.'

Luis was indifferent. 'Only the fire will purge him, Margarita,' he said. 'Only the fire will cleanse his soul, and give him a chance of standing before the gates of Heaven.'

'Meg,' she whispered. 'Call me Meg.'

As William Flower continued to burn, his charred mouth still opening and closing with words that none could hear, Meg Stannard vowed that she would bed Luis de Andrade that very day.

One

Twelve years later

A thick summer fog cloaked the bay of Aiguillon. The *Jennet* of Dunwich had slipped into the bay at dawn, and now, as evening set in, she was moored at an all but abandoned wharf in the vicinity of the island village of Charron. A tall young man paced the deck of the ship, turning occasionally to glance at the older man who stood in the stern. Some of the crew of forty sat on cables or barrels, eager to begin the work of unloading and eager to be away from this strange, remote shore.

'Maybe he's been arrested,' said the tall man, Tom Stannard, to the older figure behind him. 'Maybe they're coming to arrest us, too.'

Jack, his father, was still squinting through the dense fog, trying to make out any sign of movement ashore.

'He'll be here. There's not a royal officer for miles, other than safe behind the castle walls in Rochelle.'

Of the two men, Tom Stannard was significantly taller, but he seemed somehow less of a presence. Quiet and serious, with a pointed beard and short, straight hair cut in the old-fashioned way, he appeared older than his years. His father, though, might have a face battered and lined by countless voyages spent on deck, but his hair was as wild as it supposedly had been in his youth, and he remained stubbornly clean-shaven. Those who met the Stannards for the first time often assumed that they were brothers, and indeed, that was what age alone might have made them; in that strange, tense summer of 1567, Tom was not far off his thirtieth year, but his father was still shy of his fiftieth, having married very young. Married for the first time, at any rate.

There was a noise ashore, a noise distinct from the cries of the marsh birds and the barking of dogs. Jack Stannard's hand went to his sword hilt, while his son drew a pistol from his belt. The men on the deck stood, and looked nervously at each other.

Now there were shapes just visible through the fog. Grey, indistinct figures, like wraiths. A score of shapes, perhaps two dozen. They must have made out the equally ghostly shape of the *Jennet*, for they stopped abruptly and stood stock still.

The Stannards, father and son, exchanged another glance.

Friend or foe?

A lantern flashed three times. Jack Stannard gave a nod, and Hal Ashby, the boatswain and the most experienced and reliable hand on the ship, took up a lantern from the deck. He opened and closed its shutter five times. The lantern ashore flashed twice in reply.

Friend, then.

Jack stepped onto the gangplank and went ashore. A familiar figure came forward: a square, balding man of middling height, who sported an outrageously long and full white mustachio.

'*Bonjour, Jacques*,' said the familiar Frenchman.

'Bon jewer, Anthony,' Jack Stannard replied.

Antoine Mielle grimaced, but took the Englishman's hand nonetheless, thanking God as he did so that he had learned enough of the man's ugly offshore tongue during years of trading with Southampton and Exeter.

He nodded towards the *Jennet*. 'A good passage, *mon ami*?'

'As good as it could be – a fair wind, gentle seas, and no sea-robbers. Would that it were always so.'

'And the cargo is in order?'

'To the letter of the inventory. The secret inventory, at any rate.'

'*Bon*,' said Mielle. 'We'll begin unloading immediately.'

If the *Jennet* had been carrying her usual cargo of Suffolk woollen cloth, there would have been no urgency, and certainly no cause to unload her at such an obscure wharf. If she was carrying cloth, she would have gone straight up to one of the quays of La Rochelle itself, in the old harbour behind the Nicholas Tower. Instead, she lay amid the marshes a few miles to the north of the town, a much better place to unload a cargo that would never appear in any port book.

Mielle's men strode purposefully up the gangplank and mingled warily with the crew of the *Jennet*. Tom Stannard barked orders, and Englishmen and Frenchmen alike went to work.

'So how fares France, my friend?' asked Jack, as he and Mielle watched the hatches being broken open.

'Ah well, if I was to tell truth, then ripe for another war, I'd say. There have been riots – you know, the usual. This is France, after all. But there's also talk – serious talk – that the Queen Mother and Cardinal de Guise have persuaded the young king to join the Holy League. For certain, *mon ami*, Condé has left the court. He'll be plotting something, no doubt of it. Likes nothing better than a good plot, does the noble prince. And when whatever it is that he's plotting happens, the Queen Mother will want revenge, *bien sûr* – like all Medicis, the very first word she uttered as a babe in arms was *vendetta*. Or so they say. So sensible men must take precautions, Jacques Stannard.'

'Sensible Huguenot men?'

'All sensible men. What is Catholic or Huguenot when the times are *merde*? And then there's Alba's army, of course.'

Jack Stannard remembered the room in Westminster, all those years before, and the penetrating eyes of the mighty Duke of Alba. What an eternity it seemed since that time when everyone believed, wrongly as it transpired, that the queen was about to give child, when the old faith had flickered briefly again in England before being extinguished once more, and when Philip of Spain was King of England. Now the same Philip's vast army, paid for by the endless flow of bullion from the Indies and commanded by the same Duke of Alba whose gaze had once met Jack's, was advancing slowly along the great military road that stretched from Milan, through the Alpine passes, then along the Rhine to the North Sea, its final destination unknown.

'You have news of it? When we sailed from Plymouth, the word was that it was through the Mount Cenis pass.'

Mielle spat into the water. 'For certain, *mon ami*. But where will it go next, eh? Some say the Palatinate, some say against the Dutch. Here, we fear an order to wheel left. If Alba brings his mighty army to join with the Queen Mother, then every Huguenot man in France could feel the flames licking his balls before the winter comes.'

'In England, most men say he's marching to Brussels, to put down the riots and come to a reckoning with the Protestant lords.'

'Which he might well do, Jacques. But as I say, a sensible man takes precautions.'

With that, the first of the precautions emerged from the hold. Although they were carefully wrapped in sackcloth, there was no mistaking the shapes of the handles and long barrels of arquebuses. Dozens of heavy snaphance arquebuses, then scores of them. Mielle's men carried the bundles down the gangplank before loading them onto carts that had been driven up the causeway snaking through the marsh. Mielle himself went off to supervise the unloading, leaving Jack to oversee the work on the ship. In truth, though, Tom was more than capable of handling that, so Jack stood instead in the bows, and thought upon the irony of his situation.

Like Mielle, he, too, was a sensible man. So he went to his parish church of St Peter every Sunday he was in Dunwich, said his prayers in English, listened to the sermon in English, and took the sacrament, which looked remarkably like the sacrament that everyone had taken in the days of the old Church, but which, the Reverend James declaimed from his pulpit, most certainly did not literally become the body and blood of Christ, even if it tasted exactly the same as it had always done. Thus Jack Stannard did outwardly what the queen and her ministers wished him to do and avoided having to pay recusancy fines, but inwardly he still recited the *Ave Maria*, privately crossed himself and fingered his paternoster, and still prayed for the release of his beloved Alice's soul from Purgatory, no matter how often or how loudly Archbishop Parker and all his bishops proclaimed that there was no such place. So, yes, in his heart, Jack Stannard should have been on the side of the Duke of Alba and the Queen Mother of France, seeking to eradicate what they termed the Protestant heresy throughout Europe. Yet here he was, shipping guns to the Huguenots, the French Protestants, so that if and when the time came, they could better slaughter their Catholic neighbours.

He glanced across to Tom, who needed to perform no such mental somersaults. He had grown up chiefly in the reign of the boy king Edward the Sixth, when the Protestants had held sway, and had come to prefer the austere services, the whitewashed churches and the absence of ceremony. Tom was content to comply with whatever Queen Elizabeth, her parliament and her bishops ordered. His older sister, on the other hand—

'Jacques!' cried Antoine Mielle from the foot of the gangplank. 'We need to—'

In the same moment that he heard the nearby arquebus's report, Jack saw the Frenchman's chest seem to burst outward towards him and spout a fountain of blood. Mielle staggered forward, his face a picture of astonishment, realisation and horror. Then he fell face first into the water that lapped the hull of the *Jennet*.

'Loose the cables!' Jack commanded. 'Tom! Take the helm!'

There were sounds of battle ashore as Mielle's men fought for their lives against their invisible assailants. That was not Jack's concern, except in the sense that perhaps, just perhaps, the Huguenots might buy him enough time.

Two men joined him to free the cable securing the *Jennet* to the wharf. Slowly, so very slowly, the bow began to swing out into the stream. *Deo gratias*, a strong ebb was running, and the fog would swiftly conceal them from the attackers. Ashore, shots were being fired, and there were the unmistakable sounds of blades striking blades. There were screams as well – two, three, then more.

Jack ran to the stern, where his son held grimly to the whipstaff.

'Topsails, Father?'

'No, Tom. Sweeps, lad, the sweeps!'

'Aye, aye, Father!'

Hands ran to the hold, and within a minute or so, eight long oars were being pushed outward through small ports cut into the *Jennet*'s hull.

'On two!' cried Jack, once he knew the men were in position and ready. 'One! *Two!*'

On the command, the men below swung their blades forward, a little above the water.

'On two again! One! *Two!*'

On this next command, the men on the sweeps pushed them down into the water and then pulled back.

The exercise always amused Jack Stannard, even now, when screams and killing were still clearly audible ashore, close behind them, and their unseen, unknown enemies were still perilously close. To all intents and purposes, the *Jennet* had become an improvised galley.

The method had been born an entire sea away, out of dire necessity. Dunwich had once possessed one of the best harbours in England, but that had been all but blocked from the sea by huge storms several centuries before, which had also swept away vast swathes of the prosperous port. Over the years – even within Jack's own memory – the estuary leading to the town's quays had become ever more silted, so that it was no longer possible to bring ships up to them under sail alone. The men of Dunwich had erected warping posts so that ships' crews could haul them into harbour, but as soon as they went up, they were cut down again by the men of Walberswick and Southwold, Dunwich's immediate neighbours and inveterate enemies. The port might have closed for ever, and the ancient borough been forced to admit defeat, had not Jack Stannard remembered the galleys he had seen, including one he had once fought against, during King Harry's last war.

Southwold and Walberswick no longer cut down the warping posts, but the mariners of Dunwich kept their sweeps, and kept up their practice with them. After all, as Jack's daughter Meg said, working the oars gave the Stannard crews more muscles and better bodies than their rivals, a fact that did not go unnoticed among the maidens of the Suffolk Sandlings.

'One! *Two!*'

It was desperately hard work. True, the *Jennet* was considerably lighter than she had been several hours earlier, with most of her deadly cargo having been unloaded, but that also made her higher out of the water, so it was harder to keep consistent traction on the sweeps. But slowly, surely, and aided by the ebb, the *Jennet* inched forward, further and further into the comforting shroud of the fog, further away from the sounds of battle and death behind them.

Jack knew from earlier visits to the bay that no causeways extended further out than the one to their wharf. If they could get far enough away before the attackers could turn their full attention to the English ship, they should be safe, with nothing between them and the open sea.

That, though, assumed that the attackers did not have boats.

A shape, dark, menacing and approaching rapidly from beam-on to starboard, showed that they did. Jack saw the swivel gun mounted in its bow a moment before the weapon fired, the flash of fuse on powder providing the only point of light in the fog. The blast from the gun shattered the calm. Countless terrified seabirds took flight, filling the fog-bound bay with a cacophony of sound.

The shot smashed into the side of the *Jennet* a little forward of Jack's position, causing the entire hull to shudder. A loud cheer went up from the attacking boat. Jack reckoned he could make out well over a dozen men in it, perhaps half of them manning the oars. Were there any other boats behind, though? None had yet emerged from the fog. Hope for the best, then.

He turned to give the necessary orders, but found that his son had anticipated him. Five men, led by the burly figure of their kinsman John Holbrook, came up from the hold, each carrying a cloth-bound bundle. Swiftly, they laid them on the deck and opened them, taking out an arquebus each, part of the cargo that had still not been unloaded when Antoine Mielle fell. The two ship's boys, Hal Ashby's son Ned and an eager lad from Minsmere named Paul Battlebridge, went to work on the spare weapons, loading and priming them. Ned threw an arquebus to Jack, who nodded in thanks. Then he turned back to the rail.

The Frenchmen were reloading their swivel gun, no doubt assuming that the English ship before them was defenceless and would swiftly surrender after another shot or two. But to be sure of a hit in the fog, the attackers had to be closer than they would have needed to be in clear weather: close enough to be within arquebus range, in fact.

'God, Dunwich and the queen!' cried Jack, levelling his arquebus at the boat.

Tom, Holbrook and the others fired off their own weapons, immediately discarding them to the deck. Ned Ashby and young Battlebridge urgently handed them fresh firearms, and another salvo roared out from the *Jennet*.

There were cries of consternation on the French boat. Jack saw one man clasp his chest and fall dead over the side, and another corpse being pushed over the wale into the water. A third Frenchman was howling piteously from what had to be a severe wound. The men in the bows were still priming the swivel gun, but the men on the oars and the tiller were already bringing the boat round, retreating in the face of the unexpectedly stiff resistance from the English ship.

The swivel gun fired one last, defiant round. Jack was aware of timbers shattering to his right, and behind him, the impact forcing him off balance. He heard a loud gasp, then the strangled word 'Jesu!' and feared for one terrible moment that Tom had been hit. But as he steadied himself and turned, he saw that it was John Holbrook, his right arm, shoulder, and part of his chest gone. No man moved to assist him, the dreadful sight seeming to anchor them to the deck. But it made no odds, for Holbrook was past any assistance. His shattered body fell to the deck, and Jack Stannard thought of the four young children and his ever-cheerful wife in the little house under the lee of Hen Hill.

His widow, rather, and it would be Jack's task to tell her that she had moved from one state to the other. He already knew that he would not, could not, tell her the truth. He would tell a tale of John Holbrook dying in one of the countless accidents that occurred aboard ships;

better for her, and her children, not to know that he had died in a pointless fight against men with whom England was not at war. The Stannard ledgers would show only that a voyage trading in woollen cloth to Rochelle had turned a handsome profit.

As his crewmates reverently carried the remains of John Holbrook below decks, Jack went to stand beside his son. They said not a word to each other. Instead, both concentrated on the waters ahead, and on the fog, which was slowly lifting. There was even a hint of a breeze. Soon, God willing, they would be able to set sail, and lay their course for England.

Two

The storm struck the *Jennet* five or six leagues south-west of Ushant. At first, it was no more than a slightly darker sky and a somewhat stronger breeze. Within two turns of the glass, though, it was in full spate. The sea swelled up into a great, grey mountain range of water, the white crests crashing in on each other in a furious ferment. It was impossible to see the horizon. Huge waves smashed against the larboard beam, making the ship roll violently. As it did so, it also rose and fell between the great ridges of water. Even Jack, who had grown accustomed to such conditions over many years, felt his stomach heave as he stood upon the after deck, watching for hazards, assessing the state of the minimal sail still aloft, and listening to the ominous creaks and moans from the masts and hull.

Under his breath, he prayed in Latin to *Maria stella maris*, then to an entire litany of saints for their intercession, then to the Virgin once again. They were the prayers he had offered up in storms upon the sea every time since his first, on an Iceland voyage in the year when the queen was born. But that same queen now decreed that prayers should be said in English, and that the Virgin and the saints did not intercede between man and God, so should not be prayed to. Mindful of this, Jack began to utter the Lord's Prayer in English, over and over again. 'Our Father, which art in Heaven, hallowed be Thy name...'

All the while, the ship rolled and pitched, its timbers screaming, as the shores of Ushant, and beyond it, the murderous cliffs of Brittany, came ever closer. Jack swayed with the movement of the ship and redoubled his prayers.

Tom came up on deck, grabbed hold of the lifeline, and hauled himself over to where his father stood. 'I'll relieve you,' he shouted into the teeth of the gale.

'No, Tom,' bellowed Jack. 'I can stand another hour – two, mayhap.'

'You'll do better with some sleep!'

'And what chance sleep in this, eh? No, lad, I'll—'

A great crack cut off whatever Jack Stannard was about to say. The mainmast seemed to shudder, then to move bodily, but somehow held firm.

'Jesu,' said Tom.

'You have your wish, son,' said Jack. 'You have the ship.'

With that, the elder Stannard began to make his way forward, holding on for dear life to the rope as the sea's motion threw him every way at once, and the treacherous torrent sweeping over the deck threatened his footing with every step he took.

He reached the mainmast, and saw at once that it was cracked so badly some four feet above the deck that it had very nearly snapped clear. Jack cursed himself. The ship had been new-built, but the mast must have been in the yard at Dunwich for many years, certainly since the time of the traitor Jed Nolloth. He recalled that he had considered waiting to bring a new mast round from London or Yarmouth, but was keen to get *Jennet* to sea as swiftly as possible for a lucrative voyage into the Baltic. A false economy, it now appeared. Still, by some providence the mast was holding, and if he called up the carpenter and his crew from below, they would be able to—

A violent gust of wind and a colossal wave struck the *Jennet* in the same moment, as though trying to tear the ship in two. Jack heard a fearsome crack, saw the foot of the mainmast break apart, saw the rotten wood at its heart, looked up to see the entire timber begin to fall to starboard, stepped back instinctively, lost his grip on the lifeline, then lost his footing as another sheet of water swept across the deck. The last thing he heard before he felt his head strike something solid – before the terrible, unbearable pain overwhelmed him, and oblivion came – was Tom's scream of 'Father!'

Peter Stannard, Jack's father, was there in front of him, sitting before the fire in the lazar hospital of St James at Dunwich. But he was much younger, very nearly as Jack remembered him from his childhood, with none of the disfiguring marks of leprosy.

'You'll never be your brother, boy,' said the shade.

The old litany.

Jack made to protest, as he had done so often when the old man was alive. But it was not his father any more, and it was not St James. Instead, there in the precinct of the Dunwich Greyfriars stood Thomas Ryman, Jack's old friend and teacher, who had gone down with the *Mary Rose* in the last of Great Harry's wars.

Ryman smiled. 'Not your time, lad,' he said.

Before Jack could respond, Ryman somehow became Alice, standing before the fire in the principal room of their house, as young and beautiful as she had been in life, her body seemingly uncorrupted by so many years of death. She looked at him, cocked her head quizzically to one side as she used to do so often, then smiled.

'Not your time, Jack Stannard. No, certainly not your time.'

Not your time, not your time.

'... not your time, Father.'

Jack opened his eyes, and saw Tom bending down over him, adjusting what felt like a cloth pressed against the impossibly tight band of iron that seemed to have been forced around his skull.

Tom smiled. 'You see? I told you it was not your time.'

Slowly, Jack became aware of his surroundings. He was in the stern cabin of *Jennet*, lying upon his sea-bed. There was no band of iron crushing his head, but a piercing, fiery pain that felt very much like it. There was no storm either. The movement of the ship was gentle, the pitch of the hull easy as it rode the low waves. The scuttles were open, and Jack could see the sun's rays falling on his chart table. It was a warm day.

He tried to raise a hand, then tried to speak, but found he could do neither.

'Don't strain yourself, Father,' said Tom. 'And keep still, so that you don't loosen your bandages.' He grinned. 'You see? I did take in a little of what Aunt Agatha used to teach us, even if Meg took in so much more.'

Once again, Jack tried to speak, but failed.

'You were fortunate,' said Tom. 'You might have been crushed by the mast, or swept over the side, or struck down dead by a flying block, as your brother was. But no, Father, it was definitely not your time. You hit your head on a loose saker, even though it had been double-lashed. Then you became tangled up in a shroud that had just been torn loose by the mast, so we didn't lose you to the sea. As for the ship, thank God the timber of the mast was so rotten. It snapped free entirely, so it was easier for us to hack down the standing rigging and get the whole over the side. I thought that was the end of our good fortune. I knew we were nearing the shore, and there was nothing I could do to bring us closer to the wind. At the end, I could see the cliffs, and could hear the waves breaking on them. We must have been no more than half a league from our deaths. But, thanks be to God, that was when the storm abated. I got us into a cove on the Breton coast, we erected jury rig, and here we are, under sail and set fair for Plymouth. Then I set about tending to your stubborn old head, John Stannard of Dunwich, praying all the while that you would wake up again.'

Tom smiled, and took hold of his father's hand. Jack could still say nothing, but strangely, he could remember the words his own father had once spoken to him in the St James hospital: *There comes a day in every man's life when the roles of father and son are reversed.*

Jack Stannard realised he had tears in his eyes.

A watery dawn was breaking as the *Jennet*, still under jury rig, rounded Rame Head and made her way into Plymouth Sound. Jack Stannard, still wearing a bandage around his head, but now mobile and standing on deck, offered up silent prayers of thanks, first in Latin and then in English. He had no way of knowing whether all their lives had been saved by the old faith or the new, but at least their survival demonstrated that God had not punished him for appealing to both. And whichever dispensation had come to their aid, it had especially strengthened the hand of the true architect of their survival, his son Tom.

The vast bay stretching out before Jack had become very familiar to both of the Stannards in recent years. To the west, Cornwall's shore stretched away to the estuary of the River Hamoaze, a broad, navigable stream, albeit with treacherous rocks and shoals at its mouth. The grand new manor house of Mount Edgcumbe overlooked this channel, and was by far the most prominent building visible upon that shore. To the east, beyond the Cobbler Channel, lay the mouth of the River Plym, forming the anchorage of Cattewater, behind which lay the harbour of Sutton Pool. Between the two streams was a broad promontory, on the eastern side of which, partly hidden by the cliff, or hoe, before it, lay the town of Plymouth. Its location was marked plainly enough by the smoke issuing from its chimneys, even on what promised to be a warm summer's day.

Plymouth's castle, an old, decrepit affair, towered above the Cattewater. To the west of the castle, and only a few hundred yards offshore, lay an island, with the ruins of a chapel dedicated to St Nicholas. The flag of St George flew from this, for there was a small gun battery on the island, which was the outermost of the defences that protected the anchorage. Several vessels were in sight: some coasting traders in Cawsand Bay, to larboard; a skiff making its way across to the Cornish village of Cremyll at the mouth of the Hamoaze; and a heavily laden Portuguese caravel edging into the large harbour that lay at the eastern end of the promontory, adjoining the town. Jack could see the tops of many other masts within the harbour of Sutton Pool, and he imagined that this was what Dunwich had once been like.

The *Jennet* limped into Cattewater and anchored, attracting many curious glances from those on shore and aboard other ships.

'We are a spectacle, it seems,' said Tom, standing along-side his father.

'No matter. At least we're alive, which will most please your Catherine and the boys.'

Tom smiled. 'I think I see them yonder, upon Lambhay.'

There was, indeed, a young woman upon one of the paths by the many warehouses on the Lambhay hill, with two young boys alongside her. One was standing stock still, while the other, smaller lad jumped excitedly and waved.

'Then go, Tom. Go to your family.'

They hailed a small boat from the shore, and were rowed to the quayside. Like all its kind, Plymouth's port was a hive of activity: gangs of men shouting and singing as they loaded and unloaded ships, merchants huddled in corners arranging deals, and the all-pervasive smells of timber, tar and fish. Jack remained on the quay, watching as Tom ran to his wife and their sons, sweeping them into his arms. He smiled. It had worked well, this unlooked-for match, even if it threatened to keep Tom far from Dunwich. It was a marriage made in London, where the then-Catherine Trelawny, a laughing, buxom girl, had come with a large troop of her relations to attend the christening of the firstborn son of a cousin of hers—

A cousin who now emerged from a chandler's across the way, saw Jack, registered surprise, then raised a hand in greeting.

'Well met, John Stannard, if that is truly you beneath the bandage!'

'Well met, John Hawkins.'

Hawkins had aged poorly since their first, fleeting encounter at the strange meeting in Westminster all those years before. Although he was only a little older than Tom, there was already a substantial amount of grey in his beard, and his expression always seemed mournful, as though one he loved had just died. The only aspect of him that suggested his true age was his costume, a rich and highly fashionable black doublet with an abundance of silk trimmings; the sort of thing that ambitious young men wore in London. Hawkins was still a Plymouth man through and through, but like so many mariners, he had been sucked into the irresistible orbit of London and now lived there for much of the time. He was an ambitious and well-connected man who had recently been granted the reversion of the office of Clerk of the Ships of the queen's Navy Royal. With Jack, too, spending much time in London, they were bound to encounter each other, and had come to move in the same circles. Above all, Hawkins had married the daughter of Benjamin Gonson, treasurer and surveyor of the navy, Will Halliday's master and friend, and a man also well known to Jack. So when a marriage was proposed between young Thomas Stannard and a maternal relative of Hawkins, it seemed an obvious and felicitous alliance, of mutual advantage to all concerned. The fact that the two young people were clearly smitten with each other was an unlooked-for additional benefit.

Jack had not expected to see Hawkins in Plymouth. When the *Jennet* had sailed five weeks earlier, the Devonian was gone to London, supposedly to fit out some ships that he was being loaned by the queen for some mysterious, unspecified voyage. Clearly, Hawkins had not expected to see either of the Stannards, and had certainly not expected to see the *Jennet* in its present shattered condition. As he scanned the Cattewater from the quayside of Lambhay, he also had a keen enough eye to recognise that not all of the Dunwich ship's damage had been caused by the weather.

'You had trouble?' he demanded, nodding toward the anchored *Jennet*.

Jack nodded. 'The worst kind of trouble that Ushant can offer,' he said, 'as the size of the scar under this bandage testifies. More than that, too. Mielle's dead. One of my men, also.'

Hawkins' mournful expression became even more anguished.

'Treachery, you think?'

'Someone betrayed us, for certain. I prefer to think it was one of Mielle's men.'

Hawkins scratched his beard. 'Our friends in London will be displeased.'

'I said to you before, friend Hawkins, that dealing with any of the French, even the Huguenots, is a dangerous course to steer, no matter what profit might lie in arquebuses. I said the same to Barne, too, and your good-father Gonson.'

'It's a time for dangerous courses, my friend, with Alba on the march.'

'There's news of him?'

'In Lorraine now, or so they say. Bound for Flanders, I say.'

'Mielle thought he'd turn in to France.'

Hawkins shook his head emphatically. 'King Philip will want order in his own lands before he concerns himself with anywhere else, mark my words. The danger for us, of course, is that he might think England should still be one of his lands, and that once Alba has dealt with the Dutch, Philip will put the chance to come here before any thought of trying to meddle in France. The militias of England are good men and true, Jack Stannard, but against Alba's *tercios*, they'll just be so much carrion.'

'Surely, though, the queen has done nothing to offend King Philip?'

'The queen is a Protestant, and a woman, and has turned down his hand in marriage. Those three things alone are ample offence in Philip's eyes.'

Jack cast his eyes to the ground. It was a dire assessment, but he had no reason to doubt it; Hawkins moved in circles about the court and knew many more great men than Jack did. Indeed, he had once known King Philip, in that strange time when the Spaniard reigned in England too.

'And you, friend Hawkins?' Jack asked, raising his eyes. 'How goes it with your expedition?'

'Well. Aye, well indeed, God willing.'

Hawkins volunteered no information on the purpose of the expedition, and Jack did not press him. But he knew that Hawkins had already made two voyages to Guinea and then over to the Americas, breaking the monopolies that the Portuguese and Spanish respectively claimed over each of those shores, and it did not require necromancy to deduce that this new voyage was likely to follow a similar course. If the queen was lending him ships, then the expedition had to be a potentially lucrative one, and one that had at least the tacit approval of the highest in the land. But the Spanish in particular had paid eyes and ears everywhere, and it would hardly have behoved John Hawkins to reveal his purpose too openly, even to a man who was very nearly kin. So Jack Stannard paid his respects, and went off to join his family. Neither he nor Hawkins gave any attention to the cripple sitting upon a barrel outside the adjacent inn, so neither noticed that the fellow had been following their conversation intently.

Three

Meg poured the hot water over the thyme and ivy in the bowl, stirred, and smiled at her patient.

'God willing, Beth, this will put you to rights.'

Beth Chever, all of thirty months old, stopped coughing for a moment, but only long enough for her to muster a piercing and prolonged scream. Her mother, Anne, a seamstress of Westleton, held her close and stroked her head, but nothing availed. Meg brought the bowl over and held it to her lips. The child screamed again, but finally took a sip of the potion. She grimaced, but did not spit it out. Her mother kissed her and fussed her, so she drank a little more.

Meg smiled encouragingly, and patted the little girl's hand. This is what a child feels like, she thought. A living child. And that is Anne Chever's love for her child. Could I yet feel like that? Did I ever feel like that, in those short days?

'The cough seems a little easier already, mistress,' said Anne Chever.

'If it is no more than a cough from the chest, this should make her well,' said Meg. 'But if it is other…'

Anne Chever nodded, trying to hold back tears as she did so. Neither of them needed to give voice to the countless, deadly manifestations of what the 'other' might be.

'I will make up two jugs for you,' said Meg. 'That should suffice for three days, if you heat them as I said. If there is no improvement, bring her back to me. But if she is well, pray send the jugs back by some willing lad.'

Whether Goodwife Chever would do so was another matter. Perhaps young Beth would recover, but if she did not, it was equally likely that her mother would try one of the other reputed healers in that part of the Sandlings, or even further afield. And if Beth Chever was indeed afflicted by something other than a mere childhood cough in the chest, there was every chance that in three days' time, the little girl would be wrapped in a winding sheet, waiting to be placed in the ground.

In any event, Meg had no great expectation of ever getting her jugs back.

–

Meg stepped out of her tiny cottage in a hollow upon Dunwich Heath and closed the door behind her. She turned for a moment to take in the view to the south, across Minsmere toward Aldringham and Thorpeness. The right half of her view was flat, nearly featureless land, and the left half was sea. High grey clouds scudded across the sky, and a moderate breeze blew from the south-west. In the far distance and away to the south-east, half a dozen ships had full sail set, their courses laid for harbours far across the German Ocean. Perhaps that same wind was bringing her father and brother home safe to England from their latest voyage. Perhaps, *Deo gratias*, they were already in harbour, carousing in an alehouse and raising their tankards towards her. It was a pleasant thought, and one to hold to, rather than the thoughts of what other fates might have befallen them.

Meg turned, and as she did so, she noticed a hole in the thatch that had somehow escaped her attention until now. It looked small enough for her to be able to repair it herself. Her spinster aunt Agatha, from whom she had inherited both the cottage and the skill in healing, had never needed to call on a man for any repair to the building, and Meg was determined to maintain the tradition. Stannards were stubborn in that regard, as in so many others, and despite the surname she now bore, Meg was still a Stannard at heart.

She made her way north by the familiar path across the heath. Now, in summer, it was a glorious carpet of purple heather and yellow gorse. Thomas Ryman, an old man who had meant much to her in her childhood, had once told her that the heath resembled the cloak of a great Roman Caesar. She did not then know what a Roman Caesar was, but later, Luis had told her, and now, every time she crossed the heath, she imagined Claudius or Constantine looking out imperiously from the ramparts of the fort and city the Romans were meant to have founded at Dunwich.

She entered the town by what people still called the south gate, although it was now no more than a gap in the low, overgrown grassy bank that had once been the Palesdyke, the defence that had surrounded the town for centuries. But there was now no town immediately inside the ancient rampart, only lumps in the grass where houses had stood. There had been a parish here, but as the sea ate away more and more of Dunwich, the entire south end of what had once been termed a city was abandoned. The track on which she walked was still laughably named High Street, but the only visible buildings were still well ahead of her. There, behind the windmill, lay the ruins of the

Blackfriars, long since stripped of anything of worth, and a little further inland, the ivy-covered remains of St Mary's Temple, the old Hospitaller establishment. Then came the houses of Duck Street, now the southernmost street in Dunwich; their original location within the bounds was betrayed by the name of the decayed structure at the west end, the former Middlegate.

Meg was just considering whether to turn off and make her way to All Saints, a little way beyond Duck Street and King Street, which ran behind it, to light a candle to her mother's memory, when a young voice hailed her.

'A good day to you, Goody de Andrade!'

He was a short, grinning, freckled lad of twelve or thirteen, by name Francis Birkes, son of a cobbler over in Scotts Lane. He was not much older than Meg's son would have been had he lived, and he always reminded Meg of an eager puppy.

'And greetings to you, Goodman Birkes. What brings you out here?'

'Rabbits, mistress. More warrens than you can count in all the old foundations. And what business are you upon today, mistress?'

Meg would have chided any other boy in Dunwich for their impertinence, but she had cured young Francis of a virulent fever the previous year, and had a soft spot for the lad, especially as he insisted on addressing her by the gentlefolk's title of 'mistress'. She reckoned that he was more than a little in love with her.

'To the harbour, Francis. The Stannard account books for the last quarter need making up.'

Not a few in Dunwich thought it strange beyond all measure that a woman should interest herself in such things, let alone actually do such work, but Francis Birkes was not yet of an age to form prejudices and preconceptions. He merely nodded, as though what Meg de Andrade had said was the most natural thing in the world.

'And are the Masters Stannard returned from their voyage, mistress?'

'No news as yet, alas.'

'I shall pray for them, mistress.'

Meg doubted it. Francis Birkes was probably the least godly youth in Dunwich, although there were many other contenders for that dubious distinction. On the other hand, he wanted more than anything else not to have to follow his father into the cobbler's trade, but to be taken on by the Stannards and sail the seven seas with them.

She made to move off towards the town, but Francis seemed to forget all thought of rabbits and trailed along beside her.

'There's a coal ship from Newcastle just docked at the Dain quay, mistress, and I heard some of her crew a-mardlin' to the lads ashore. They say the Queen of Scots has been locked away in a castle on a lake. They say everyone in Scotland calls her a whore and a murderess, for conspiring in her husband's murder and then allowing the man who killed him to bed and marry her.'

'Lord Bothwell,' said Meg, who, like every woman in England, was secretly fascinated by the extraordinary doings of Mary Stuart. 'I'm not sure if it was a case of her allowing him, Francis.'

'Well, that's what they say, mistress. But do it mean she couldn't become queen here, if Elizabeth was to die? Men in the alehouses – some say she's the next heir, others say not because she's a papist.'

Meg knew perfectly well that no one was within earshot, but she still stopped and glanced around urgently, then placed her hands on Francis's shoulders.

'You must never talk of our sovereign lady but with respect, Francis Birkes, and you must never, ever talk of her death. Never. Do you understand me? Do you promise me?'

The lad nodded gravely. Meg patted him on the head, but felt an utter fraud as she did so. For one thing, she recalled her father and grandfather upbraiding her younger self on many occasions for equally incautious talk about the monarch of the day. For another, she had her own, very private feelings about the precise status of Mary of Scotland in relation to her cousin Elizabeth.

'Go along now, lad,' she said, as kindly as she could. 'Go and snare a rabbit or two, and don't pay any heed to the drunks in the alehouses.'

The boy complied, and Meg made her way into the body of the town. She exchanged greetings with acquaintances and distant kin, stopped to speak at length to old Mother Watson, widow of one of the sometime bailiffs, and then made her way across the open area of clifftop that was now all that remained of the market square of Dunwich. She could remember when it had four sides, and when the town's greatest church, St John's, stood on the easternmost of them. But it had fallen into the sea during a Christmas Day service in the old King Henry's time, a disaster that she had barely escaped with her life, and now not a trace of it remained.

She wondered how long her present church, St Peter's, a few yards to the west, would survive the onslaught of the sea. Not that she cared for the building itself, nor for the worship conducted within; it had always been smaller and more nondescript than St John's, but now, like almost every church in the land, it was bereft of its statues and images of the saints, of its rood screen and its colourful wall paintings. Instead, its interior was whitewashed and bleak, a plain so-called communion table standing in the middle as a pale replacement for the altar that had stood at the east end. There was no music, no joy at all to the worship – nothing but interminable and gloomy sermons in English, the glorious mysteries of Latin now no more than increasingly distant memories. But her Luis lay in the graveyard of St Peter's, and the thought of his bones being swept away by a great wave formed her most persistent nightmare.

She passed through the other end of Palesdyke at the Guilding Gate, skirted Cock and Hen hills and the ruins of St Francis's chapel, and finally arrived at the harbour. Apart from the coal ship Birkes had mentioned, no other vessel lay at any of the quays. The port was so much quieter than it had been in her childhood, and she remembered her grandfather telling her how much busier still it had been twenty or thirty years before that. But men were working at the largest of the Stannard warehouses, loading carts full of German goods for the markets of High Suffolk, and they all acknowledged her with waves and smiles.

One of them, Hugh Ebbes, smiled particularly broadly and called out a cheery greeting. Ebbes made no secret of his ambition for her hand. Meg was flattered, for he was a handsome man with a strong body. But he was penniless, and while, one day, she might perhaps bed him for her own gratification, marriage was out of the question. A pity: at least Ebbes was interested in her and not daunted by her singularity. Several of her suitors in the nine years since Luis's death had been put off by her reputation for plain speaking, some by the rumours that inevitably attached themselves to women who healed, others by her extraordinary liking for numbers and ledgers, and yet others by the discomfiting fact that she could actually read and write.

The only other man who was seemingly undeterred by all this, and had made a serious offer for her hand, was a jobbing painter of Norwich, one Philip Grimes by name, who had fallen in love with her after encountering her by chance one day at the market in Saxmundham. Grimes was a handsome and good man who was loyal to the old faith, the principal quality Meg looked for in a potential husband. Had they met in another time, she would certainly have accepted him; but with the churches whitewashed, no more demand for the painting of rood screens or statues of the saints and the Virgin, and the Suffolk gentry determined to have their portraits painted by fashionable Flemings in London, he could only live from hand to mouth, and Meg's father was reluctant to take on a son-in-law who might be eternally dependent on his wife. Even so, Meg could not find it in her heart to reject Philip Grimes outright, partly because she prayed that his fortunes would turn – as they were sure to do if the true Church was restored once again in England. In the meantime, though, Meg de Andrade remained a widow, possessed of the most exotic surname in the Sandlings.

She made a cursory check of the loading of the carts, then of the condition of the principal warehouse, before moving on to the old boat shed. This had been abandoned for years, for no craft had been built at Dunwich since the time of Jed Nolloth, a shipwright and once a trusted friend of her father and grandfather, who had taken Southwold's gold and betrayed Dunwich and the Stannards in the foulest manner imaginable. The shed was very dark and stank of damp wood. As her eyes adjusted, she saw the familiar sight of ancient worked timbers, some intended for top timbers, some for futtocks and knee timbers. There were larger pieces too, their purpose or function now long forgotten. There was one exception to this: a large, nearly rectangular piece, poorly whitewashed and thick with dust; but there were now only two people alive in the world who knew why it was the exception. Meg's father was one, and she the other.

She walked over to it, placed her left hand upon it, and with her right, took out an object that had once been beloved of every man, woman and child in England. Now, though, it was proscribed and derided, while the wooden object upon which her left hand rested was even more illegal. If her part in its preservation was to become known, Meg de Andrade might face prison, or worse.

She crossed herself, fingered her paternoster, and began to repeat the *Ave Maria* under her breath. As she did so, she recalled the dreadful image that lay beneath the whitewash, the image that had hung for so long above the rood screen in the doomed church of St John. She remembered vividly the penetrating red eyes and terrible black wings of the colossal devil, looming above the churches and houses of Dunwich as they were swept away by the sea, seeming to gloat over all the poor people about to be drowned. She remembered when it had been renowned for miles around. It was perhaps the most famous artefact the town possessed.

For this had been – this *was* – the great doom painting, the Doom of Dunwich itself. And Meg Stannard, the widow Margaret de Andrade, was its guardian, solemnly

44

tasked with the duty by her father amid the ruins of St John's church, the day after most of it fell into the sea.

It had lain in this dark corner, the memory of its glory forgotten by all but her and a handful of the faithful, for the best part of a quarter century. When Queen Mary was proclaimed, Meg hoped that the Doom might emerge triumphant from its hiding place and be hoisted high once again. But John's church no longer existed, as its last ruins now perched precariously on the edge of Dunwich cliff. That left just two churches in the town: St Peter's, now nominally her parish church, and All Saints, where her mother was buried. But William James, the rector of St Peter's, was a reformer, put in during the reign of the heretical boy-king Edward, and although he complied reluctantly with the restoration of the Mass and the other requirements of Catholicism, he was not prepared to have the Doom installed in his church.

By contrast, Edrich, then the rector of All Saints, was sound enough in faith, but he was a markedly timid man. He protested that his church was too poor a place for such a great treasure, but in truth, he feared an influx of the faithful from all over Suffolk and beyond, swelling his congregation and making more work for him. So the Doom had remained in the boat shed. Then, after Queen Mary died, it swiftly became apparent that her successor would have no truck with such symbols of what her jackals called popish idolatry. But Meg was patient. She would wait for the reign of the new Queen Mary, when she knew she could easily sway Walkinson, the present rector of All Saints, who was besotted with her – a state of affairs that he managed to conceal from his wife and six children. Until then, the Doom would stay safe...

She was so deep in her thoughts that she was unaware of another.

'Good day, sister,' came a voice from behind her.

She started, but had the presence of mind to pocket her rosary before turning. He was framed in the doorway, but she did not need to see his face. The weak, reedy voice was enough.

'And good day to you, brother Ned,' she said.

'What brings you in here?' he asked.

'Before he sailed, Father told me he was thinking of having boats built here again,' she lied. 'I have a mind to make an inventory of the timbers we have, to see what size and type of craft might be best. But what brings you to the harbour? The alehouses have been open for hours.'

She sensed his discomfort, and prayed that he had no suspicions about what she might have been doing. But Ned Stannard was comfortably the most stupid of her three half-brothers, as well as the least fervently Protestant. Had it been George or Harry, she might have been more concerned, although Harry, the only one of them that she liked, was surely unlikely to betray her. And if it had been their sister Mary, Meg might already have been in dread for her liberty, even though the girl was the youngest of them all.

'Shall we talk in the light, sister? I can barely see you in here.'

She followed him out. In daylight, Edward Stannard cut an unimpressive figure. Just past his nineteenth birthday, he was tall but strikingly thin, the consequence of a wasting sickness some years earlier. His face was pale, his yellow hair already thinning, and he had a marked squint. His mother had marked out his brothers for great things, but she despaired of Ned, who was too lumpen even for the Church. This alone made Meg feel a certain sympathy for him. Anyone or anything that caused Jennet Stannard to despair was an unwitting ally of Meg de Andrade.

'So, Ned, what brings you to this land of demons and monsters?'

'It is a harbour, sister, nothing more. But Mother told me to speak to you.' Ned, who would not have recognised a jest if it slapped him on the cheeks, did not meet his half-sister's eyes once. 'She thinks I should become involved in our trades and businesses. She thinks I should learn the state of our affairs. She thinks you should teach me the ledgers – show me bills of lading and the like – so that I might help you with your work.'

Meg nearly laughed, but somehow kept her face straight. The notion of her stepmother wanting to do anything to help her in any way was as likely as the sun and the moon changing places, but then the same could be said of the prospects of poor Ned being able to count much beyond the number of fingers on his hands. No, Jennet Stannard had some scheme or other in mind, and it would undoubtedly be to Meg's disadvantage. Fortunate, then, that she had chosen the worst possible instrument for her stratagem. True, Ned was the only instrument her stepmother had at hand, but that did not alter the case.

Meg smiled innocently at her half-brother.

'Of course, dear Ned,' she said, 'it will be good for you to be so occupied. As you'll see, the keeping of the books and papers is a very easy task. Very easy indeed. Why, it must be, must it not, for a poor simple woman to have done it unaided for so very long?'

47

Four

Ah the sighs that come from my heart,
They grieve me passing sore;
Since I must from my love depart,
Farewell, my joy, for evermore.

Jack Stannard and Will Halliday exchanged a smile before
they began to sing the next verse, Jack in a lyrical tenor
line and Will in his deep bass.

I was wont her to behold,
And taken in arms twain,
And now, with sighs manifold,
Farewell, my joy, and welcome, pain!

They had first encountered Cornysh's love song when
they sang together in the chapel choir of Cardinal College.
At the age they were then, their interest in maidens only
just burgeoning, phrases such as 'taken in arms twain'
and 'sighs manifold' told of as yet unknown and exciting
delights, almost but not quite within reach. At any rate,
such songs, prohibited in the sternest terms by their po-
faced choir master, were more thrilling than the countless
settings of the *Kyrie* that formed the staple of their days.

Their audience, there in the principal room of Will's house, was a small one. Marion, Will's wife, grew plumper every time Jack saw her, and the hair spilling out from beneath her coif was now largely grey. She was a sensible, intelligent woman, who had been an ideal helpmeet for her husband during their years of marriage. Jack envied his friend in this. She sat by the two youngest of their seven surviving children, Lettice and Elizabeth. The former was clearly bored beyond measure, despite her valiant attempts to hide it, but the latter, a lively youngster of eight, was entranced.

Will's house stood on Aldgate Street. It was close by the church of St Andrew Undershaft, and the two men's music-making was but a pastime until the bells rang three, when they would leave in answer to another man's summons: a summons that had not a little air of mystery to it.

The house was quite new, thin but tall, as was the fashion in London, with three storeys above the ground floor. Rich furnishings and Flemish tapestries provided further evidence that Will Halliday had come a very long way from the impecunious young clerk he had once been. Even so, Jack could not envy him. For his part, he was always glad to escape from London, and was still discontented that a summons to meet a man of some importance, as Will termed him, had delayed his plan to take the Suffolk road as swiftly as he could, having left Tom at Plymouth to oversee the repairs to the *Jennet*. Dunwich's peace and quiet might have been born of decay, but it was always a blessed relief after London.

Ah, methink that I see her yet,
As would to God that I might!

There might no joys compare with it
Unto my heart to make it light.

The two men proffered a bow to their audience. Marion and Elizabeth clapped enthusiastically, Lettice politely.

'Truly, the Chapel Royal's loss is our gain,' said Marion Halliday.

She knew that it had once been the dearest ambition of her husband and his friend to join the exclusive number of the monarch's own choir, but fate had set them both upon very different courses.

'I still live in hope,' said Jack, laughingly.

At that moment, the first bell of Undershaft tolled, followed closely by the slightly more distant bells of St Katharine Cree and St Katharine Coleman. Jack looked sideways at Will.

'We must go.'

'Of course,' said Marion. 'God be with you both.'

Will kissed her, followed by his daughters. Then he and Jack made their way out into Aldgate Street, cut across to Lyme Street, and turned onto Lombard Street at St Dionis Backchurch. It was a warm, dry afternoon, and their journey provided Jack with a perfect reminder of why he disliked the great city. The streets, even those that might be termed side roads, were full. Hawkers and beggars lined their sides, the former bawling out their wares and the supposedly astonishingly low prices they wanted for them, the latter pitifully imploring passers-by for alms. Between them passed a throng of people of all stations and descriptions, from well-dressed men and women of rank to apprentice boys in little more than rags. Carters and men on horseback struggled valiantly to make their way through the press. Dogs fought with cats, and rats scurried hither and thither amidst the pungent dung that covered almost the entire length and breadth of each street. Pigeons, crows and jackdaws swooped on anything that could possibly be construed as food. Will evidently loved the bustle, but it merely reinforced Jack's opinion. Oh, for the quiet, nearly deserted streets of Dunwich.

Once again, he asked Will for the identity of the man they were going to meet, but once again, his friend was elusive upon the matter.

'It would mean n-nothing to you,' said Will. 'Although in a way, he is nearly k-kin to you, Jack.'

'Kin? How can that be?'

'Well, your wife is a c-cousin to Sir George B-Barne, who was Lord Mayor, is she not? This man married Barne's daughter. T-true, she died, but there may be a c-canonical degree involved somewhere.'

'But what else is he, Will? You make him seem a man of mystery.'

'In a way, he is. He sets out to k-keep his affairs p-private. But Secretary Cecil r-rates him, and many speak of him as a c-coming man. Master Gonson for one, and others of the Council of Marine Causes, too – Sir William Wynter says this fellow will be a great man one day. He has been a Member of P-Parliament, and has been in Scotland with Throckmorton, the ambassador. I've heard whispers that he was somehow involved in the intrigues surrounding Queen Mary's d-downfall. He is t-trusted with c-confidential matters by the highest in the land. The very highest, if you t-take my meaning.'

Jack shivered involuntarily. Once, he had been within a few yards of King Henry the Eighth of famous memory. He had briefly held the confidence of Lord Admiral Lisle, as he then was, who later became Duke of Northumberland, the man who ruled the kingdom and tried to deny the crown to its true queen, setting the Lady Jane Grey in her place. He had once been in the same room as the dreaded Duke of Alba, in those strange days when Philip of Spain reigned as King of England. But those had been mere chimeras, fleeting moments that had never been repeated. He was an Icarus who had flown too close to the sun, and had rightly been burned. Now, though, he was about to meet a man who seemingly had the confidence of Queen Elizabeth herself. Perhaps Icarus was about to take flight once again.

They came to the Pope's Head, a large, rambling old hostelry opposite St Mary Woolnoth, close to where Lombard Street and Cornhill came together. The court-yard was full of drinkers, moneylenders rubbing shoulders with carters and lawyers, and apprentices leering at bawdy wenches and having their interest returned in full measure. The two men made their way into the range on the far side, climbed two flights of stairs, negotiated a warren of corridors, and came at last to a closed door at the very back of the rambling tavern. Will knocked on it, and a clear, confident voice responded from within.

'Come.'

They entered. The room was small, but light and airy, with several chairs and a table. The man before them was in his middle thirties, Jack estimated, although his hair was already running to grey. His beard and moustache were immaculately trimmed, the ends of the latter being turned upward in a manner that might have been ludicrous in a man with less of a presence. His body was not large, but firm and broad enough, and was clothed almost entirely in black, making him appear very nearly Spanish. Yet it was his eyes that caught Jack's attention. Although, at first sight, the bags under them gave an impression of tiredness, Jack realised that the eyes themselves were anything but tired. Indeed, it was hard to see if this man ever blinked.

'Halliday,' said the man.

'M-Master Walsingham, permit me to name John Stannard of D-Dunwich.'

'John Stannard,' said the man, appraisingly. He spoke quietly but firmly, with no trace of an accent. 'I understand, though, that you have always been known as Jack? My sometime good-brother Barne says as much, and he is acquainted with your wife, who ought to know your given name. I shall call you Jack, then. For my part, I am Francis Walsingham. Please, let us be seated. Some wine?'

Jack and Will both nodded. Walsingham took a jug from the table and poured two goblets. Jack noticed that he did not take one for himself.

The three men sat.

'So, then, Goodman Stannard,' said Walsingham, 'you had a noteworthy voyage, I gather.'

'I prefer them less noteworthy, Master Walsingham.'

'So I imagine. A shame about Mielle… he was a useful man for us in those parts. But there are others, of course. And your ship? It is still at Plymouth? It can be repaired?'

'My son will see that it is. It should be a matter of no more than a few weeks.'

'And your plans for it, once the repairs are complete?'

Jack frowned. Why should this man, this supposedly influential man, take such a minute interest in the *Jennet* of Dunwich?

'To see if cargoes are offered at Plymouth, or one of the ports thereabouts. If not, to have my son bring her back round to London or Dunwich, then to one of our usual trades.'

Walsingham nodded, and pursed his lips.

'I have a different proposition for you, Jack Stannard. A very different proposition. You know John Hawkins of Plymouth, I am told.'

'I do. He is kin to my son's wife.'

'And you know he is about to embark upon a distant voyage?'

'I do.'

Walsingham rose, walked to the window, looked out over the scene below, then turned back to face the two men once again.

'Master Halliday here, and Master Gonson, Master Barne, and others too, all tell me that you are a man of discretion, Jack Stannard. A man who can keep confidences. I trust their judgement, and I intend to tell you confidences of the highest nature. But I am also told that you are a God-fearing man, Stannard of Dunwich.'

'I endeavour to be so, Master Walsingham.'

'Well, then, you should not object to offering me an additional assurance.' Walsingham took up a substantial book from the table, and walked over to Jack. 'The New Testament, Goodman Stannard. The words of Our Lord. I ask that you swear on it that you will not divulge anything said in this room. Can you do that?'

Jack felt as though he was being led into a trap, but did not know how, or why. Even so, he rose, placing his right hand upon the book and his left upon his heart.

'I do so swear, so help me God.'

Walsingham returned the book to the table.

'Very good,' he said, 'although perhaps you might have preferred a Latin version?'

Jack's head swam. No man knew what prayers he said in his thoughts, or what faith he kept in his heart. *No man.*

He glanced at Will, but his friend's face was as shocked as his own must have been.

Walsingham sat once again, and raised a hand.

'The queen has decreed that she will not make windows into men's souls,' he said. 'Your faith is no concern of hers, and no concern of mine, John Stannard – no concern for now, at any rate. But your ship is quite another matter. You see, your friend Hawkins is embarking upon a voyage that will take him to the shore of Guinea, perhaps thence to the Carib Sea. It is intended as a mere trading expedition, but it has been proposed by two Portingal adventurers of good repute and experience. Substantial profits are anticipated, especially as these Portingals claim to have certain knowledge of—

'But no, that is beyond the point for this discussion, I think. Nevertheless, as I say, large profits are expected. For that reason, many very considerable men of the court, the Common Council of London, and so forth, have invested in this voyage.' Walsingham's tone suggested that he, too, was one of those investors. 'Indeed, the queen's majesty herself is loaning Hawkins two of the royal men-of-war, which are being made ready in the River Medway as we speak. But there are, shall we say, sensibilities. I am sure you are aware of them, Master Halliday.'

Will, still startled by Walsingham's intelligence of his friend, faltered in his reply.

'M-M-Master W-W-Walsingham…'

'Take some of your wine, Master Halliday.'

Will did so, and then attempted to speak again.

'P-Portugal claims a monopoly on t-trade with Africa, and S-Spain a monopoly on t-trade with the Americas. Both c-claim that the Pope g-granted it t-t-to them in a t-t-treaty—'

'Tordesillas,' interrupted Walsingham, 'in the year 1494. A line drawn upon a map. A line drawn down the middle of the world, with all newly discovered land on the east side of it given to Portugal, all to the west to Spain. The arrogance of it, made doubly so because the Pope who made the treaty was a Borgia, one of that foul, incestuous breed of murderers and fornicators. That foul *Spanish* breed. And as it transpired, of course, Spain's share proved to include vast seams of gold and silver, the foundation of all its overweening power. So the Spanish are eager to exclude all others from the Indies, whatever their reason for going there, lest such interlopers become a threat to the flow of bullion into King Philip's coffers.'

'Yet Englishmen have t-traded with the Americas in r-recent years,' said Will, gaining in confidence. 'Many of the g-governors and m-merchants are eager to do so. But King Philip and his m-ministers are set against it. They do not give the b-bullion as the c-cause, of c-course. Instead, they stand upon their p-privilege, and upon the letter of the t-treaty.'

'Aye, very true, Master Halliday, and there's the nub of it,' said Walsingham. 'Those of the court and city who invest in the voyages of Hawkins and his kind – why, even the queen's majesty herself – are keen for them to proceed. Indeed, for them to be more frequent, and larger, as this next voyage will be. But such voyages come with a terrible risk, Jack Stannard. For if Hawkins makes a mistake, if he somehow offends the Spanish, if he overreaches himself, then the consequences might be unthinkable. There may even be war with Spain, and with Alba's army soon to be a mere few miles across the sea from England's shore, God knows what the outcome of such a war might be.'

'A terrible prospect,' said Jack, 'but I do not see how it concerns me, Master Walsingham.'

Jack was truly baffled, although inwardly, he felt a certain thrill to be addressed as an equal by such a seemingly important man as this, and to be talking of such weighty matters of state, the likes of which were usually so very far above his purview. Perhaps in Purgatory, or Hell, or wherever his diseased soul had finally gone, Jack's father was finally proud of him.

Walsingham went to the table, brought back the jug of wine, and refilled Jack's and Will's goblets.

'There are men who place the risk of war above the chance of profit,' he said. 'England is not ready for a war. We are too weak. Thank God that France is bitterly divided and on the brink of another war with itself. What happens upon the coast of Guinea is of little concern to me, or those I represent – whatever happens, we will not have a war with Portugal, which has a child king and is even weaker than England. But Spain... we cannot have a breach with Spain at any price. So, John Stannard of Dunwich, I want you to sail with Hawkins, in the ship you already have at Plymouth. It will be a royal command, but he knows you, he is kin to your son, so he will have no cause to suspect or object. Doubly so, as there will also be a letter from his good-father, Master Gonson, who is one of the major investors in the voyage.'

Jack saw Will smile. This, then, was partly his doing. Jack knew that a few years earlier, his old friend had attended the wedding of John Hawkins and Benjamin Gonson's daughter.

'All I ask,' continued Walsingham, 'is that at every opportunity, you urge caution upon Hawkins. If there is any quarrel with the Spaniards, seek to pacify it. If there is any incident, record the facts of it. When you write home, and when you return, tell the truth, so that we do not depend only upon the word of John Hawkins as to what has transpired. Those who think as I do want a man we can trust sailing on this voyage. A man of good judgement. A man we can depend upon. A man who, of course, will be amply rewarded for his work. Will you be that man, Jack Stannard?'

Jack's thoughts raced. To act the spy went against every instinct in his body. He knew nothing of Guinea, or the Carib Sea, or the Indies. He had never sailed the great ocean, and did not have the first idea of how to do so. Such a voyage would mean months, perhaps years, away from Dunwich, and Meg, and...

But Walsingham had talked of ample reward. What was more, if Jack succeeded, then Walsingham and those who thought like him would know his name, and would know him to be a dependable man. He might even come to the attention of the queen herself.

He thought again of the great ocean, and of the Carib, and the Americas beyond it. Yes, like every seafarer contemplating a voyage in unfamiliar seas, he felt a sense of fear. But every seafarer also felt the thrill of the unknown, the prospect of new sights to be seen, of new knowledge to be gained: the irrepressible urge to know what lay beyond the horizon.

It was also true that such a voyage would, indeed, mean months, perhaps years, away from Dunwich. Years away from his wife.

'Yes, Master Walsingham,' he said, raising his goblet in a toast, 'I will be that man.'

Five

Tom Stannard and the men of the *Jennet* had spent a hard day stepping her new mainmast up at the mooring by Spike Point, and were intent upon a prodigious quantity of ale. Tom felt a little guilt at this, as his Catherine and the boys saw him little enough, but it was important to keep the men content, far as they were from their own homes in Dunwich. So they were drinking their way around the taverns and alehouses of Plymouth, coming at last to a small alehouse hard against the wall of the old and decayed castle, high upon its hill overlooking Cattewater.

The Suffolk men were just seated upon stools, and a serving lad was bringing over their tankards, when Tom realised that their choice of hostelry might have been a mistake. Across the room, a large group of Devon men, all sailors by the look of them, were far gone in their cups, and casting suspicious or hateful looks toward the new arrivals. Tom recognised a handful of them. They were all men who sailed with Hawkins, or formed part of the large circle of bragging, strutting fellows who trailed after every successful captain, hoping for advancement and riches. One, of his own age and curly-haired, he knew a little, and knew for a boastful creature, full of his own importance. He was a distant cousin of Hawkins, had sailed with him to Guinea and the Americas, and had a swagger about him.

It was this curly-haired fellow who commenced proceedings.

'So foreigners drink here now,' he said loudly. It had taken Tom many months to comprehend how Devon men spoke, and for them to comprehend him, but even in drink, this man spoke with surprising clarity. 'Strangers overrun our Plymouth, as God is my judge. Not just all the French and Flemings and Portingals and the rest of them – worse than any, I say.'

The men around him growled approval. Tom looked around the men of the *Jennet*, silently imploring them not to rise to the bait. They were good fellows, some of whom he had known since his childhood, and they complied.

'Suffolk,' said the man, warming to his theme. 'What is this "Suffolk", eh? Where is it? I'll tell you, my boys. The Devil's arsehole, that's where it is.' There was laughter at that; the Devon men plainly loved this fellow, and were hanging on his every word. 'And there sit the Devil's turds. I'll wager they're papists to a man – didn't Cardinal Wolsey, that great Satan, hail from Suffolk?' There were a few nods of assent. 'Are they even Christian, though? I hear they worship statues and fuck their sisters since they can no longer get choirboys.' More laughter, and the raising of tankards. 'Whatever they are, they're not English. Devon is the true England, boys, the very beating heart of England; we know that for sure, don't we?'

One of the Suffolk men, an angry young foretopman named Mark Ferris, made to rise, but Tom put a hand on his arm and restrained him. The bold fellow was not finished, though, not by a large margin.

'And that one. Stannard. What sort of name is that, eh? Stannard of Suffolk. A papist, I'll wager again, from a land of papists, heathens and worse. Even dares to fuck a kind of kinswoman of mine—'

One last plea for restraint rose up in Tom's thoughts, but was overwhelmed by a tidal wave of red fury. The dagger was in his hand in one moment, flying across the room in the next, buried in the wall just beside curly-head's in the third. By then Tom was already halfway across the room, followed by the rest of the men of Dunwich. The Devon men rose as one to meet them.

With his eyes and thoughts still raging, Tom had little sense of what was happening around him, even less of time. One man stood between him and his tormentor, but Tom lowered his head and charged like a bull into the man's stomach, driving him over a table, which overturned. He tried to pick himself up, but before he could do so, curly-head leapt on him from behind, his fingers seeking to gouge out his eyes. Tom wrestled him to the ground, forcing him onto his back, then freed his right hand enough to land a punch upon the fellow's jaw. His opponent broke away and stood up, feeling his chin. All around was carnage. Stools were being broken upon skulls, blood and teeth flew, men cursed and screamed. It was impossible to tell whether Suffolk or Devon was prevailing.

Curly-head came at Tom again, swinging a punch at his head. Tom avoided the blow by swaying cleverly. He had been a feeble child, ever reminded of the fact by his sturdy elder sister, but he had remedied that by learning the art of the fists from German and Flemish sailors on the quays of Dunwich, then testing himself by wrestling in fairs from Lavenham to Thetford to Lowestoft. Now he counter-attacked, kicking at curly-head's shin, a blow

61

that connected. His assailant staggered backwards, but steadied himself and came again. Tom caught the glint of a blade, and knew that curly-head had drawn his dagger. Tom could handle himself with a knife, but his own was still stuck in the wall. So he circled, his arms outstretched. Curly-head thrust forward and stabbed, making a gash across Tom's left forearm. But the move put him off balance, and Tom swung round with his right, seizing curly-head's arm and pulling it upwards, leaving the dagger pointing harmlessly at the roof. The two men came together, sweating and breathing heavily, curly-head snarling obscenities through his teeth. He tried to punch at Tom with his left hand, but nothing he did could make Tom weaken the pressure on his opponent's right arm.

The blade fell from curly-head's grip, landing noisily upon the thinly-strawed floor of the alehouse.

Tom immediately followed up his advantage, swinging a sharp left uppercut into curly-head's face. The man fell backwards, a torrent of blood flowing from his nose. Tom paused, trying to get his breath, and took the chance to look around him. It was clear that the men of the *Jennet* had prevailed. The Devonians were being pressed back toward the door, many of them nursing broken limbs and bloodied noses. Curly-head saw it too, and also began to retreat.

'This is not finished, Stannard of Suffolk,' he snarled. 'This has barely started.'

Tom managed a smile, and nodded.

'The only true thing you've said this day, Frank Drake.'

Catherine Stannard tended her husband's wounds solicitously, if not entirely sympathetically, being of the opinion that a man approaching thirty and with significant responsibility for the Stannard trades and monies, not to mention two young sons, should know better than to involve himself in alehouse brawls. The chubby six-year-old face of Adam Stannard, their elder son, was serious at the best of times, but now its mask of disapproval would have done credit to the sternest Puritan preacher. Four-year-old Peter, though, was evidently delighted by this proof of his father's martial skill, and wanted to know precise details of the fight.

'These are not matters for one of your years,' said Catherine.

'But Mother—'

'Enough, Peter Stannard!' she said.

'But Mother—'

The Stannards' servant, a widow named Yeo, whose accent was very nearly impenetrable, came into the room, and Catherine gestured for her to take the boys away. Before she did so, though, Widow Yeo handed a letter to Tom, who recognised his father's hand at once. He broke the seal and unfolded the paper.

'Well, Thomas?' said Catherine. 'What is it to be? France again, or does he want you to take *Jennet* back to Dunwich?'

Tom could not read quickly, certainly when compared to his sister Meg, so he found it comforting that his wife could not read at all. But as he studied his father's words, his frown deepened.

'Thomas?'

'There is to be a voyage,' he said, finally. 'A long voyage.'

'Where, then? Spain? Italy? Muscovy?'

'Guinea at the very least. Mayhap the Americas too. With Hawkins.' Tom smiled grimly. 'No doubt with Drake too, in that case.'

'The *Americas*? With cousin John? In God's name, why?'

'Father does not say in so many words. He talks of it being the wish of men of influence – not named – and a likely source of great profit for us.'

Catherine Stannard stood, folded her arms, and pouted.

'But those voyages take many months, Tom! Years, perchance! I will have to live as a spinster or a widow for all that time!'

He stood and went to the window. It was possible to see the mastheads of the ships in the harbour, and to hear the cries of the seabirds and those who worked the quays. He struggled to suppress the guilt he felt within. Yes, he was condemning Catherine to the life once lived in convents, but how would he, Thomas Stannard, endure so long a time in the company of men alone? He prayed that he would be strong, and not tempted into the most grievous of sins. The sin he had fallen into once, a very long time before.

Finally, he turned, crossed the room, and took his wife in his arms.

'We have weeks, mayhap months, before you become anything akin to a spinster or a widow, Catherine Stannard. Ample time for me to give you enough memories to make that tolerable.' He kissed her.

'Memories, Thomas Stannard?' She smiled. 'Memories of what, pray?'

He cupped her breasts, then began to undo the ties of her kirtle.

'Let me show you,' he said.

Six

There was a popular saying in the alehouses of Dunwich. 'There are no mountains in Suffolk,' some wit or other would comment, gravely, before pausing for effect. 'None, at any rate, but Goodwife Jennet Stannard.'

This was always certain to raise a hearty laugh among those assembled, no matter how many times they had heard it before, and even if they were still relatively sober. Some, including the lady in question, had accused Meg de Andrade of coining the jibe, but Meg always kept an entirely straight face and said nothing.

Whatever the truth of that matter, there could be no disputing another truth, namely that mountains tended not to move. In that, Jennet Stannard lived up to the jest at her expense. Since the growth of her girth and bosom, occasioned by six births and an unfailing liking for the largest cuts, she had rarely ventured beyond the Palesdyke. She, who had once gone frequently to London to visit her cousin Sir George Barne when he was an alderman and then Lord Mayor, now rarely ventured even as far as Blythburgh market. That being so, Meg boggled at the intelligence brought to her by Francis Birkes, who had overheard it in the Pelican in its Piety. Her stepmother had hired a particularly well-appointed cart, this being intended to carry her to the great Bungay fair, a good three-hour journey from Dunwich.

Curious.

Meg thanked God for another undoubted truth about mountains: namely, that if ever they should attempt to move, it was well-nigh impossible for them to do so discreetly. She also thanked her father for his foresight in teaching her to ride. It meant she felt no qualms about hiring a horse to carry her to Bungay and back, recruiting an eager Hugh Ebbes as her escort. Thus equipped, she rode out of Dunwich by way of St James Street, passing the now ruinous leper hospital where her grandfather had spent his last years, and made for the ancient road through the Westwood to Blythburgh, and thence north-west to Bungay.

–

Jack Stannard made enquiries after the man he sought at the Steelyard, but the Germans of the Hanse League who congregated there looked at him as though he were mad. One, though, was a little friendlier than the rest, and finally directed Jack to Queenhythe Dock. He walked the short distance west along the Thames by way of the quays, feeling more at home there than he did in Aldgate Street and the other environs of Will's house. This was his world. Although only small craft usually plied here, just upstream of London Bridge, the grey-brown river was full of activity. Barges were being loaded or unloaded at the wharves, while others waited in the stream to take their place. Sailors and dock workers bawled at each other in a score of tongues. On the quays and wharves, the smells of tar, pitch, oil and dead fish pervaded all. Out in the middle of the river, though, very different craft plied back and forth. The familiar skiffs of the Watermen's Company carried important men – and the occasional important woman – upstream and downstream, between Westminster and the City. There were also a few private barges, splendidly gilded and adorned with flags, carrying the even more important where they pleased.

Jack came at last to Queenhythe, the old dock close by St James Garlickhythe. Ahead, the huge walls and towers of Baynard Castle loomed above all. There were several vessels within Queenhythe, but he sought the largest, a foreign caravel that must have struggled to get through the bridge.

'Ho, there!' he cried. The ship, heeled hard against the quayside, appeared to be deserted. There were several large holes in the inboard, larboard side of the hull, sealed temporarily by tarpaulins. 'Ho, I say! I seek one Bruno Cabral!'

There was no response. Jack boarded the ship, and repeated his call once again. Finally, there was a rustling below decks, then a head emerged into daylight. Jack assumed at first that the man must have been coated in tar. It took him a moment to realise that it was not so; that this, in truth, was the fellow's natural skin.

'Cabral?'

'Who seeks him?'

The black man's voice was a deep growl, his English nearly perfect but with a strong Portuguese accent.

'I am John Stannard. Are you Cabral?'

The man climbed up fully onto the deck. He was of the same height as Jack, but far more strongly built, his shoulders broad and square. His shirtless chest bore the scars of ancient wounds.

'I am Bruno Santos Cabral. John Stannard, then. So you are the man Senhor Halliday spoke of. The man who sails for Guinea with Hawkins. The man I was told to expect.'

'I was told you are a good pilot for those waters, and for the crossing of the ocean if it comes to it.'

Cabral was looking Jack up and down, as though assessing a horse at a market. 'You were told right.'

'And you are willing to take the voyage?'

Cabral shrugged. 'Your Senhor Halliday offers generous terms. And as you see, my ship will not be earning money for a long time. So yes, I am willing.'

'And you can ride? My ship is at Plymouth, but Master Halliday will arrange post horses for us. We can be there in three days if you can ride, longer if you cannot.'

'I can ride.'

Although entirely different in appearance, and far less garrulous, Bruno Santos Cabral somehow reminded Jack of a Genoese he had once sailed with, Valente by name. There was a certain air of confidence about such men, some strange alchemical force that they exuded.

'Good. Then you will break bread with me at the Three Cranes, that we may know each other better?'

'I will not.'

Jack was taken aback by the man's directness and apparent disregard for civilities. Perhaps, though, this was a Portuguese fashion; he had encountered very few of that nation before that moment.

'Why, in God's name, if we are to spend days together upon the road and months together upon the ocean?'

For the first time, Bruno Cabral smiled. 'Exactly that, Senhor Stannard. If we are to spend days together upon the road, then months together in the same hull, we will have ample time to come to know each other better, I think.'

Beneath the town's churches and the ruins of its castle, Bungay's water meadows were full of cattle. There had to be thousands of the beasts, their cries and stench overwhelming all else. Meg de Andrade had never seen so many animals in one place, but neither had she seen so many Scotsmen. The drovers who had brought the cattle down from the north, from some benighted place named Galloway, were everywhere, filling the taverns, carousing in the streets, spending their new-found money at the countless stalls that filled every open space in the town. Not a few aimed lewd suggestions in Meg's direction, but she laughed off most of them, and the ferocious countenance of Hugh Ebbes deterred the rest.

They stabled their horses at a large inn by one of the churches, and went inside for a jug of ale and some cheese to recover themselves after the long journey. Meg had little fear of being detected by her prey; her stepmother's bulk meant that she would be seen long before she could see, while her escort, Meg's vapid half-brother Ned, would never leave his mother's side, her very existence seeming to depend on the presence of an attendant who could listen to her incessant complaints and be ordered about at her every whim. That role was usually occupied by the youngest of the half-siblings, Mary, but she was confined at Dunwich by a bad summer cold. Meg had not offered to treat her.

'You go south along the river, then work your way back into the town,' Meg said to Ebbes. 'I shall do the same to the north.'

'It might not be easy to find you, goodwife, the throng being so great,' said Ebbes.

He was evidently revelling at being in the presence, and the confidence, of the most eligible widow in Dunwich. Like every other man of the town, too, he knew precisely how things stood between Meg de Andrade and her step-mother.

'No fear of that, Hugh, for you'll have all the time you need to find me. She doesn't run like a hound, after all, so like as not she'll be in the same place where you spy her for some time afterward.'

Ebbes smiled, and attempted to engage Meg in pleasantries that might further his hopeless cause, but she had ears only for the old Scots drover just across the room, who was declaiming to all who would listen that the Queen of Scots had miscarried of twins in her island prison, then been deposed by her Protestant lords and forced to sign an instrument of abdication. Her lover, Bothwell, the Duke of Orkney, had fled the country, and was said to be in Denmark. Thus it seemed that Scotland had a new king, James the Sixth, a babe in arms, with the Protestant lords in true control of the kingdom.

Meg frowned. This was not what she wanted to hear. If the Doom of Dunwich was to be brought out of its hiding place and raised high once again, signifying the return of the true faith to England, then this Mary had to be England's queen. By hereditary right, and in the eyes of God, she already was, by undoubted and legitimate descent from Harry the Seventh, the woman now known as Queen Elizabeth being naught but the bastard of the Boleyn whore, conceived in a sinful state of bigamy. But Meg, like almost all of the very many in England who thought that way, knew well enough to keep her thoughts on the subject very private indeed.

Instead, those thoughts returned to the more immediate task. She realised that Ebbes was still prattling, so she cut him short as amiably as she could, and they left to commence their search, taking different directions once outside the tavern.

As a child, Meg had always loved fairs. Every year, she insisted on being taken to the great horse fair at Halesworth. But it was at Halesworth fair, eight years ago, that her Luis, who seemed to have no more than a cold, fell to the ground at her feet and was dead even before she could stoop down to touch him, aged no more than twenty-four. She had not gone to a fair since. Walking through the crowded streets of Bungay, though, and being part of a large, happy crowd, brought back memories of better days. She even bought a sweetmeat and ate it lustily.

An hour passed, and she began to curse herself. Her stepmother could have perfectly legitimate reasons for being in Bungay, after all; had she not talked of grazing more cattle on Dunwich cliff? If so, she had to buy them somewhere, and there was no better place than this. And did not cousins of hers own land hereabouts? What, too, if by mischance, Ned spied Meg before she spied him, unlikely though that might be? While riding from Dunwich, she had prepared a tale of an assignation with Philip Grimes, just in case. But that sounded feeble beyond measure, he being in Norwich, or so she believed, with no possible cause to come to Bungay. Such a tale might placate Ned, but Jennet Stannard would see through it in an instant—

The very thought of the name seemed to conjure the presence of her stepmother. Meg saw her from a distance, waddling like a vast duck, with Ned at her side. They were moving away from the crowds, heading up an empty alleyway. Meg swiftly crossed the road and followed them. Memories came to her of endless games of hide-and-seek with her brother Tom in the streets and lanes of Dunwich. Despite her height, Meg had always been excellent at hiding and remaining undetected. Tom, exasperated, sometimes accused her of being in league with witches, who spirited her away to their realm.

Her brother and stepmother emerged from the alley and disappeared. Meg hurried to the end and peered cautiously round the corner. Strange: the two had separated. Ned appeared to be making for an alehouse on the other side of a patch of open ground, while Jennet was moving slowly towards the vast building that dominated this part of the town. It was a castle, the walls decayed and ivy-clad. Entire towers had collapsed into piles of rubble that no man had ever bothered to clear. The ancient place seemed to be entirely empty.

Jennet Stannard walked between the double drum towers of the gatehouse and disappeared from sight. Perhaps, Meg thought, she had gone to a hidden place to answer a call of nature, although the notion of the mountain squatting and then being able to rise again unaided seemed beyond all comprehension.

There was a movement – yes, a man, coming toward the gatehouse from the other direction.

Her stepmother with a lover, and a much younger one too? It was an even more unlikely notion than that of the mountain pissing in the ruins of a castle. But if Meg could prove adultery, and persuade her father to put the bitch aside...

The man was closer now, and Meg realised that his face was familiar. For a moment, she struggled to place it.

Then she did, and felt a cold chill run down her spine.

Stephen Raker.

The first time she'd seen him, at Aldeburgh fair, his significance was not explained to her. His was a face to register, she was told, and to be wary of. But gradually, over the years, she'd wheedled more and more of the story out of her father and her grandfather, the last leper of Dunwich.

Stephen Raker, sometime bailiff of Southwold, one of the most ardent advocates of overturning the ancient privileges of Dunwich so that Southwold might rise in its stead.

Stephen Raker, the man who had tried more than once to kill her father, believing him guilty of the judicial murder of the man whom Raker had always, but erroneously, believed to be his father.

Stephen Raker, Jack Stannard's secret brother.

Her uncle.

She was suddenly aware of a movement behind her, turned, and looked into a familiar face.

'Hello, sister,' said Ned Stannard.

Seven

The mystery fleet came into Plymouth Sound upon a strong south-westerly breeze, its course set directly north-east, heading for the Cobbler Channel and Cattewater. In truth, Tom Stannard reflected as he watched its progress, the only mystery about it was its purpose; its identity was clear enough. The flags and pennants streaming from its staffs and mastheads were well known to all English seafarers. They were the colours of the Spanish Nether-lands, so this was one of the many fleets that belonged to Philip, King of Spain and erstwhile King of England. But those colours should have dipped in salute to the St George's flag flying from the gun battery on St Nich-olas Island, and they did not. So the English squadron, anchored in the mouth of Cattewater, was watching anxiously, guns already primed. Tom stood upon the high poop deck of the flagship, the vast and ancient royal warship *Jesus of Lubeck*, one of two dozen or so men who attended the admiral, John Hawkins. He kept a consider-able distance from Hawkins' kinsman, Francis Drake.

'They know the law of the sea,' said Hawkins, gruffly. 'They know they must salute the queen's flag. So why do they ignore it? I ask. Do they think they can insult us so, in our own waters?'

'Mayhap they intend to attack us,' said Drake, casually.

His words brought a stunned silence to the deck of the *Jesus*. Men looked at each other and shook their heads. It was an impossible thought. England and Spain were at peace, and they were on an English ship, in an English fleet, in an English harbour. But, much as he resented Drake, Tom Stannard admitted to himself that he could see no other possible explanation for the oncoming fleet's strange course.

For his part, Hawkins crossed to the ship's rail, raising a hand to indicate that he wished to be alone. For two or three minutes, he stared out at the Spanish fleet. Then he turned back to address his men.

'Run out larboard batteries on *Jesus* and *Minion*! Break out half-pikes, bills, swords and arquebuses! Clear for battle!'

Trumpets sounded, drums beat, men ran to their stations and took hold of weapons as they were brought up from the armoury below decks. Edward Dudley, a gruff old soldier who commanded the other soldiers, ordered his men into position. Below decks, there was a colossal din as gunports were heaved open and the great culverins of the *Jesus* were run out. Tom had heard that in any sort of a sea, the huge ship was a nightmare – slow, crank and leaky. But none of that mattered in the Cattewater anchorage. Lying at single anchor, her larboard beam to the approaching enemy as the tide flooded, she was a formidable floating fort, and the same was true of the *Minion*, the smaller royal warship also loaned to the Hawkins expedition by the queen. For a moment, Tom considered the possibility of returning to the *Jennet*, but she had only just come off the careen and was still a good half-mile up the Plym. No, the business would be done here, at the entrance to Plymouth's harbour. He drew his sword and awaited the Spaniards.

Still the Flemish ships came on. They were now well within sight of the St George's flags flying from the southern ramparts of Plymouth Castle, high on the hill above Lambhay, and from the mastheads of Hawkins' ships. But there was still no lowering of their own colours, no acknowledgement of the Queen of England's right to such a mark of respect in her own waters.

Aboard the *Jesus*, men offered up prayers, all the while holding firmly to their weapons. For his part, Tom prayed for the queen, his wife, his sons, his father and his sister. Then he looked intently at Hawkins, trying to imagine what he would do if he were in the admiral's position.

Hawkins was staring at the bows of the leading Spanish ship, judging distances. Then, very slowly, he raised his sword.

'Upon my command, master gunner!' he shouted.

Another wait. Tom counted to ten, and then again—

'Give fire!' cried Hawkins.

The larboard culverins of the *Jesus* roared out, followed a few moments later by those of the *Minion*. Tom had never experienced a broadside from a great man-of-war before. The noise seemed louder than the mightiest thunder he had ever known. Despite its colossal size, the hull of the *Jesus* shook as the cannon recoiled, and the entire ship seemed to move bodily to starboard. Then the cloud of smoke enveloped him. But just before it did so, he saw splashes from the ship's hail of shot spout from the sea, no more than a few dozen yards ahead of the most vanward Spaniard's bow.

The broadside seemed to have no effect whatsoever. The Spanish ships still came on, seemingly intent on sailing straight into the inner harbour and destroying Hawkins' squadron.

Tom watched as the guns were reloaded and run out again, men shouting, officers barking orders. Once again Hawkins raised his sword, judged the distance, and waited for his moment. Then—

'Give fire!'

The culverins of the *Jesus* and the *Minion* roared out once more. This time, though, there was a clear difference in the result. When the gun smoke finally rolled away from the deck of the *Jesus*, Tom saw several holes in the hulls of the leading Spanish ships, and tears in some of the sails.

The next broadside, if there was one, would be a killing affair. But it was not to be. The vanward Spanish ship hoisted a signal flag, loosened its sails, and began to alter course, luffing up towards St Nicholas Island. The entire fleet behind it followed suit. As they turned, the ships furled their topsails and lowered their flags.

The Spanish fleet was finally saluting England, and England's admiral, John Hawkins.

—

The Spanish fleet came to an anchor between Mill Bay and St Nicholas Island, well to the west of Cattewater, and a longboat soon cast off from its flagship. In addition to its crew, it bore three men, one of whom, by his dress, was evidently some sort of high dignitary. Hawkins, meanwhile, donned his best clothes, and lined up two files of soldiers and sailors armed with pikes and arquebuses, clad in tunics bearing the royal arms, in the waist of the *Jesus*, in an impressive show of martial might. Tom Stannard and other officers and gentlemen of the expedition massed upon the quarterdeck, looking down upon the Spanish emissary as he came aboard. Hawkins' personal trumpeter, standing by the admiral's side and attired in a splendid tabard, sounded a brief call, and the files of soldiers and sailors came to attention with a crash of arms. Hawkins himself, though, turned away and walked a few paces, entirely ignoring the emissary.

The Spaniard, his face a mask of rage, made directly for the English commander, all diplomatic niceties evidently forgotten.

'Hawkins,' he said loudly, and in good English, 'what is the meaning—'

He was cut off by the trumpeter, who sounded a shrill note. The sound stopped the Spaniard in his tracks, but it was also the cue for Hawkins to turn and advance. His face, if anything, was even more furious than that of his guest.

'Baron Wathen, Lord of Campveer,' he said, 'you dare to complain of England's welcome? What fleet is this, and why does it disturb Queen Elizabeth's peace? Why did you ignore the normal courtesies of the salute? Why did you sail on, as though to attack these, the queen's ships of her own Navy Royal, lying in the queen's own harbour?'

Edward Dudley, dressed in half-armour and standing next to Tom, leaned over and whispered to him. The younger Stannard had gone drinking with Dudley on two occasions since his father had gone to London; the amiable old soldier had a fund of entertaining stories, even if he was rather too fond of stressing his alleged distant kinship to the queen's favourite, Robert Dudley, Earl of Leicester.

'Campveer's a Fleming,' Dudley said. 'He and Hawkins know each other of old. No love lost, if you ask me.'

Tom nodded. He could see the Flemish admiral's bluster falling away from his face with every second that passed. Even so, he rallied, and essayed a response to his English counterpart's onslaught.

'I disturb no peace, John Hawkins! My fleet is at sea to meet His Majesty the Catholic King himself, who at this very moment is upon a voyage from Spain to Flanders. We sought merely to take refuge from the inclement weather in a friendly harbour.'

Hawkins stared at the Lord of Campveer, then turned away again, made another walk of a few paces, and turned back once more. If anything, his face was even redder than before.

'What do you take me for, Baron? Do you take me for a landsman, or even for some tavern wench that does not know east from west? I can read the elements as well as you, and I have had kinsmen at sea this very morning, out fishing far beyond Eddystone. This is not weather to make a fleet seek refuge in harbour, Lord of Campveer! This is nothing to trouble the rawest lubber, let alone men like you and I, who have sailed these seas all our lives!'

'I... I—'

'*No*, Baron! It is a fiction! And your tale of King Philip being at sea – I name that a fiction too, sir! If the king had sailed, do you not think that Plymouth would have heard of it long before now? And I know the king, Baron. I served him, when he was the king here. He was my master. No man loves King Philip more than I. But I tell you this. He has sent Alba to Flanders, so why in God's name would he also go there himself?'

Edward Dudley nudged Tom.

'Hawkins served Philip?' said the old soldier. 'I had not heard that. He has not told me that. Is it true?'

Tom nodded, for this was a tale he had heard from his wife, Hawkins' kinswoman.

'It is. At the time of his marriage to the late Queen Mary, and afterwards too. But see, Wathen did not know that either.'

The Flemish admiral attempted to cover his confusion. 'But I maintain, Captain Hawkins, that to open fire upon the ships of a friendly nation—'

Hawkins stepped closer to Wathen and bawled directly into his face. 'As I would open fire upon the ships of any nation that showed such flagrant disrespect to the queen's flag in these, her own waters! I say you know the time-honoured custom of the sea well enough, Lord of Campveer. So why did you not salute, eh? Why did you not salute the queen's flag until my culverins compelled you to?'

Wathen of Campveer said nothing. Hawkins stood close in front of him, staring directly into his eyes, but still Wathen was silent. Then the English admiral smiled, turned on his heel, and signalled to his trumpeter, who struck up the familiar notes of the glorious old Agincourt hymn. Hawkins went below, and Baron Wathen, Lord of Campveer, admiral of Flanders, was left to make a shamefaced departure from the deck of the *Jesus*.

–

Later, in his large and well-appointed cabin, Hawkins held a council with his captains and other officers. In truth, it was less of a council and more of a celebration, with wine, ale and laughter in abundance. Hawkins even had his personal band playing jaunty tunes, while his pages, including his own nephew Paul and a small, serious black boy, went around the cabin, refilling goblets and tankards. The admiral moved easily through the company, and he came at last to Tom Stannard.

'Well then, cousin Thomas,' he said, 'what did you make of it, eh? More drama in a day in Plymouth than Suffolk's shore has seen in a century, I'll wager.'

'True, no doubt, cousin Hawkins. But what was it all for? What was Wathen about?'

Hawkins smiled, but it was a bitter, reflective smile.

'I told him I knew King Philip, and I did not lie in that. So I know exactly what Wathen was about, as I was telling Frank Drake just now. Someone discovered the true purpose of our voyage – at a guess, de Silva, the Spanish ambassador, although who informed him is quite another matter. Of course, he informed the king, and Philip, being the man he is, would not hesitate. Wathen's fleet was sent to destroy us in harbour before we could sail, before we could become any sort of threat to Spain's monopoly of the American trade. No doubt about it, Tom Stannard. But their intelligence was incomplete, for they did not know we had brought *Jesus* and *Minion* around from the Medway. They could not have expected our broadsides, so when he saw such great ships in the Cattewater, and when we opened fire, Wathen must have known that Philip's little scheme had failed. All he could do then was to try to bluff, bluster and lie. But, of course, it could not conceal his responsibility for the failure. His pride's responsibility, at any rate.'

'His pride? How so?'

'The Achilles heel of all Spaniards, even Flemish ones – they taught the story of Achilles and his heel in Suffolk? Good. But yes, his pride. Consider this, Tom Stannard. If Wathen's ships had furled topsails and dipped their flags to the battery on St Nicholas Island, we would have had no cause to suspect them. I would not have ordered our batteries to be manned and the crews to be armed. They could have sailed straight into Cattewater and blasted every one of our ships into driftwood. But no, Spanish pride meant they saw no need to salute a flag they were about to attack. And that, my friend, gave us as sure a warning as if King Philip himself had written me a letter setting out his intentions.'

'But why should the king wish to do such a thing, thus risking a war with our queen? Just what is the true purpose of our voyage, cousin Hawkins?'

John Hawkins tapped his nose with his finger.

'In good time. Remember, Wathen and his ships lie just across the bay. Even now, his spies might be swimming under the stern, listening for careless talk.'

With that, John Hawkins patted Tom on the shoulder and went off to talk to the mayor of Plymouth.

Eight

Jack Stannard and Bruno Cabral rode through the Coxside gate of Plymouth, straight into the main body of a frantic hue and cry. Men, some armed and helmeted, were running up and down the streets of the town, hammering on doors, searching alleyways, shouting and bawling. At first, Jack thought there must have been a murder; surely nothing else could have drawn such a throng. Just then, though, he spotted a vaguely familiar face whom he recognised as one of Hawkins' under-officers. This fellow recognised Jack in turn.

'Ho, Mark Willis!' cried Jack. 'What's afoot here?'

'Cap'n Stannard. You've not heard, then?' Willis looked suspiciously at Cabral.

'I've been on the road from London these four days.'

'Aye, well, the two Portingals have vanished. Killed, some say, but the admiral says they've fled.'

At the mention of the English word for his countrymen, Cabral looked up. 'Portuguese? Which Portuguese?' he demanded.

But Jack knew.

'The two who proposed the expedition in the first place?'

'Aye,' said Willis, 'them.'

'These Portuguese,' said Cabral. 'What were their names?'

84

Jack had passed on to his new companion as much information as Walsingham had told him, namely that the Hawkins expedition had been instigated by two Portuguese merchant adventurers, who'd come to England with a scheme for trading upon the Guinea coast in contravention of the monopoly granted to Portugal by the treaty of Tordesillas. Walsingham never mentioned their names, and despite Cabral's curiosity, Jack could tell him no more.

'One was Luis, I think,' said Willis. 'The other had a strange name – started with H, though.'

Cabral shook his head. 'Antonio Luis and Andre Homem,' he said. 'These were the men responsible for this expedition? These?'

Willis nodded.

'*Filho da puta*. Then I must see your Admiral Hawkins. At once, Jack Stannard.'

An hour later, in the great cabin of the *Jesus*, John Hawkins listened in silence to Cabral's words.

'Luis and Homem,' said the Portingal. 'I met them, what, five, six times? Yes, they were merchants, but not men of good reputation. They made enemies in Lisbon, and were forced to leave there. They claimed to know the Guinea coast – above all, to know where to find gold mines. They took their story to the regent, the Cardinal Enrique, but he laughed them out of court. Then they went to the French, who sent out an expedition, but that got no further than fighting a feeble battle with the garrison on Madeira. So they went to the court of King Philip, where again they got short shrift. So, at last, they came to England. Is that the tale they spun to you, Admiral Hawkins? The tale of the gold upon the Guinea coast?'

The normally confident John Hawkins was quiet and glum.

'I always suspected them,' he said, slowly. 'I've sailed to Guinea twice, and talked to enough men there to know that these tales of gold mines somewhere just beyond the coast are naught but dreams. But to some of our merchants in London, and to some of those about the court – even to the queen herself – a tale like that was irresistible. They needed an admiral who knew the coast, so behold, your humble servant.'

'More fool England, then,' said Cabral, sharply.

Hawkins, normally so vocal in defence of his native land, was silent, even shamefaced.

'There's no trace of them?' said Jack.

'None,' said Hawkins. 'They don't know the land, and would be found easily upon the roads. But they were flush with gold generously advanced them by some of our sponsors, so I reckon they paid some shipmaster or fisherman to take them over to Brittany. I always sensed they never wanted to come on the voyage, and now I see why.'

'Their bluff would be called,' said Jack.

'As you say.'

'Then surely the voyage can't proceed?'

Hawkins looked at Jack, then at Cabral. For the first time during the interview, there was a ghost of a smile upon his lips.

'Oh, it can proceed, all right. Not with the same purpose, it's true. There'll be no gold mines, for sure. But there's another purpose that might yet satisfy all those so-great men who've invested money in this. More than satisfy them, God willing. But if that's to happen, gentlemen, I must write a difficult letter. Aye, a very difficult letter. A letter to the queen.'

—

The beginning of autumn in Dunwich was heralded by another great storm, which swept in from the east, rattling window shutters, blowing down a crumbling wall in the ruins of Blackfriars, and taking another few inches from the cliff in St Peter's parish. Meg de Andrade sat in her cottage in its hollow upon the heath, listening to the wind howling, moving a little nearer to her fire, and praying that her thatch held. It was markedly difficult to concentrate on reading *In Praise of Folly*. In any case, she had one ear alert for the elusive sound that some swore they heard on nights such as this, and that she was convinced she had heard often in her childhood, and even sometimes since. It was the sound of distant bells, tolling a lament. Every man, woman and child in Dunwich would swear upon the Bible that they had heard them, and that they were the bells of the town's drowned churches, still ringing out beneath the waves that had overwhelmed them long ago.

But that night, Meg could not hear even the faintest trace of a toll upon the storm. Perhaps, in the heretical realm of the usurper Elizabeth, the submerged bells of Catholic Dunwich no longer rang out. Instead, she stared into her fire, and began to reflect upon other things.

It had been the strangest of summers since that day at Bungay fair. Her stepmother had said nothing to her. Was Ned really so stupid that he had accepted her unlikely tale of a clandestine meeting with Philip Grimes, and then acceded to Meg's entreaties not to tell his mother? Was he even privy to the knowledge that Jennet Stannard had met with Stephen Raker, the sworn enemy of both the Stannard family and the borough of Dunwich? True, in recent weeks there had been angry looks and barbed remarks aplenty from her stepmother and her familiar, Meg's half-sister Mary, but there was nothing new or strange in any of that. Ned had continued to make a half-hearted effort to learn about the Stannard accounts, presumably at Jennet's insistence, for he gave no sign of it being of his own volition.

Meg had written of all this to her father, but he seemed to show little interest, even in the strange meeting between his wife and his murderous half-brother. But then, Jack Stannard would not be returning to Dunwich, as Meg and the entire town had expected. Instead, he would be setting out on a lengthy and perhaps dangerous voyage to distant lands, by way of unknown seas, and Tom would be going with him. God knew how long they would be gone. Meg de Andrade prided herself that she depended upon no man, but even so, she felt a certain unease that her father and her brother would be so far away, and for such a time.

There was an even louder gust of wind. Meg laid aside *In Praise of Folly*, tightened her grip on her rosary, and began to mutter the *Ave Maria* again.

Her father had left clear instructions that in his and Tom's absence, the management of the family affairs would devolve upon her. This was all well and good, she thought, but with the two of them gone for many months, if not longer, that management might become uncertain. Ned was no threat, but his oldest brother George was a very different case; almost since the day of his birth, he had been a ferociously intelligent but devious little cub, so it was no surprise that he had shown a considerable aptitude for the law, and was even now completing his studies at the Middle Temple in London. If George needed a strong arm, it might be provided by his other brother, Harry, a soldier and member of the Yeomen of the Guard, the personal escort to the queen. Add to the mixture Goodwife Jennet's mysterious dealings with Stephen Raker, and Meg sensed the brewing of a particularly noxious potion.

A thought struck her. It was laughable and immodest, perhaps even treasonable, but once it entered her head, she could not drive it out.

Were Mary of Scotland and her bastard cousin Elizabeth really so very different from Meg herself? Of course, their stations were far more exalted – better skirts, for one thing – but they, too, were solitary women, contending against the schemes of other women and above all of men, many of whom believed that it was unnatural for a mere woman to bear any authority at all.

Meg recalled that, when she was a child, she had often imagined herself as a queen. Well, in one sense, perhaps that was exactly what she had become.

As the wind rose higher still, she began to laugh at the thought. She laughed louder and louder, as though in competition with the storm, and finally tears of mirth flowed, emulating the torrents of rainwater spilling from her roof.

–

The easterly storm that battered Dunwich was no more than a strong breeze by the time it reached Plymouth, making it an ideal wind to carry the fleet to sea. The *Jesus of Lubeck* led the way, her profusion of flags and pennants making a proud show as she sailed out through the Cobbler Channel. Her fore- and aftercastles towered high above the water, and with all sails set upon her four masts, she gave at least an outward illusion of raw power. Immediately astern of her was the *Minion* – older, smaller, but still warlike enough. Then came the *William and John*, the largest of Hawkins' own ships; or rather, his family's ships, for it bore the names of himself and his trusted brother. The *Swallow* was not long returned from the Guinea coast, and was now returning there, with the smallest of the Hawkins ships, the bark *Judith*, following in her wake. Whatever John Hawkins had written to the queen, and whatever her reply had been, the expedition was under way at last.

Last of all, the *Jennet* of Dunwich edged out of Catte-water. As she caught the breeze off the land, Tom Stannard ordered more and more sail set. His father was well content to leave such decisions and commands to his son, for in many respects, Tom was the better ship handler, as he had demonstrated during the storm off Ushant, and Jack was shrewd enough to admit it. Bruno Cabral stood alongside Tom, learning the feel of the ship in anticipation of the distant waters where he would be in charge of her navigation.

For his part, Jack leaned on the starboard rail, watching the familiar sights of Plymouth falling away one by one. There were tiny, distant figures upon the Hoe, too far away to be distinguishable, but Jack knew their number would include Catherine and his two grandsons. He wondered whether he would ever see them, or England itself, again. Once again, he felt the nagging doubt that came to him often in his dreams, and almost as often in his waking hours. Were it not for Francis Walsingham's secret instructions, there would be no need at all for Jack to be on this voyage. Tom was more than capable of commanding, especially with Cabral at his side; and Jack knew that if he really wished not to sail, it would be an easy matter for Will Halliday to convince Walsingham that Tom Stannard would make just as dependable an informant as his father. Jack was an old man, nearly fifty, with aches in his bones that had not been there three or four years before, and although he could still stand a watch, so could a dozen or more younger men in the *Jennet*'s crew, especially Hal Ashby, who was likely to be a shipmaster in his own right in three or four years' time. Jack would be consuming victuals and occupying space, essentially out of nothing more than vanity – his urge to see the strange, fabled shores of Guinea and the Americas.

Then there was the other issue, the one he had spent weeks attempting to dismiss from his mind: Meg's intelligence that his wife had met with Stephen Raker. A part of Jack chided himself for not returning to Dunwich to get to the bottom of the matter, but he could not believe it amounted to anything. Jennet might be many things, but surely not even she would dare to conspire with Jack's greatest enemy against the interests of their family. Besides, Meg was clever – by far the cleverest woman Jack Stannard had ever known – and resourceful, and more than capable of handling her stepmother.

Whether she was capable of handling Stephen Raker might be another question entirely, though. A notion suddenly occurred to Jack. Had he dismissed the problem of his errant wife and Stephen Raker because his urge to be upon the voyage overrode all other things? Was it a form of madness, which had made him ignore what should have been his principal concern? Had he made the most dreadful mistake of his life?

That was the troubling thought in Jack Stannard's mind as his very last sight of England's distant shore disappeared below the horizon.

Nine

The storm blew up when they were four days out of Plymouth. In its duration and intensity, it made that which the *Jennet* had encountered on her return from France seem like a gentle summer breeze. Worse yet, it arrived very suddenly, little more than a half-glass separating relative calm from a potentially ship-killing gale. Sheets of water lashed across the deck. The ship pitched, yawed, and rolled, the timbers screaming and creaking in protest. Thunder that was surely loud enough to herald the apocalypse shook the skies, and jagged bolts of lightning rent the heavens. The wind played the shrouds like the strings of an impossibly loud, shrieking lute, the sails beating like its accompanying drum.

'Reef the foresail!' barked Jack, his face stung by the howling wind and dagger-like rain. 'Take in all other sail! Faster, lads, in the name of God! Make all fast! Make fast, I say!'

As he shouted his commands, he tied a rope around his waist and secured the other end to the mizzen mast. Instinctively, but very quietly, he began to murmur the *Ave Maria*, confident that Cabral, the only man near him, would not be able to hear. But even in such extremity, it would be better to be careful. He fell silent, but still said the prayer in his mind.

Below decks, Tom ran backward and forward, bawling commands to double-lash the guns, ordering spare men to man the pumps. All along the hull, on both sides, he knelt down, feeling the caulking, checking for any leaks. The *Jennet* was a fairly new ship, well built by Dunwich men whom he had known since his childhood. God willing, she was secure, and would remain so.

Confident that all was in order below decks, he returned above. The moment he emerged from the hatch, he was knocked from his feet by a brute of a wave. The roll of the ship sent him sprawling across the sodden deck. He could see the wale approaching, and beyond it the grey wall of the sea and oblivion...

He reached out with both arms, but there was nothing – then his right hand caught a rope that had not been made fast, and he clung to it for dear life. The hull began to roll the other way, and Tom lifted himself, catching the horrified expression on his father's face as he did so. The son had barely escaped the fate that the father had only just avoided off Ushant.

'The boats, Father!' cried Tom as he reached Jack.

'I know. But great God, what can we do?'

Tom looked astern. The *Jennet*'s longboat and pinnace, being towed behind the ship, were being tossed like corks upon the fearsome waves. One moment they rode high upon the crests, as though they were trying to leap into the sky like seabirds; the next, they plunged down into the depths. Every wave threatened death to the two men that each boat contained. The storm had struck so suddenly that there had been no time to haul them in, especially when the priority had to be securing the ship itself.

Tom stared out. The four men in the boats were good men. Dunwich men. Philip Holt, the coxswain of the longboat, was a friend from his childhood. Tom had courted his sister and might well have asked for her hand, had she not died of griping of the guts, aged eighteen, despite Meg's best efforts to save her.

'Starboard the helm, two points!' he cried, although whether the *Jennet* really would come two points closer to the wind, God alone knew. 'Watch on deck, ease foresail, then stand by to come aft!'

The men huddled under a tarpaulin in the waist, just forward of Tom's position, emerged from their cover, grabbed the lifeline that led forward, and adjusted the foremast yard and running rigging. While Tom shouted orders for other men to come up from below, Jack remonstrated with his son.

'If we're too beam-on,' he bawled against the gale, 'then just one great wave—'

'I know, Father. I know as well as you. But I have faith in the *Jennet*, and in God.'

As the *Jennet* turned, even by the very slight amount that Tom had ordered, the waves crashed principally against her side, rather than the bow. While this made the ship roll even more violently, it created more of a lee, giving slightly calmer water to the two boats. That, in turn, gave the watch on deck a chance to haul on the tow ropes, Hal Ashby screaming 'Heave!' even as towering waves broke over them all.

Tom and Jack watched from the stern rail. The pinnace was nearer, and minute by minute, she came nearer still. The two men aboard, brothers named Garwood, waved their arms desperately, shouting words that were instantly carried away by the storm. But still the pinnace came closer. Tom took hold of a rope, secured one end to a stanchion, and braced himself to throw the line.

The first effort fell agonisingly short.

The second touched the bow of the boat, but the elder Garwood, scrambling forward, just failed to catch it.

The third throw was taken, and the rope made fast. The brothers, looking like a pair of creatures from the deep, hauled themselves up, and were helped aboard by their shipmates.

The longboat, though, was a different matter. Further astern to begin with, she was also less weatherly than the pinnace. With the latter cast loose, more men grabbed the longboat's tow rope, but the wind suddenly veered. Tom saw Philip Holt raise both arms heavenward, as though reaching out for some invisible lifeline, or else to implore God to welcome him into Heaven. In that moment, a wave crashed into the longboat, fully beam-on, and over-turned it. Tom thought he caught one last glimpse of Holt's hand, grasping desperately above the water, but then it was gone.

Tom gripped the ship's rail tightly. His father put a hand on his shoulder, then turned to shout to Hal Ashby and the men on the tow rope the order that Tom was incapable of giving.

'Belay!'

–

The fleet had scattered as soon as the storm began, its ships deliberately increasing the distance between each other to reduce the risk of collision. For a while, the lofty hull of the *Jesus* was still visible, swaying drunkenly upon the great waves. Jack could easily imagine the scene aboard:

the chain pumps working incessantly, the carpenter's crew toiling to seal the gaps as her caulking failed and leaks burst through the hull, the soldiers and gentlemen volunteers spewing copiously over the lower decks. She was a very old and very high ship that had never been built for seas such as these, and she rode them like a pig. As the last sight of the maintop of the flagship disappeared behind the towering waves, both Stannards wondered whether they would ever see her, or John Hawkins, again.

They had little time for such thoughts. The storm blew relentlessly for three days and three nights, the sea an unremitting cauldron of ferocious waves. Not an inch of the *Jennet* above decks was dry, and precious few inches below. With no work to be done on the sails, nor upon the upper deck, the men huddled below, trying but usually failing to find a relatively dry corner and to snatch a few moments of sleep until their next shift on the pumps came around. Jack and Tom took turns on deck, but in truth, there was little a ship's captain could do, either. There were no stars visible to navigate by, no other ships to avoid, no course to order other than that dictated by the screaming wind, but also, thankfully, no ship-killing coast within hundreds of miles. There was nothing for it but to run with the wind, praying that the storm would soon blow itself out.

Bruno Cabral came up on deck from time to time, and by the middle of the second day, the two Stannards were confident enough in him to let him stand watch alone, giving them both slightly longer sojourns below, in the relatively large cabin at the stern that the three of them shared. They developed a pattern: while one was on deck, a second attempted to sleep, while the third oversaw, and often assisted in, the back-breaking work at the pumps.

In the middle of the second night, Jack climbed to the upper deck, took a firm hold of the sodden lifeline, and made his way aft to relieve Cabral. There was no lessening of the storm. All around, thunder growled viciously. The ship still moved insanely in several directions at once, the masts creaking ominously, and the hull groaning in protest at the constant assault from the evil, white-crested waves, so much more frightening at night, like a mighty army of the dead ceaselessly battering at the walls of a castle.

Cabral greeted him with no more than a nod.

'No break?' shouted Jack, into the wind.

Looking about, he already knew the answer, but some part of him hoped that Cabral, who had sailed far more distant seas than any Stannard, might have detected just a hint of a change.

'None,' said the Portuguese.

'So be it. When you go below, say a prayer for us, Bruno Cabral.'

The taciturn Cabral nodded again, untied himself, took hold of the lifeline, and made to go forward. Then, he seemed to have a thought, and turned back to face Jack, leaning close to ensure he could be heard.

'You talk in your sleep, Jack Stannard,' he said. 'You say a name often – Alice. Now, I know Alice is not your wife. The ship is named for your wife, Jennet. But men in the crew have told me who Alice was, and I see how things stand. I had a wife, once. She died. You are a braver man than me, or a stronger, to take a second.'

'You choose a strange time and place to talk to me of my wives, Senhor Cabral,' bellowed Jack.

'Not strange,' said Cabral, who seemed not to need to raise his voice so much to be heard above the wind. 'Where else, and when else, can we know for certain we are not overheard? So I tell you this now, that you may think upon it. *Minha amigo*, it is not only Alice you name as you sleep. You mumble prayers – *Maria stella maris*, and others. Prayers in Latin. And I have seen you take out a paternoster and finger it when you think no man is looking. So I know that we share a faith, Jack Stannard. You may sail with heretics, and you may pretend to be a heretic, but in your heart, you are still loyal to Rome.'

Jack felt as though he had been struck down by one of the lightning flashes that lit the horizon. In that moment, the wind, rain and spray stinging his face meant nothing. He could say nothing. He thought he was so careful, that this was so secret…

Cabral looked at him steadily.

'You are safe, Jack Stannard. Bruno Cabral does not betray others. He certainly does not betray one of his own. *Dominus tecum*.'

He turned, and made his way below decks, leaving Jack to the storm and his thoughts.

You talk in your sleep, Jack Stannard.

Walsingham had known, or at least suspected, that Jack was still a Catholic at heart. But Jack was convinced that, before Bruno Cabral, only three living people could know that. Two were his son and his daughter; that was, his oldest son and firstborn daughter, Alice's children. But the third was the woman who had shared his bed in Dunwich until she became too vast to do so.

-

Just after midnight during the third night, Jack and Tom were on deck together. For an hour, they had been looking at each other, not daring to say a word, not daring to hope. Instead, they watched and listened, turning one way and then another, looking aloft and then astern. The sea was still a foaming swell, the ship still rolling and pitching as if set to overturn at any instant, but there was a difference.

It was Tom, younger and thus by nature more hopeful, who gave voice to both their thoughts.

'Easing, for certain, and backing northerly,' was all he said.

Jack made no reply, although he knew his son was right. Another hour, and every man on the ship knew it. For the first time in many hours, there were smiles below decks, and good humour. Men who had not eaten for days devoured a hearty repast of lyngs cod, poor john and stale bread, washed down with Plymouth beer. The *Jennet* moved just a little less violently, the wind blew a little less hard, the rain became gentler and then, praise God, intermittent. Cabral came up on deck, then a few of the bolder men from below, with Hal Ashby the first of them. Another turn of the glass followed before Cabral hesitantly and wordlessly pointed to the heavens. Jack and Tom followed the direction his finger pointed to, and the younger man actually grinned.

It was a star.

A little after dawn, with the blessed sun rising and starting to warm the larboard side, the *Jennet* became a true ship again, rather than a mere wooden ark wholly at the mercy of the wind and waves. Hal Ashby's whistle blew, men clambered up the standing rigging with a rare eagerness, the foresail was properly unfurled, and the other sails were set. The English ensign was broken out at the stern, although there was no ship within sight to see it. Lookouts went into the tops, but made no report. A clear and empty sea surrounded the *Jennet* all the way to the horizon.

The Stannards and Bruno Cabral held an impromptu conference on deck. Their view of the stars during the small hours had been too broken by the last clouds of the storm to enable clear fixes with their cross-staffs, but the general situation was clear enough: they were being blown southward upon a favourable breeze, and God willing, they would make landfall at the rendezvous set by Hawkins when the fleet was last assembled. Whether that fleet still existed was known only by—

'Sail ho!'

Ned Ashby, the young lookout in the crow's nest upon the main, had the keenest eyes on the ship.

'Where away?' cried Jack.

'Starboard quarter, ten leagues, maybe fifteen!'

The three men went to the ship's rail and strained their eyes toward the horizon. At first, the only thing apparent was a tiny shape in the very far distance. Slowly, though, it became clear that it was a ship, with distinguishable masts and sails.

'A Portingal or a Spaniard?' asked Tom.

'Too large to be a caravel,' said Cabral. 'Maybe a Spaniard, although she's too lofty for a galleon.'

'High-sided, for certain,' said Jack.

The courses of the two ships closed, and all the while, the Stannards' confidence rose. But it was young Ned Ashby, high in the maintop, who settled matters.

'She's breaking out her colours! It's... it's... aye, no doubt of it, it's the cross of St George!'

Cheering began on the deck of the *Jennet*. Tom Stannard punched the air, his father smiled, and Bruno

Cabral remained impassive, looking out intently at the vast, battered but fast-approaching hull of the *Jesus*.

Ten

'Tenerife,' said John Hawkins, standing at the highest point of the aftercastle of the *Jesus*. 'You know it?'

'I sailed here once, in sixty-two,' said Tom Stannard, standing beside him. 'I've been no further south nor west than this.'

'Aye, well, you'll better that by some way this time, cousin. If we survived that storm, and if we can find our other ships, then I think we can truthfully say that God smiles upon us, eh? They're not in Santa Cruz, though. I thought they would be. No matter. There are several good anchorages in these islands, so God willing, they'll have run into one of the others. Time, then, to think of hailing our friendly and generous hosts, Tom Stannard.'

The island ahead was mountainous, its highest peak topped with what looked to be a thick coat of snow. Cliffs and steep grey-green slopes rose from the sea to harsh black hills a little way inland. Other islands were in sight – Palma to the west and Grand Canary to the south-east, according to Bruno Cabral's charts – but it was for Tenerife that Hawkins conned the three ships of his fleet that had found each other thus far, the *Judith* having appeared three days before.

Before the fleet entered the bay of Santa Cruz, in the north-east corner of the island, Tom returned to the *Jennet* and found Cabral, who had been sailing these seas since childhood, with the watch on deck. Jack stood alongside him. Tom conveyed to his father Hawkins' instructions for anchoring, and Jack smiled.

'Our admiral is short on trust, then,' he said.

'He is right to be,' said Cabral. 'Spaniards. Never trust one of them, I say.'

As the English ships entered the bay of Santa Cruz, they dipped their ensigns and fired guns in salute to the red and yellow flag of Philip, King of Castile, Aragon, Mallorca, Sardinia, Naples, Sicily and Jerusalem, erstwhile King of England, duke and count of more territories than most men could enumerate. It was all perfectly correct, perfectly innocent, yet when the three vessels dropped anchor, they did so in positions where – entirely coincidentally, of course – they were masked from the fire of the Spanish gun batteries ashore by local merchant ships lying inshore of them.

The familiar process of sending boats ashore to replenish the fleet's water casks got under way immediately, and one of the boats from the *Jesus* also bore letters from Hawkins informing the governor of his entirely peaceable intentions and inviting old friends among the local merchants aboard for supper that evening; this became known to the Stannards on the *Jennet* because a boat also came across to them, requesting their presence. Thus it was that, a little after the bell was rung to mark the end of the second dog watch, Jack and Tom Stannard, attired in their best shirts and tunics, were rowed over to the flagship, leaving Cabral on watch in the *Jennet*.

Hawkins, it seemed, was already among friends, laughing uproariously in the midst of a half dozen Spaniards on the upper deck. The Stannards moved on in search of company, and found it with Robert Barrett, the sailing master of the *Jesus*, a stocky, red-bearded young Cornishman with a face marked from smallpox. Sailors from the flagship's crew and Hawkins' young pages, all liveried like court flunkeys, moved about the deck charging and recharging the fine Venetian wine glasses that Hawkins must have unstowed from the hold. The admiral's band provided constant music; verily, the flagship was a floating English manor house, with its lord lavishly entertaining his guests.

'Our admiral seems to be in easy company,' said Jack.

Robert Barrett nodded. 'He has been here before, remember, more than once.' Barrett had a strong but easily intelligible accent. 'Men don't forget John Hawkins. He's also markedly generous with his gifts, so they have even more cause to remember him. See those two? The older man, Pedro de Pontes, is father to that one, Nicolas. When Hawkins first sailed to the Indies, they supplied him with a pilot and letters of introduction. Some Spaniards have no difficulty with the notion of trading with the English. Would that their king and his ministers thought the same way.'

There was a disturbance near them. Edward Dudley pushed his way through a gaggle of gentlemen volunteers from the *Judith*, making his way directly for Tom Stannard. The old soldier, so out of place among the loud young men all around him, was sweating and agitated.

'Stannard,' he said, 'Thomas Stannard. I must speak with you. Alone, if you will.'

Tom exchanged a glance with his father, who nodded, and the two men went up to the highest part of the poop deck, which was deserted.

'What's the issue, Captain Dudley?' said Tom.

The older man was clearly fighting to restrain a considerable inner rage.

'I've no right to ask it,' he said. 'But there's no other – all the rest are Hawkins' choices, Hawkins' men…'

'No other what?'

'No other candidate, Tom Stannard. To be my second. In a duel.'

—

Tom paced the sun-baked beach below a great cliff, and wondered why he had agreed to participate in such utter folly. That was what his father had called it, and he was undoubtedly right. But when Tom had learned the cause from Edward Dudley's lips, and heard the names of those involved, a mist had come over his eyes, much as it had in the days when he would take on far larger and more experienced fighters in the Suffolk fairs, simply to prove a point to his older sister.

Dudley was a few yards away, swinging and thrusting with his sword, practising his steps and his feints. It seemed that since sailing from Plymouth, he had become involved in a running argument with a certain George Fitzwilliam, a great favourite of Hawkins. The cause of the argument was obscure. Fitzwilliam seemed to have cast some aspersions on the name of Dudley, of which the old captain was inordinately proud. There was a suggestion that he had reminded Dudley of the executions for treason of two men to whom he claimed kinship – King Harry the Seventh's tax-gatherer and Edward the Sixth's Lord Protector – but the final straw seemed to have been a drunken, ribald suggestion from Fitzwilliam that the current great Dudley of their time, the queen's favourite, the Earl of Leicester, had not only taken Her Majesty's much-vaunted virginity, but had fathered several secret bastards upon her. That, it seemed, was the moment when Edward Dudley had issued his challenge.

Tom had encountered George Fitzwilliam on a few occasions, and entirely disliked him, so none of what Dudley said came as a surprise. Fitzwilliam was the sort of arrogant young man who was unjustifiably proud of what was, in truth, a mediocre lineage, and who bragged much of the admiral's confidence in him. It was hardly surprising – and, in Tom's opinion, the final nail in his coffin – that Fitzwilliam should be a boon companion of Francis Drake.

'Boat coming in from the *Jesus!*' cried Dudley. 'At last, the damn rogue's coming to pay for his insults. Coming to meet his fate, by God!'

But as the boat neared the shore, it was clear that it did not contain Fitzwilliam. Its passenger jumped out into the shallow water and strode up the beach, punctiliously offering a salute to Dudley.

It was Francis Drake.

'Captain Dudley, sir,' he said. 'The admiral's compliments, but he would have you attend him in his cabin aboard the flagship.'

'My compliments to the admiral, but I have an appointment. I shall gladly attend him after it is concluded.'

Drake smiled. 'The appointment has been cancelled, Captain. But it is precisely that of which the admiral wishes to speak.'

Later, aboard the *Jesus*, Hawkins insisted on speaking to Dudley alone. But he indicated that Tom and Drake, together with his servants, should wait immediately outside the door to the flagship's great cabin, so it was easy to hear every word spoken within.

'Now, Captain Dudley—' said Hawkins in a conciliatory tone. But he was given no chance to finish the sentence.

'An affair of honour, Hawkins!' bawled Dudley, who had spent the boat trip back from Tenerife growing angrier with every stroke of the blades. 'By what right do you interfere?'

'By my right as admiral,' said Hawkins, a little more loudly, 'acting with the authority of the queen's majesty. I laid down instructions just after we sailed from Plymouth, Captain, as you may recall. No quarrelling between us, and no disobedience to the admiral's command. You have served for many years, Dudley, and fought in wars. You know the importance of obedience to commands, and to higher authority.'

'If I saw any authority worthy of the name, Hawkins, I'd defer to it.'

'Careful what you say, Captain. Remember who I am, and what office I hold.'

'Aye, of which you don't waste a second of any day reminding us.'

There was a pause, which caused Tom and Drake to glance coldly at each other, then Hawkins tried a different tack.

'We can't appear disunited before the Spaniards, Captain, least of all on their own soil. Wait for the shore of Africa, man, then you can have your affair of honour, and I'll act as the judge.'

Dudley began to yell. 'Oh, you the judge? And what a fair and neutral judge you'd be, John Hawkins! Why don't you just show your true colours and act as second for your bumboy Fitzwilliam?'

Those outside the door of the great cabin heard the unmistakable sound of a hand slapping a cheek. Tom stepped toward the door, but Drake laid a hand on his arm and shook his head. But the next sound from within was that of a sword being drawn from a scabbard, followed by a cry from Hawkins.

'Murder! In God's name, murder!'

Now it was Drake who made for the door and burst through it, followed immediately by Tom and two of Hawkins' servants.

The sight before them was astonishing. England's admiral was bleeding from a gash in the right side of his face, above the eye, but he was parrying a furious attack from Dudley, who seemed utterly oblivious to the others who had now entered the room. Dudley was so enraged that he made no attempt to keep up a guard, and as the horrified onlookers watched, Hawkins wounded his assailant in the arm. Tom and Drake then sprang forward, pinned Dudley's arms behind his back, and disarmed him.

Hawkins leaned heavily on his chart table, panting for breath and wiping blood out of his right eye. But he was still the commander, and still able to give the orders that had to be given.

'Take Captain Dudley away, and place him in irons on the orlop deck. Two guards to keep watch over him. A trial to be convened this afternoon. Make it so.'

The scene on the upper deck of the *Jesus* was solemn, as befitted a court of law. All hands of the flagship, and representatives of the crews of the other two ships in the company, had been mustered to witness the proceedings. Jack had come across from the *Jennet*, and now stood alongside his son, who had given him a summary of the proceedings thus far. A gaggle of the gentlemen volunteers stood a little way from them. Drake was there, and so was George Fitzwilliam, looking ashen-faced.

There was an audible gasp as Dudley was led onto the deck, in chains and still wearing his torn, bloodstained garments from the morning. Then Hawkins appeared, attired in a fresh outfit and wearing a bandage across his forehead and right eye. He nodded to Robert Barrett, who read the charge.

'You, Captain Edward Dudley, are charged that on this day, the twenty-fifth day of October in the ninth year of the reign of our sovereign lady Elizabeth, whom God preserve, you did mutinously attempt the unlawful killing of John Hawkins, esquire, admiral of this fleet set forth with Her Majesty's authority for an expedition unto the shores of Guinea and the Indies.'

Barrett stood aside, and Hawkins stepped forward to stand directly in front of Dudley.

'How do you justify yourself, Captain Dudley?' he demanded.

Tom caught Dudley's eye, and saw at once that all the confidence and bravado had gone. Something very different had taken their place.

Dudley looked away, and suddenly slumped to his knees before Hawkins, weeping profusely.

'Sir, it is very true,' he said. 'I have had time to think upon it, and know that what I did was wrong. I am truly ashamed of it, sir, but I know that this proceeding, this court, is nothing but what I deserve. I have had command of men, and if any had ever drawn a blade on me and wounded me, I would have ordered them hanged. It is the right punishment, and it is entirely your right to inflict it, Admiral Hawkins. I did what I did. I am guilty as charged. All I can do, sir, is throw myself upon your most gracious mercy.'

With that, he prostrated himself upon the deck, and touched Hawkins' feet.

Tom and Jack exchanged a glance. The younger Stannard had expected Dudley to remain unrepentant, but his frank admission of guilt had clearly won over many of the men on deck. Two or three were even in tears, while George Fitzwilliam looked away, out across the sea toward the mountains of Tenerife.

'John Hawkins, the man, forgives you in an instant,' said Hawkins. 'But I am not merely John Hawkins the man. I am admiral of this fleet, and thus an ambassador of the queen's most excellent majesty. By attacking me, you have endangered this fleet, and these men. Worse, you have done it under the very guns and flags of a foreign power. There are those who would call such an act treasonable. You are a knowledgeable man, Captain, and thus you know the fate that has always befallen those who commit such affronts to the laws of God and England.'

'My life is in your hands,' said Dudley, simply.

'Bosun!' cried Hawkins. The boatswain of the *Jesus* stepped forward. 'Fetch an arquebus. Two balls, if you please.'

The boatswain saluted with two fingers to his forehead, then ran below to the armoury. Hawkins turned once again to Dudley.

'Make your peace with God, Edward Dudley,' he said, 'for you are about to look upon His face.'

The words finally broke Dudley entirely. The old soldier's body was racked with sobs, and his collapse affected many of those on the deck of the *Jesus*. Men fell to their knees weeping, raised their hands in supplication to their admiral, and called out for mercy.

'Aye, mercy!' cried Tom Stannard.

'Mercy, in God's name!' added Jack. Tom knew that, in his pocket, his father would be thumbing the beads of his paternoster.

Francis Drake, a little way away, merely smiled, and murmured words that few but the Stannards heard.

'Just shoot the old bastard,' he said.

The boatswain returned from below decks. Solemnly he loaded and primed the instrument of execution, then handed it to Hawkins.

The admiral addressed Dudley once again.

'Are you ready?' he demanded.

'I am done with the world,' replied the old captain, 'and I am ready to receive the punishment that you have appointed for me.'

John Hawkins steadied the gun's rest upon the deck, then pressed the arquebus to Dudley's temple.

He put his finger to the trigger.

Eleven

No man breathed.

Hawkins' gaze, looking down the barrel of the arquebus, was fixed upon the prone figure of Dudley, whose brains were about to be shattered and spread across the deck of the *Jesus*.

Tom Stannard bowed his head, not wanting to look upon the horror. Jack, though, kept his eyes on Hawkins. Thus he saw the admiral look across to the carpenter of the *Jesus* and utter a simple command.

'Free him.'

As the carpenter stooped to remove Dudley's chains, Hawkins took the old soldier by the hand and raised him to his feet.

There was a gasp of disbelief from the men mustered on deck. Then wild cheering erupted, caps were thrown into the air, and men slapped each other on the back.

'Hurrah for the admiral! God bless the admiral! Hurrah!'

Jack and Tom were among the few close enough to Dudley and Hawkins to hear what passed between them.

'But I must die for what I have done,' said Dudley, sobbing. 'I wish to die, unless you can help me to forget the memory of my deed. Release me only if you forgive me, Admiral.'

Hawkins' response was gentle.

'It is done, my friend. I forgive you gladly. All record of what has passed this day will be expunged. Now, come. We shall drink and talk.'

At that, Hawkins led Dudley toward the great cabin of the flagship, passing close to the Stannards. Jack nodded approvingly to the admiral; this, he thought, was a good and godly act, and the wild, seemingly endless cheering of the crew bore witness to it. By showing mercy, by turning their anger at Dudley into pity, Hawkins had united the crew, and reinforced their loyalty to him. There was a stamp of greatness about it, thought Jack.

Tom, though, was noticing the expression on the face of Francis Drake. It was furious.

—

The *Jennet*'s pinnace lay upon the beach before Santa Cruz. Tom had command of the shore party tasked with replenishing the ship's water casks; men were rolling the empty casks up to the watering place, next to a small chapel, then rolling the full ones back down to the boat. It was hard, sapping work, even though the sun was not fully up, and the men of the *Jennet* were all stripped as far as decency would permit. A small gaggle of young girls and older matrons stood under the shade of some trees at the head of the beach, their whispered asides and laughter suggesting that they were frankly appraising the bodies of the Englishmen. Tom waved at them, and a few blushed. Others, though, called out brazenly, and some of the Dunwich men posed provocatively before them. One such was Hal Ashby. He had a firm, brown body, Tom thought, which reminded him of Hugh Ebbes back at Dunwich, apart from the large old scar across Hal's belly—

No.

Tom chided himself, and turned to look out to sea, to where the English fleet lay beyond the Spanish merchantmen. Such thoughts only made him feel ashamed. He was a happily married man, and every day he thanked God that being in that blessed state, and his delight in his wife and sons, kept him from the thoughts and dreams that had plagued him since he was young. When the Reverend James at St Peter's preached upon Leviticus 18 or 20, the young Thomas Stannard used to shift uncomfortably upon his stool. So when it was proposed that he should marry Catherine Trelawny, he rejoiced that his soul stood at least some chance of avoiding eternal damnation.

'Idling, Stannard of Suffolk?'

Drake's unwelcome, insinuating voice made him turn abruptly. The man could not have been in his thoughts, and yet his appearance at that precise moment seemed more than a coincidence.

'Don't you have the casks for the *Jesus* to attend to, Drake?'

Drake smiled. 'All in hand. Remember the *Jesus* is a proper man-of-war of the Navy Royal, and my cousin runs her as such, so men know their places. Unlike that shabby excuse for a hull that you and your father cherish so much, and your crew that does what it pleases.'

Tom took an angry step forward, but then saw that the eyes of most of the men from the *Jesus* and the *Jennet* were upon him. So soon after the admiral's very public treatment of Edward Dudley, it would be unutterable folly for Tom to fight with Francis Drake in front of the crews.

'Shabby she may be, Drake, but she rode the storm better than the great wreck you call the *Jesus*.'

Out of the corner of his eye, Tom could see some of his men moving closer to those from the flagship. Whatever his own feelings in the matter, neither he nor Drake could afford a repeat of the fight in the Plymouth alehouse. That being so, he essayed a broad smile, although he suspected the effect might be ghastly.

'But come, Frank Drake,' he said, as merrily as he could, 'we're Englishmen ashore in a foreign land. The admiral, kin to both of us, has made clear that he won't tolerate any disunity in our fleet. For my part, I intend to complete the lading of our casks, then to try my Spanish on some of the ladies yonder. What say you?'

The Devon man's face changed, the mischievous, baiting mask giving way to profound disapproval.

'Fornication, Stannard? Fornication with *papists*?'

Drake looked around, saw the two parties of men waiting for the slightest excuse to lay about each other, then shook his head and turned away, gesturing for the men of the *Jesus* to accompany him. Tom watched him go. He had no intention of committing fornication with anyone, that day or any other, but he had often heard it said in Plymouth that when it came to matters of the flesh, Francis Drake was as rigid as an Old Testament prophet. Better, then, for him to regard Tom as one kind of sinner rather than another.

–

'It's happening,' said Tom. 'Hawkins said it would, and he was right.'

Jack screwed up his eyes, and peered into the darkness. It was an hour or so after dusk, and all had seemed quiet in the harbour of Santa Cruz. But then he saw what he thought was a movement...

Yes, there could be no doubt of it. For a bare minute, no more, the light from the candles, lanterns and fires of the town was hidden as some dark mass moved in front of them. The mass could only be the hull of a ship, and the ship could only be one of the vessels that had lain between the English fleet and the guns of the Spanish batteries. Forewarned by his friends among the merchants of Tenerife, Hawkins, and thus the captains of his ships, knew that at dawn, the governor of the island would give orders to his gun batteries to blow Queen Elizabeth's ships out of the water.

But Hawkins was ready, and the Stannards and their men aboard the *Jennet* were ready. The watch on deck was already crowded around the foot of the shrouds, eager to get aloft. Jack left the command to Tom, at whose signal the men climbed up to the yards to ready the sails. Others hauled upon the capstan, pulling up the *Jennet's* anchor from the depths. Once the anchor was clear of the water, the sails were unfurled and sheeted home. The breeze was not a strong one, but it was good enough. Through the darkness, they saw the white sails of the *Jesus* ahead crack and then fill sufficiently to move the great ship forward, the lantern at Hawkins' stern showing the way for the *Jennet* and the *Judith*. Jack studied the trim of their own sails, thought of ordering a slight change to the foretopsail, then held his tongue. This was his son's command, and Tom, standing at the rail shouting clear, crisp orders to the men, had become a more than capable shipmaster. Jack felt a surge of pride that this should be so.

–

The fleet moved only a very short distance down the coast, then dropped anchor again. When dawn broke, they were well out of range of the guns of Santa Cruz. The Stannards watched with some amusement as a boat bearing the oversized ensign of the governor of Tenerife went out to the *Jesus*, no doubt to deliver a protest about the English fleet's inexplicable snub to Spanish hospitality. They learned later that Hawkins had been equally polite, and equally disingenuous, in his reply. Nevertheless, the lesson was clear. When, a few days later, the entire fleet sailed for the coast of Africa, the other ships separated by the great storm having been discovered at the neighbouring island of Gomera, it did so with a clear understanding that henceforward, it should assume itself to be in a state of war with Spain.

That assumption loomed large in the next letter that Jack Stannard wrote to Francis Walsingham, ready to be forwarded in any friendly vessel the *Jennet* encountered that might be returning to European waters.

Twelve

His first sight of the fabled continent of Africa should have thrilled Jack Stannard. In childhood, his teacher and later friend, Thomas Ryman, had told him tales of Prester John, King Solomon's mines and the Queen of Sheba. He had dreamed of it as a land of mysteries, giants and monsters, of riches beyond measure and dangers beyond imagination. There should have been towering cliffs topped by vast statues erected by ancient empires, and waterfalls emerging from forests of trees taller and greener than any in England.

But there was none of this. Instead, Africa was a dull, flat, grey shore, the surf breaking upon the interminable beach just as it did in more familiar waters. Thus Jack Stannard's first impression of Africa was that, as a coast, it seemed somewhat less interesting than Essex.

Bruno Cabral now had charge of the ship's navigation, and had laid out a portolan chart upon the barrel of a saker to explain their location to Tom.

'We have made landfall to the north of Cabo Blanco, Thomas Stannard, so we will be somewhere in this vicinity. An empty shore, with no harbours of refuge. Little trade. Hawkins knows this; he has been here before. So we will coast southward until we reach the cape, then strike south for the Senegal river and Cabo Verde. That is where he expects to take his slaves.'

Jack knew full well the principal purpose of the voyage; that was, its revised purpose, since the two Portuguese merchants had vanished from Plymouth and Hawkins had obtained the queen's permission to continue the expedition with a revised and, arguably, rather more dangerous objective. But Tom, who had not travelled southward as far or as often as his father had, still seemed convinced that they would engage principally in the familiar sort of trades, the selling of cloth and the like, and found it difficult to comprehend the notion of a cargo that breathed and spoke.

'There is profit in this – the taking of slaves?'

'Great profit,' said Cabral. 'Why do you think the French, and now you English, seek to take some of the trade from we Portuguese? The Spanish colonies in the Indies need men to work their fields and their mines. Great numbers of men. Where can they get them in the numbers they need? Africa is the only place. So the Spanish permit the Portuguese, and only us, to ship slaves across the sea, but if a ship of any other nation comes to the Indies, the Spanish there will gladly ignore their king's prohibition and buy from its captain, so great is the need for men. Hawkins knows this. He has made two voyages to this coast, and made great profit. This time, he hopes for even more.'

Tom nodded, but he was still thoughtful. His father, watching the exchange, knew that expression of old.

'But Master Cabral,' said Tom. He seemed to think better of his question, but then asked it anyway. 'Master Cabral, are these not your people?'

By this time, Jack Stannard had known Bruno Cabral for a period that could be measured in months, and he had never seen the Portingal angry. Now, though, Cabral stood upright, puffed out his chest and leaned forward towards Tom, his eyes blazing.

'Are you like a Turk or a Muscovite, Tom Stannard?' he said, coldly. 'Or are you like a Frenchman or a Spaniard? No, you are not. Do you claim kinship to them? No, you do not. Do you speak their languages? No, you do not. Likewise, I do not claim kinship to those fellows ashore – the fellows that we seek. I was born in Lisbon, as was my father, and his father before him, and so on back to the time of Sancho the Pious. I am a Christian, with hope of salvation through Our Lord, while they are brute beasts who worship false gods, so they are damned to hellfire by their ignorance. In that, my Catholic bishops and your heretical prelates are as one. So just because my skin is the same colour as theirs does not mean I am like the people ashore, just as you are not like any of those I have named.'

He sniffed. 'And let me tell you this: even if that were not so, they are losers in war. In Europe, we pride ourselves that our wars have rules, do we not? We pride ourselves that we have honour, and all that accompanies it. We have heralds in fine tabards reading proclamations. We have trumpeters to accompany them. But at the end of a battle, what do you see? Thousands of throats being cut to spare the trouble and expense of prisoners. I witnessed this myself at Muscat and in Ethiopia, in my country's wars with the Grand Turk. On the shore yonder, too, many of those defeated in war are slaughtered. But others are enslaved, just as they would be if there were no Portuguese, French or English at all upon this coast. I swear upon the grave of my mother that this is true. So they still live, Thomas Stannard, and if they are taken by people like us, they have a chance to become Christians and attain salvation. Where, then, is the greater honour, and the lesser *hipocrisia* – what is your English word? Ah, *sim*, cant. Where is the lesser cant, Thomas Stannard?'

Jack looked on with some amusement. His son's expression was one he had often worn in childhood, when his older sister Meg chided him for some real or alleged misdemeanour. Tom, abashed, turned and looked out to sea, toward the endless coast of Africa, and pondered Bruno Cabral's words.

–

The English attacked two hours before dawn. The long-boats cast off from the ships, their oars muffled. From the *Jennet*'s boat, Jack and Tom could see the white flag flying from the stern of Hawkins' barge, the signal for the rest of the flotilla to follow. Like the men in all the other boats, the Dunwich crew were clad in warlike fashion in leather jerkins and helmets, and were heavily armed with arquebuses and crossbows. Cabral had been left behind to command the ship; in the unlikely event of a surprise attack, his superior knowledge of the local waters might pilot the *Jennet* to a safe haven.

They had sailed down the coast from Cabo Blanco, where they had seized three small Portuguese caravels that had been abandoned by their crews after an attack by French raiders. Then they continued their voyage, passing the mouth of the Senegal river, constantly sending boats out to look for possible landing places. At last, just to the north of Cape Verde, they seemed to have found the ideal location: a broad beach bordering a sheltered anchorage with twelve fathoms of water. It was this beach that the Englishmen now stormed.

The boats grounded upon the strand and the men leapt ashore, every one of them obeying Hawkins' order to maintain complete silence. The men of *Jennet* came ashore next to Edward Dudley and his contingent of soldiers, and Tom exchanged a nod with the old warrior, now unshakeable in his loyalty to John Hawkins and evidently intending to make the most of his reprieve. He also caught a glimpse of Francis Drake, but the two men did not acknowledge each other. The two hundred or so Englishmen, nearly half the entire manpower of the fleet, formed up in good order and began to march into the hinterland.

'It seems too good to be true,' whispered Jack to his son.

'Hawkins is confident. He says he knows where the village is, that we simply surprise it at dawn, then just carry off the people. He says he did such things many times on his previous voyages.'

Jack made no reply. He was not complying with Hawkins' order to stay silent; rather, he was thinking of his own shore in Suffolk, of how unlikely it would be for a landing party of enemies to surprise one of the villages a few miles inland. But he knew how Hawkins would respond to that, for he had heard him say the like several times in the great cabin of the *Jesus*, echoing the words of Bruno Cabral. *These people are not like Englishmen. They are savages, little better than brute beasts.*

At dawn, though, he was lying upon a slight ridge among sand dunes, looking down upon the native village that stood exactly where John Hawkins had said it would. The place was a rough affair of small huts, standing in the shade provided by a grove of palm trees. It was entirely silent, with not a living soul to be seen.

Thus far, at least, it was both good and true, as Hawkins had predicted.

The white flag was waved from the admiral's position, and the English charged, screaming and bellowing as they ran down the slope into the village. Jack felt the old thrill of battle's blood rush as he lifted the sword in his hand and cried, 'for God, for Dunwich and for England!' But as he came into the village, he slowed, then stood stock still and looked around him, as did Hawkins, Drake, Dudley and the rest. The huts were empty, but there were still warm embers in the fires—

There was a whistling sound, and Jack was aware of a man crying out near him. He turned, saw it was Tom, saw the arrow protruding from his upper arm, and in the same moment heard the cacophony of rage as hundreds upon hundreds of near-naked natives burst out of their cover among the trees and dunes, shooting arrows and slinging short spears against their assailants. Intent on aiding his son, he barely noticed an arrow bounce off his jerkin.

'Tom…'

The younger man pulled the arrow out of his arm and flung it to the ground.

'A scratch, Father, no more. Come on, we've a battle to fight!'

Hawkins, too, had been struck by an arrow in the arm, albeit just a glancing blow that had not entered his flesh. As with Tom, the wound was not impeding him in the slightest. He and Dudley were barking orders, and the English were rapidly taking up a rough defensive formation to meet the onslaught. The first arquebuses gave fire, and crossbow quarrels struck the chests of unclothed natives with terrible results. Still the villagers came on, yelling their war cries. One reached Jack and thrust his spear forward with more hope than skill or force. Jack swung his sword nearly from his shoulder and cut deeply into the man's neck, causing a torrent of blood to spurt out onto the sand. Now more and more of the formidable English weapons were firing, and the momentum went out of the native advance. Hawkins raised his sword and shouted an order to charge.

'Remember our purpose, men!' he cried. 'If you can, capture them instead of killing. God for England!'

The Englishmen pressed forward, firing all the time, but the natives were now more cautious of their enemy's weapons, and kept themselves close to the limit of both sides' range.

'Damnation!' cried Hawkins to Dudley, and to Jack, who had come to their side. 'They'll not stand and fight like good Christian foes!'

'If we keep up this sort of attack,' said Dudley, 'we'll exhaust our ammunition.'

'Whatever we do,' said Jack, 'we won't much reduce their advantage in numbers. And if we take captives, we'll have to detach men to guard them.'

'Aye, that's so,' replied Dudley. 'It's only a matter of time before some of our men start to fall, and if they weaken us enough, they've the numbers to overwhelm us, no matter how skilfully we wield our swords, bows and guns.'

Hawkins cast a quick glance around the scene, then nodded.

'Aye, well, I don't fancy my story ending here, at the hands of these sorts of fellows. Signal the retreat – we fight our way back to the boats!'

In truth, it was as easy a journey as it could be with hundreds of natives screaming abuse every step of the way but staying at too great a distance to do much damage to the English force, and vice versa. Long before Hawkins' men reached the beach, many of them were laughing, shouting prime Anglo-Saxon obscenities back at their assailants, and even baring their arses. By the time they got to the ships, many of them were singing, as though they had won a great victory over Frenchmen or Spaniards. But as they met in the great cabin of the *Jesus* to take stock and lay fresh plans, Hawkins and his officers, including the two Stannards, knew that the expedition had been an utter failure. They had taken only nine captives, a pitiful number. Worse, every village along the coast for many miles to the south, and probably far inland too, would now be alert to their presence on the coast, as the constant sound of distant drumming suggested. But the gloom among the English commanders would undoubtedly have deepened had they known the sequel to the failed attack on the nameless village.

–

The sickness took hold two days later. Aboard the *Jennet*, Tom had the watch upon deck. Jack and Cabral were below, dozing upon their sea-beds, when one of the ship's boys, Bradlow, burst into the cabin, bawling that Captain Stannard was unwell. Jack sprinted to the upper deck, followed closely by Cabral. Tom was leaning hard upon the starboard rail, gripping his throat and making strange gulping noises. He was sweating even more profusely than all the other men upon the upper decks.

'Tom, lad!' cried Jack, running to him and taking hold of his shoulders. 'In Jesu's name, what's the matter?'

Tom could evidently say nothing, simply pointing to his mouth, which he seemed unable to open.

'I have seen this upon this shore,' said Cabral, calmly. 'The savages' arrows must have been poisoned. It brings on spasms where men cannot open their mouths or swallow.'

But Jack had already come to the same diagnosis through observation. He snatched up a small belaying pin, told Cabral to hold Tom, and began to try and force his son's jaws apart. All the while, men of the watch on deck looked on, horrified.

'Come on, lad,' said Jack. 'Alice, intercede for me. Mary, Mother of God, intercede for me!'

Tom's face was turning purple. Jack no longer cared what any might make of the prayers he uttered, and despite Cabral's warning glances, he began to recite the *Ave Maria*. At last, the Virgin and all the saints seemed to hear him, and Tom's jaws parted sufficiently for Jack to be able to thrust the belaying pin between them. Tom gulped in air, and Jack and Cabral slowly led him below, finally laying him upon his sea-bed in the stern cabin.

Perhaps a half-glass passed before Tom reached up and removed the belaying pin from his mouth. 'Will it return?' he asked.

'It will,' said Cabral bluntly.

'And will I die?'

Jack looked intently at the Portuguese, waiting for his answer. But Cabral simply stood and said, 'I shall go to the flagship.'

As Cabral left the cabin, Tom gripped his father's hand, as he had done so often when he was a little boy.

'Oh Christ in heaven, Father, it returns – I can feel it...' Without another word, he took up the belaying pin himself, and thrust it between his teeth.

–

Tom had two more attacks before Cabral returned from the *Jesus* some hours later. By now, word was all over the fleet: more than a dozen men were sick, including John Hawkins and Edward Dudley, both of whom had been scratched by arrows. The natives, whose weapons had seemed so feeble, were far from being the lambs to the slaughter that most of the Englishmen had assumed they were. Although the arrows were pitiful things, incapable of penetrating a stout leather jerkin, the slightest touch to flesh made them deadly. The spasms, which made the victims choke, would get progressively worse, and within days, if not sooner, they would die.

Jack spoke to Cabral on deck, out of his son's earshot. The fleet was continuing southward under an easy sail, the unending featureless coast well away to larboard.

'Well?' he demanded.

'I spoke with one of the captives,' said Cabral. 'He had a little Portuguese, and I know a few words of some of the tribes on this coast. There is a cure.'

Jack grasped his hand and kissed it fervently.

'Thanks be to God! *Deo gratias!*'

'But it is not certain, Jack Stannard. It depends on how much poison is on the arrowhead, how strong the mixture is, how deeply the arrow has penetrated...'

Jack's face fell. He recalled Tom standing there in the village, the arrow buried deep in his arm. Hawkins, Dudley and some of the others had only been scratched.

'I must try,' he said.

'Of course. It is garlic, nothing more. Rub a clove of garlic deep into the wound. God willing, it will draw out the poison, and your son will be well. If not...'

Jack was already gesturing for young Bradlow to go below to search the ship's victuals, and an hour later, he was at Tom's side, pressing a clove hard into the arrow wound in his arm, quietly murmuring all the old Latin prayers as he did so. Tom seemed calmer at once, less feverish, but then his face went into spasm once more, and Jack hastily resorted to the belaying pin.

This was his moment of deepest despair. The garlic had failed. Tom would die, and they would heave his body over the side, weighted down by a cannonball, to lie for ever in this strange, hostile sea, so very far from Dunwich or his wife and young sons in Plymouth. With Tom gone, Jack would be a dead man too, although he might still live and breathe for whatever remaining time God had allotted him.

By the next turn of the glass, though, Tom's spasm had subsided. By the one after that, he had not had another, and word had come from the *Jesus* that both Hawkins and Dudley lived, and were well. By dawn of the following day, Tom Stannard was standing his watch, and his father was lying upon his sea-bed, weeping unashamedly.

Thirteen

*The Jennet, at anchor off the shore of Sierra Leone
Christmas Day, the year of Our Lord 1567*

Meg, my dearest child,

*A Portingal ship here is sailing for Madeira,
and then intends for Nantes and Bridport, so I
have convinced her master to take letters for me,
trusting in God that they might reach the intended
recipients. First, I wish you joy of the season,
remembering it is twenty-three years now since
you were mercifully spared when John's church of
Dunwich was consumed by the sea. I know the
season will be long past by the time you receive this,
if ever you do, but consider my blessing a promise
of many joyous Yuletides yet to come before our
fireplace in the old house. It is hard to think of
fireplaces here, where we seem to live every day
in the very heart of a furnace, the heat lying like
a great weight upon the land. Every day of this
voyage persuades me further that it was folly for
me to sail upon it, and that, God willing, when I
finally return to England, my seafaring days will
be behind me.*

*I pray you have received my last letter, which
told you of your brother's sickness and recovery,*

Deo gratias. Since then, we have continued south along the coast of this benighted place. The eight deaths from poison that we sustained at Cape Verde put fear into the hearts of all men, and whatever Hawkins says to them, most remain persuaded that the native people have witchcraft and necromancy on their side; they are thus reluctant to undertake other attacks ashore. This fear has been reinforced by the reports of scouting parties, who talk of seeing the remains of men who have been eaten by other men. Kyrie eleison, daughter.

At the mouth of the great river called Gambia, we encountered some French ships under letters of marque, and persuaded them to part with a prize they had taken from the Portuguese, a good ship of 150 tons and eight guns. Hawkins has named this the Grace of God, and has placed his kinsman Francis Drake in command of her. Perhaps Tom has spoken or written to you of this man, who is kin to Hawkins on the other side of the family from Tom's Catherine. They do not agree well, this Drake being a proud and brash fellow, but he is a great favourite of Hawkins, and I have told Tom that he should tread carefully. You will know in the fullness of time whether he does or not.

Our fleet has undertaken several expeditions in search of slaves. The coast is a maze of muddy channels and swamps, and none of our ships have been able to go inshore, so we have sent out parties in boats. I have gone out twice, Tom thrice, but it is a thankless business, with not one captive to show for it. These expeditions are commanded by a fellow called Robert Barrett, sailing master on the Jesus, a man much in Hawkins' confidence. Only one of his efforts is worthy of record. Hawkins sent him with three boats to examine a place called Cacheo, some distance up a mile-wide river, where we had certain intelligence of three Portuguese caravels laden with slaves for the Indies. Barrett attacked with only forty men, but somehow secured the ships, the Portingals fleeing ashore, although they had no slaves aboard them. Hawkins sent three ships upstream under Drake and Dudley to support Barrett – I volunteered the Jennet, but was refused – but their men were attacked by a great host of savages recruited by the Portingals, six or seven thousand against two or three hundred of our men. But no matter the numbers, Meg, naked men against trained Englishmen with arquebuses and no shortage of ammunition are akin to naught but chaff. Barrett and his men, covered by Dudley's soldiers, made their way back to their boats, their wounds no worse than scratches – and thanks to God, these people seem not to know of the poisons that their kind further north employ.

Now, Meg, it is true that Barrett, Drake and Dudley got their men safe away, but as in our first expedition ashore, a retreat can never be termed a victory, no matter how men brag. What is more, we have no commission to take Portingal ships, and our country is not at war with Portugal. Your half-brother George can tell you better than I that our seizing of these Portingal hulls makes us pirates, and no fine words can clothe that. I said this to our admiral, but he laughed. I find it far from a laughing matter, for I am loath to have the odious appellation of pirate spoken in the same breath as the name of Stannard.

Since the action at Cacheo, we have sent parties up more rivers, negotiated with native kings who despise their neighbours and wish nothing more than to see them taken by us as slaves, and by one means and another obtained a hundred and fifty of these wretches. In truth, daughter, it has all been a tedious business upon this vile shore, where the heat is nearly unbearable, the swamp presses in on all sides, and insects swarm by day and night. To amuse you, then, I enclose a drawing of the great beast, the hippopotamus, which I have now seen many times, and which the more credulous of the men fear as some sort of demon. Indeed, I witnessed one of them come up under a pinnace, drive in the planks and timbers, and sink the boat in an instant. We saved most of the men, but two perished. So the hippopotamus is clearly not a beast to trifle with, and I have done my best to record its likeness, though I know your friend Grimes would have done much better.

Meg, do not, I implore you, show this drawing around Dunwich and claim it as an image of your stepmother.

No man can deny the truth that thus far, our voyage is a failure. Perhaps the gold mines that the Portingal adventurers spoke of never existed, and even if they did, perhaps we would never have found them. But since Plymouth, Hawkins has boasted of the money to be made from slaves, how easy it will be to find them upon this shore, and how much gold we will be paid for them in the Carib. Thus far, though, as I say, we have taken only a hundred and fifty, and that will be insufficient even to recoup the expenses of the voyage, let alone turn a profit for all those great folk who have invested in it. As yet, none of these slaves have been placed aboard the Jennet, and I pray that they will not be for some little time yet, as the captains of the other ships are telling me what trouble they are put to in guarding and feeding them.

Meg, it is a strange business, whatever Cabral and Hawkins say, which is that if we did not take and sell slaves, the Portingals or French certainly would, as they have been doing for many years. I have seen enough already to know that they are not wrong in this. But they also say that by this means, profit will accrue to England, and thus to the righteous causes of Queen Elizabeth and the Protestant faith. You may imagine my thoughts upon this matter, daughter, for truly, some may be slaves of the body, but others are slaves of the soul. Still, mayhap profit will yet accrue to the name of Stannard, and to Dunwich, which may still rise once more in consequence. Yet for this to be so, we must take far more than a mere hundred and fifty slaves, and we must take them here or hereabouts, for otherwise we will be forced into what Cabral calls the Bight of Benin, where the Portingals have impregnable castles and where the winds are so contrary that we might never be able to beat back for the Indies. I fear, then, that upon this matter, God has turned his face against us, and that we shall return to England, if we ever return at all, in ignominy and failure.

There is much else I would say, but I must stand my watch shortly. Know this, though. I have thought much upon the matter of your stepmother and Raker, and see now that I was wrong to dismiss it as lightly as I did. I have thought of writing to her, but fear that such a course might make matters difficult for you. As it is, I am dispatching other letters along with this one, and though these might not make matters wholly right, they will, God willing, grant you greater security against that man's schemes.

So, Meg, I pray you to put my friends in remembrance of me, and to keep me in your prayers, as I shall keep you in mine.

May the God of your mother guard and keep you, my dear daughter.

Your loving father

Meg – one final matter, before I apply seal to wax. I entreat you to write to Will Halliday in London, to see if he has had receipt of my letters to him. If he has not, then I beg you to send him this message. He is to tell our friend from the Pope's Head that the eggs remain unbroken, the horses remain in their stables, and we have encountered no griffins. Those exact words, Meg, no other. One day, I pray that I will return to explain it all to you. Until then, be safe, be true, be faithful.

Jack sealed the letter, added it to the pouch containing the others, and handed it to the lad who was to take it over to the Portingal ship. As he did so, he heard something of a commotion on deck, and went out from the stern cabin to see Tom exchange frosty greetings with the newly minted Captain Francis Drake, who was just coming aboard.

'Ah, Captain Stannard the elder,' said Drake, seemingly in good cheer and doffing his hat. 'I give you joy of the season.'

'And to yourself, Captain Drake.'

In truth, there was no sense of the Christmas season. It was not yet eight in the morning, but the sun's heat was already overwhelming, and the slightest movement made men run with sweat. Awnings stretched over the deck of the *Jennet*, as they did over those of the other ships, and a few men who had been on watch during the night were stretched out beneath them, hoping for a blessed conjuncture of shade and even the merest hint of a cooling breeze.

'What do you want here, Drake?' said Tom, testily.

'Mere good neighbourliness, Captain Stannard,' replied Drake. The fight in the Plymouth tavern seemed entirely forgotten, on the one side at least. 'The admiral and I have been somewhat concerned that God is not praised aboard your ship – how can I put it? – quite as fulsomely as He should be.'

Tom and Jack exchanged a glance, but it was the father who responded.

'We call the men to prayers each morning, as the admiral's instructions enjoin,' said Jack. 'I am not a man much versed in scripture, but I do my utmost to lead respectful worship.'

'No doubt you do, Captain Stannard, no doubt you do. But with respect, men's souls need more than a few rote prayers each morn. Aboard the flagship, we have a psalm, the Lord's Prayer, the Creed and a sermon at the start of the forenoon watch and the end of the second dog.'

'Do you keep a bishop aboard the *Jesus*, then?' said Tom, mischievously.

'From what I have seen of bishops,' said Drake, 'we are better placed. Blessed indeed, one might say. We have two godly men who preach with all the knowledge and fervour of any at Paul's Cross. Mayhap I join with them from time to time – my father was a man of the cloth, so I can essay a passable sermon.' Even if you struggle to essay modesty, thought Jack. 'So, my friends, I am come with the admiral's authority to invite you to a service of thanksgiving aboard the flagship for our blessed saviour's nativity.'

Two hours later, Jack, Tom, and all but a bare ship-keeping watch from the *Jennet*, commanded by the unashamedly Catholic Bruno Cabral, were assembled in the capacious waist of the *Jesus* to hear one of Drake's friends, a squat, ugly fellow named Harry Newman, preach with a full measure of Lutheran venom. Hawkins alone was seated, and protected from the sun by an awning. A Spanish viceroy could hardly have appeared in more state, nor been more indifferent to those in the waist of the ship, who had barely any cover.

Tom Stannard listened intently to Newman, though, as did many of the men in the congregation. This was the line that Church and state expected of Englishmen, after all, and Tom was perfectly content with it. Jack, though, wished to cry out against the travesty of it all, but kept silent. That a mean fellow of no standing, and not ordained, should dare to preach the word of God, and to offer up seemingly endless prayers for the life of Elizabeth...

Slowly, Jack's inner rage subsided, and he concentrated a little more upon Newman's interminable rant – for he would not distinguish it with the name of sermon. As he did so, he felt a growing sense of discomfort. Newman had taken what seemed to be a random and inappropriate selection of texts – Peter, Romans and Titus upon giving obedience to rulers; Ephesians 6, justifying slavery; Revelation 17, against the Whore of Babylon, defined by Newman, as by so many of his kind, as the Pope; and so on. It was hardly cheering Christmas fare, and not what Jack was accustomed to in Dunwich. Worse, Newman also had an uncomfortable habit of seeming to stare directly at Jack, as though he was the one sinner in the congregation to be singled out and threatened with eternal hellfire. Damn his eyes, then. Jack stared back, defiantly.

Newman finally finished, but there was no respite, though some of even the sturdiest foremastmen were struggling in the enervating heat. For now Francis Drake himself stepped forward, and embarked upon what could only be called a tirade, extolling the virtues of Queen Elizabeth, 'that fair, blessed and righteous virgin', and denouncing the Pope in familiar terms. He had certainly learned much from his father, and spoke even more clearly and passionately than Newman had.

'And so, my friends, I tell you this!' he cried, his eyes scanning the congregation. 'England will carry the banner of true reformed religion forth across the world! England, God's chosen nation upon earth! We will put to flight all ignorance and popish superstition, wherever it may be! We will bring the truth to all nations and peoples, aye, even to the heathens of these very lands! Under our blessed Queen Elizabeth, the new Deborah, the new Judith, we will humble the pride of Spain, and all nations of the world will come to know and fear the name of England!'

Many of Drake's and Hawkins' Devon men cheered at that, and even a few of the loyal men of the *Jennet* nodded vigorously. Jack saw Tom stifling a laugh, and was close to smiling himself.

High words, Frank Drake, he thought, when what we are really about is the getting of gold, pure and simple, and by whatever means.

But Drake had not finished yet. Of course he had not.

'But my friends, be wary of serpents in our midst! Recall Matthew Chapter Twenty-Seven, the terrible lesson it contains. Be vigilant, friends, for our England has enemies within!'

Matthew 27: the story of Judas and the thirty pieces of silver.

Jack Stannard looked at Drake, and realised that the Devonian was staring directly at him, with Hawkins nodding sagely at his side.

Fourteen

'Boat ho!' cried the lookout in the crow's nest of the *Jesus*.

'Damn your eyes, boy,' shouted Hawkins from the quarterdeck., 'stay awake up there! I see it already! We all see it!'

The flagship lay at anchor in the middle of the fleet, still moored at the mouth of the Sierra Leone river. It was three weeks after Christmas, and the prospects of the expedition were no better. From time to time, one or two ships had been dispatched to investigate this or that estuary, but every one of these expeditions had returned empty-handed. Time was against the English. The cloying humidity had given way to a brisk, dry easterly wind, filled with sand from the great desert that Cabral said lay far inland. This, though, would soon give way in its turn to even less bearable heat and great storms. The fleet needed to be away from this terrible shore, but it still had only a fraction of the cargo it required to turn a profit.

These thoughts had dominated the discussion between Hawkins and his captains in the great cabin of the *Jesus*, and they were still at the forefront of most of these men's minds as they stood upon deck, watching the strange native canoe riding the surf as it came out to them. It seemed to be no more than a great tree trunk, hollowed out and rowed by a score of near-naked savages, bearing two men in headdresses who appeared to be passengers.

Jack Stannard stood alongside Hawkins. The strange affair on Christmas Day felt almost like a bad dream; since then, the admiral had seemed to go out of his way to take Jack into his confidence. True, Francis Drake had almost entirely avoided the company of the two Stannards, but that was due in part to Hawkins favouring his kinsman's small ship for most of the brief expeditions to hunt for slaves. The *Jennet*, though, had never been sent out at all.

The canoe came alongside, and the two passengers stepped aboard the *Jesus*. Cabral came forward to act as interpreter, with Jack continuing to stand by Hawkins' side. First one of the emissaries, then the other, embarked upon what was clearly, in any language, a set speech, made up of a concoction of Portuguese and native words that Cabral seemed to navigate with little difficulty.

'They are ambassadors of Sheri, King of Sierra Leone, and Yhoma, King of Castros, both of the Sapi people,' he said. 'They salute the most excellent admiral of the King of England.' Hawkins made to say something, but Cabral smiled. 'They have not heard of your Queen Elizabeth. Indeed, they have not heard of the notion of a woman holding power in her hands.'

'Then explain it to them,' said Hawkins, 'and tell them that on behalf of Her Majesty Queen Elizabeth, I bid them welcome.'

Cabral uttered a string of words, only one of which Jack recognised: Isabella. The two emissaries looked at one another, evidently struggling to comprehend the idea of a female ruler. But they swiftly recovered their confidence, and began a lengthy discourse, which Cabral summarised rather than attempting to translate word for word.

'Their masters are at war with two rival kings, Sacina and Setecama by name, from a nation that has been invading the Sapi lands from the east. These have been driven back, but have fortified themselves within a town they call Conga. It is a strong position, and their enemies have many men within it. Kings Sheri and Yhoma have attacked it many times, but have failed with all. They have witnessed the weapons of the white men, and believe they will win if you choose to ally yourselves with them to take this town.'

Hawkins looked around at his captains. Jack reckoned they were all having the same thought, for it did not take Hawkins long to turn back to Cabral.

'Ask them what we get in return.'

Cabral posed the question, and the two emissaries broke into smiles as they provided their answer.

'Captives,' said Cabral. 'As many as can be taken.'

Once again, Hawkins turned to his captains.

'One throw of the dice, gentlemen,' he said. 'That is all we have. We cannot remain on this coast more than a matter of days, we cannot go south into the Bight of Benin, and we know there is nothing to the north. Aye, I'd hoped a cargo might appear that would be ripe for the taking and fall into our laps, but that's not going to be so. God knows, I don't want to attack a fortress and risk any of our men's lives, but it seems to me that God has also presented us with an opportunity we can't refuse. These little kings want English guns for their war? Then I say they shall have them.'

There was a growl of approval, and Jack found himself joining in.

—

'No, Tom!' said Jack Stannard.

142

'It's decided, Father. I cannot withdraw without being accused as a coward. Rightly accused.'

'But why, in God's name?'

'Isn't it obvious? Have you not said as much yourself? Would you not go in my place, if you were twenty years younger – even ten? There's been no chance of glory for us, and no chance of profit either. Drake and all the Devon men despise us as foreigners. But Hawkins is fairer, and listened to my case. Cabral, myself and ten of our men as part of the force of ninety that Barrett will take upriver to attack Conga. It makes sense.'

The two men, father and son, were arguing in the stern cabin of the *Jennet*. With the sun, tide and wind as they were, the space was blessedly cool, albeit at a temperature that would rarely be found even on the hottest days in Dunwich.

Jack did not reply, but turned to look out across the sea. Tom studied his father. He had aged since the beginning of the voyage; there was no doubt of it. Not long ago, he would not have been so cautious. Tom thought back to the Bay of Aiguillon. It seemed an eternity ago, yet it was only a few short months. The Jack Stannard who had fought off the French there had been altogether a bolder, more certain creature than the one who stood before him now.

'And if you perish?' said Jack, without turning back to face his son.

'You will still have two grandsons left alive, to teach and make into seamen.' Tom did not even think of mentioning his half-brothers George, Harry and Ned; they were lost to the sea, and in so many ways to their father, too. Nor did he mention his doubts that Adam would ever want anything to do with the Stannard trades. Even at his tender age, the lad rarely lifted his nose from the Bible, even though he could only understand one word in every three. Peter – laughing, impudent Peter – was a different matter.

Jack Stannard turned, then walked over slowly to his son. He reached out and embraced him firmly.

'Aye, well, so be it, then. May God go with you, son – no, forgive me, but I have to say it the old way. *Dominus tecum*, Tom.'

The younger man smiled. They were the words he had rebelled against throughout the reign of the late Lady Mary, the words he had sworn never to utter again, but knowing that this might be the last time they saw each other upon earth, he would not deny his father this comfort.

'*Et cum spiritu tuo, Pater.*'

–

An hour later, the *Jennet*'s boat, commanded by Tom, was second in the little fleet under Robert Barrett that slowly made its way up the Sierra Leone river. The sails, nearly useless against this easterly breeze, had already been abandoned, and men were at the oars, straining against both the current and the incessant heat. Both sides of the river were utterly featureless, the monotony broken only by the sight of elephants walking slowly along the banks and sometimes stepping into the water to cool themselves, much to the alarm of some in the English boats. The sights and the discomfort confirmed Tom's opinion that this was a vile and thankless place.

After another hour, a small party of natives appeared on the northern bank, and exchanged the signal agreed between the emissaries and Hawkins. The English boats pulled in to one of the few relatively open landing places, and the little army stepped ashore. They were a very little army indeed, and as they entered the native camp, Tom became even more aware of the fact. The path into the camp was lined by hundreds upon hundreds of natives, all nearly naked, all armed with spears, bows and clubs. They eyed the English party with what seemed to be a mixture of curiosity, suspicion and contempt.

'If they should turn on us...' said Tom to Cabral.

The Portuguese nodded. The stares directed at him were of a very different kind, and he knew that if the native kings changed their minds, he would probably suffer a very different fate to his white companions. He said nothing, choosing instead to return with interest the stares of the more brazen natives.

The Englishmen were led to the largest of a small cluster of mud huts. The interior was blessedly cool but very dark, and it took Tom's eyes a few moments to adjust.

The two kings sat upon stools in the centre of the hut, flanked by dozens of old men who were presumably their ministers and courtiers. Some things were the same the world over, Tom thought, as he joined Barrett in bowing to royalty. King Sheri was the older and larger of the two, very fat and wearing the skin of what had once been a great cat of some sort. His ally Yhoma was a much younger man, strongly muscled and with tightly curled hair. Barrett launched into a brief but flattering speech that would have done credit to Richmond Palace, with Cabral providing the translation to the two monarchs. They, in turn, extended their greetings to the general of the mighty King Isabella, and ordered a toast in palm wine, which Tom found both unexpectedly strong and surprisingly pleasant.

The formalities over, detailed negotiation began. This was painfully slow, with everything having to go through Cabral, and it swiftly became clear that there had been some misconceptions on the English side. The two kings did not simply want a bombardment of Conga from the river, with the falconet swivel guns that the Englishmen had brought up in their boats; they also wanted Barrett's men to assist them in an assault on the landward defences of the town, and expressed clear disappointment that Hawkins had sent so few men.

The critical moment came when, through Cabral, Barrett asked how many warriors were defending the town.

'Six,' came the reply.

'Six? Hundred?'

Cabral asked for clarification, and King Yhoma said something in his own language, which the Portuguese pilot evidently had difficulty with. King Sheri said something else, and Cabral turned to his English companions with a curious expression upon his face.

'No,' he said. 'Six thousand.'

Tom was taken aback, but Robert Barrett merely nodded.

'Stubble to our swords,' he said, 'and more than enough captives to fill our decks ten times over. A mighty windfall indeed for our investors and for England, thanks be to God.'

'As you say, Captain Barrett,' said Tom, 'but if we do capture the town and take that many prisoners, how do we ninety men guard them for the passage back to the fleet?'

Robert Barrett was a devout man, of the sort who fervently believed that God would provide in all eventualities, but the expression on his face suggested that he knew at once that Tom Stannard was right, and that something other than divine intervention would be required.

'In that event,' he said, 'we'll send to the admiral for reinforcements. In the meantime, I say we should test the defences of this place for ourselves. These are heathen savages, Stannard – what sort of fortress could they build that would hold for even an hour against godly Englishmen, eh?'

–

Tom's experiences in the next two days proved incontrovertibly that the answer to Barrett's rhetorical question was not that which the shipmaster of the *Jesus* had anticipated. Conga was vast, even by English standards, and its defences would not have been discreditable if they had surrounded one of Queen Elizabeth's greatest fortresses. When they first approached the town, King Yhoma arranged a demonstration, ordering forth a cohort of a hundred of his men. These obeyed without the slightest hesitation, even though they must have known the fate that awaited them. As the group ran toward the defences, the ground suddenly gave way, and a dozen of them vanished. Tom could hear terrible screams, and Cabral commented casually that the defenders would have placed sharpened stakes in the bottoms of countless hidden pits. More stakes, bristling like some vast hedgehog, lay between the attackers and the wall, and the few who got as far as that final barrier were mown down by arrows fired from the top of a wall more than ten feet high, assembled from huge tree trunks lashed together. Behind the wall, the drums of the defenders beat out a constant rumble of defiance, while the men on the rampart gave strange, piercing yells that unnerved the English attackers.

Robert Barrett now ordered his arquebusiers into position, and a score of Englishmen let loose a half-dozen volleys. But these struck the enormous wooden wall and did no harm; the tops of the heads of the defenders, all that could be seen at that range, were far too small and distant to be realistic targets. Tom could hear the falconets from their boats in the river firing on the far side of the town, but within an hour, word came from these, reporting that their shot had had no effect at all on the defences or the defenders on that side.

For the rest of that day, and all of the next, Barrett persevered. The English probed at every stretch of Conga's defences, at every corner and quarter, but the upshot remained the same, and finally he admitted defeat. He did so with considerable reluctance; he had known John Hawkins rather longer than Tom Stannard, and knew exactly how the admiral would react to yet another summons for help.

–

Barrett's concerns were borne out. When he arrived before the walls of Conga that evening, with Dudley, Drake, several gentlemen volunteers and another hundred men – the most that could be spared without compromising the safety of the fleet – Hawkins was in a foul temper, and spared little time in taking out his frustrations on the officers of his vanward.

'Sweet Jesu, Rob,' he snapped at Barrett, 'we are *Englishmen*! We follow the true reformed faith! These fellows do not even wear clothes, and they worship stones and skulls!'

'Cousin,' said Tom, in as mollifying a tone as he could manage, 'the position is very strong.'

'The defences are of wood,' said Drake, loftily. 'Now, that might still be what you use in Suffolk, but in Devon, we have long been accustomed to stone. Are you seriously saying that we Englishmen cannot overcome walls of wood and naked savages?'

'Captain Stannard is right,' said Barrett, but Hawkins was evidently in no mood to listen, Drake even less.

'No,' said Hawkins. 'Damnation, we can spare no more time, and must be away from this coast! This place will fall, and it will fall tomorrow, as God is my judge! You, there! Cabral!'

The Portuguese stepped forward, and bowed his head slowly in a gesture that Tom considered a perfect blend of respect and contempt.

'Admiral.'

'Go to our allies, these jumped-up little kings! Tell them to deploy all their forces on the morrow, for we attack at noon!'

'As you say, Admiral.'

As dawn broke, and the two armies of their allies prepared for the attack, even Drake could not disguise his admiration. The thousands of warriors oiled their skin, then danced and chanted to the rhythm of their drums. Tom thought of his father, the sometime choirboy of Cardinal College, Ipswich, downstream aboard the *Jennet*. Without doubt, he would have been impressed by the singing of these heathen natives.

When the sun was high enough in the sky, the native regiments moved forward to the edge of the bow's range from the wall. A trumpet sounded, the boats in the river opened fire with their falconets, the attacking army charged forward, and the English contingent landed on the tiny area of riverbank available to them. Tom walked forward in the van of the English contingent, close to Hawkins, who was urging his men to ever greater efforts. The admiral, seemingly ignoring the heat, was dressed incongruously in his best armour, including a splendidly decorated and immaculately polished breastplate. The defenders responded furiously, sending down a hail of arrows, but these were very different from the bolts that had slaughtered the French at Agincourt. No more than light darts, they bounced off the men's leather jerkins and did no greater damage than inflicting wounds akin to insect bites; having seen men struck by them more than two days earlier, Tom was confident that these arrows were not poisoned, and thus were little more than inconveniences. Within an hour, he had taken perhaps half a dozen hits, but continued to fight his way forward.

At Hawkins' command, the English assault was concentrated on one small part of the defences on the river side of the town. Barrett's boats had already weakened this during the previous days, and with more craft, and thus more guns, at his disposal, Hawkins could now mount a sterner and more persistent attack. When a trumpet blew, the boats ceased fire and the English ashore stormed forward. The natives on the ramparts howled and shot off their arrows, but the bombardment from the boats and the steady fire from the arquebuses slowly weakened their resolve. Soon, the men at the front of the English formation reached the rampart itself, and Tom found himself hacking at it with his sword, slashing through the ropes that held the great tree trunks together.

Another blast of the trumpet, and the English attack withdrew slightly. The guns on the boats in the river fell silent.

Tom returned to Hawkins' position on the riverbank, joining Drake, who was casually pulling an arrow out of his arm, and Dudley, whose cheek was bloody.

'All right, lads,' said Hawkins, 'all right. We have our breach. Time for God's righteous flame, the fire of England itself!'

A ragged cheer greeted his words. The arquebusiers, their work done for the moment, moved to the rear on Dudley's command, and their place was taken by the cross-bowmen, who had been held back deliberately. Behind them, the pikemen formed up, their weapons lowered for an adjustment to their usual method. Several blazing cauldrons had been set up on the riverbank, making the place even more hellish, and from these the crossbowmen lit fire arrows.

'For God, Elizabeth and old England!' cried Hawkins, raising his sword and then sweeping it downward with a shout of 'Loose!'

The crossbowmen fired high. Their arrows cleared the rampart easily, landing in the dry palm-leaf roofs of the mud huts within Conga. Tom clearly heard the screams of women and children, but the crossbowmen had already reloaded, and without waiting for a fresh command from Hawkins, they fired at will.

Another three volleys followed, by which time much of the nearest part of Conga was well ablaze. Now the pikemen advanced. But their weapons were not capped by the usual deadly spearhead; instead, they bore flaming bell-shaped containers filled with pitch. The trumpet sounded, and the English advanced into the breach, supplemented by several files of the native kings' armies. Still the defenders of Conga resisted ferociously, but without the rampart to shelter them, they were easy targets for the arquebuses and swords of the English, as well as the throwing spears and arrows of the attacking army. Worse for them, the pikemen now fanned out, and began to fire more and more of the huts that the crossbowmen had not been able to reach.

For a moment, perhaps even an entire minute, Tom found himself shoulder to shoulder with Francis Drake as two or three dozen defenders rushed them. He cut and thrust, but took no pleasure in the business. His foes had no strategy, no guile, and no answer to a sword wielded by a man who knew how to use it. His blade sliced easily into native flesh, severing limbs, hacking through ribs and collarbones, taking off heads. He felt as though every inch of him was drenched in blood, and he could see that Drake was the same.

'A Suffolk man who can use a blade as well as a Devonian,' said Drake, panting for breath in a brief lull as their assailants fell back to regroup. 'So you know how to fight and kill after all, Tom Stannard.'

'I learned from my father,' gasped Tom, 'and he learned in turn from a man who was at Flodden, Marignano and Pavia. A man who went down with the *Mary Rose*.'

'That so? Well, then. We must talk of it one day. Take your guard, though, Stannard of Dunwich, for here they come again!'

So it went on. More and more it seemed to Tom as though he were fighting through Hell itself, for the flames from the burning huts made the day even hotter, and the smoke stung his eyes. Now, too, there were unearthly screams from the far side of the town, as though the dead themselves were wailing from the depths of their eternal torment. It took him a moment to realise that this could only be the war cries of their allies' main army, which must have finally breached the rampart on the other side of Conga. It was the age-old story in sieges: make one breach, and no matter how many defenders remained, they were doomed nine times out of ten. He caught a glimpse of Hawkins, but heard him more readily than he saw him.

'Stay together, my lads! Keep formation, damn you! No looting now! God is with us! To God and the queen be the glory! The day is ours!'

As he heard those words, Tom Stannard watched one of the allied natives chase a naked boy of about Adam's age out of one of the burning huts, then skewer the hysterical child upon the point of his spear, exulting as he did so.

So this, it seemed, was victory.

Fifteen

It was a hard winter in Dunwich. Blizzard followed blizzard, and thick snow often carpeted the heath for days on end, making it impossible for Meg to leave her isolated home, let alone reach the town, even to attend the pale imitation of Christmas Mass that the law now enjoined. But she had learned from her late aunt Agatha, who had possessed the cottage before her, so there was always enough food in the building for two or three weeks, and enough wood for the fire for just as long. One snowstorm confined her to the cottage for six days, but at the end of that time, and although it was still bitterly cold, there was enough of a break in the weather for her to set out upon the path to Dunwich, and for traffic to begin to move more freely on the roads around the Sandlings.

Unknown to her, it was the very day, and the very time, when, four thousand miles to the south, her brother was attacking the walls of Conga.

Meg followed her usual route toward the Palesdyke, but as she neared it, she saw a curious sight. A lone rider upon a large, sleek black mare was turning in through the barely discernible gap that had once been the south gate. The man appeared well dressed, with a sword at his side, but he was hooded, and she could not see his face. Curious, she thought: there was no road to the south gate, and had not been for very many years, if not centuries. All travellers from outside the town entered by Middlegate or St James Gate, and it was inconceivable that anyone could have ridden through the thick gorse on the heath, especially with so much snow lying upon it. So whoever this rider was, he must have deliberately chosen to skirt round the town, avoiding the usual entrances, so as to enter unobserved. It was very unlikely that any citizens of Dunwich had yet ventured out of their houses, and if any had, they would almost certainly be going in the opposite direction of this, either to the churches or the harbour.

She followed the rider.

A little further on, he turned off the path and coaxed his reluctant horse through the thick snow toward the ruins of Blackfriars. He seemed not to be aware of Meg's presence behind him. Close by the monastic remains, he dismounted, tethered his horse, then walked into what had once been the refectory building. Meg followed, giving the horse a wide berth in case it should alert the rider to her presence. She pressed herself against the refectory wall, then edged along it until she came to a former doorway. Slowly, silently, she looked through the doorway.

Empty.

Very carefully, she stepped through into the roofless building—

A man's arm hooked around her neck, squeezing the breath out of her. She punched out, but he was pressed up behind her, and she could muster no force. Instead, her hands went up to his arm, to try to break his grip, but he was relentless, threatening to choke the very life out of her. She could feel his breath upon her neck, and could even see it as little clouds upon the icy air. Then his other arm came around, and his hand fondled her breasts. She screamed, but she knew the vast old walls of Blackfriars would deaden the sound long before it reached the houses of Duck Street.

The man's hand moved down, across her stomach. Then he suddenly thrust it between her legs and grabbed at her. She screamed again.

'I could have you, here and now,' said the man, whispering coldly into her ear. 'And oh, there would be such pleasure in being inside Jack Stannard's daughter, every which way I pleased. So very much pleasure.'

As suddenly as he had gripped her, he released her. She stepped forward and turned toward him, but she already knew who he was.

'But I am a God-fearing man,' he said, 'and as such, mindful of canon law. So I will not commit incest upon you, niece.'

Stephen Raker pulled back the hood from his head. His grey hair was close-cropped and little more than stubble, but he also sported a large and well-groomed grey beard. He was fleshier than her father.

'I will not call you uncle,' said Meg, trying to conceal the fact that she was shaking.

Raker laughed. 'I am grateful, Margaret Stannard – no, your pardon, Widow de Andrade. You see, there are already more than enough chinless youths and mewling brats in Southwold who call me that. Families, eh?'

She stared hard at the man's face. It was difficult to see any resemblance to her father, his brother, but there was something about him that reminded her of her grandfather, even though she could not remember him before the leprosy ruined his features.

'You are bold to ride into Dunwich,' she said as her breath steadied and her heart grew calmer. 'There are many in this town who blame you for the deaths of loved ones, and would gladly see you dead. Many who would gladly kill you themselves. I am of that number.'

Raker shrugged. 'Times change,' he said, simply. 'But I have no interest in being in the heart of your precious town, niece, which is why I took the route I did. My interest is here, and here alone.'

'Blackfriars? What interest can you have in a ruin?'

'Your stepmother hasn't told you? Christ's holy wounds, she's more discreet than I imagined. Why, niece, we are set to become neighbours, you and I, for I have a mind to buy this place.'

'*Buy* it? Buy Blackfriars?'

'Just that. Curious, how it has remained unsold all these years – ah, but then I suppose a buyer might be deterred by the notion that it might fall into the sea before their son could inherit. I have no sons, so I have a mind to build a house here, niece. What think you to that?'

Meg had no reply. After all, the notion of Stephen Raker building a house at Dunwich Blackfriars was precisely as unlikely as that of her standing there engaged in a superficially civil conversation with the man who had once tried to kill her father.

Raker began to walk around, his boots crunching through the virgin snow, inspecting the ruinous building with a proprietorial air. Meg, though, remained rooted to the spot, trying to take in what she had heard.

Finally, she managed one question.

'What part does my stepmother play in this?'

'She really hasn't told you? What a curious family you Stannards are. If I'm to acquire this place, I need an intermediary in Dunwich, someone with knowledge of the town, and there are precious few who'd be willing to undertake such a role for any man of Southwold, let alone any named Raker. Your stepmother, though, is an incomer, and thus has little prejudice against either.'

'You would not dare to even think of such a thing if my father and brother were here,' said Meg. 'And whatever else she might say or do, my stepmother swore at the altar to obey my father in all things.'

Stephen Raker smiled. 'As well, then, that your father and brother are upon such a distant and lengthy voyage, is it not?'

Something was very wrong, but Meg could not quite grasp it. She watched Raker poke his head into dark corners and push aside piles of rubble so he could see what lay behind. *Something was very wrong.* Not even Jennet Stannard would do something so certain to enrage her husband and stepson – to ensure that when they finally returned from sea, there would be a reckoning that could not possibly end well for her.

Of course.

Meg cursed herself for her slowness, but now that she had thought of the answer, it was obvious.

'What does my stepmother get in return?'

'Mmm? Oh, that's between me and her, I think. And between you and her, if you choose to ask her, and she chooses to tell you. But it isn't just a matter of Raker and Stannard, Meg. Think of this – if I build a house here and become a burgess of Dunwich, then it ends the conflict between our towns. All those long centuries of undeclared war at a close. Peace will reign, as Our Lord enjoins. What could be worthier, eh?'

Raker smiled at her, but Meg did not believe a word that this man, her uncle by blood alone, had spoken. She did not trust him, and she certainly did not trust her stepmother.

She mumbled her excuses, and Raker bowed and said something complimentary in return, which she immediately forgot. She walked out of the ruins of Blackfriars in a daze, and thought for a moment of returning to her cottage, bolting the door behind her, and rejecting a world that seemed to have gone insane.

Instead, she turned north. Her younger self would have gone immediately to her former family home and berated her stepmother. But the widow Margaret de Andrade was not quite as impetuous a creature as the young Meg Stannard had been, and that was due in part to Luis, her husband of only two years. No man could have been further removed from the popular view of Spaniards, and especially young Spaniards, as being hot-blooded and impulsive. Had he been walking beside her that day, treading through the snow there upon Dunwich cliff, he would undoubtedly have urged her to be very sure that she had all the facts, a proper plan of campaign, and a way of extricating herself from any unforeseen difficulty, before she confronted Jennet Stannard.

That, then, was exactly what she would do, and that, in turn and firstly, meant going to talk to Harry Chever, master of the small Stannard ship *Gerfalcon*, presently lading at the Dain quay for a voyage to London.

Sixteen

'They are killing my Negroes!' cried Hawkins. 'They are slaughtering my profit!'

The Englishmen stood in the middle of Conga, arrayed in defensive formation. All around them, the armies of the two kings ran through the town, the warriors screaming and slaughtering indiscriminately. A few women were carried into huts to be raped, but most, and all of the children within sight, were simply impaled on spears. Many were then hacked or torn to pieces. Some who avoided this fate managed to reach the English line and surrendered themselves, but even though the number of captives swiftly swelled to several dozen, it was still nothing like enough to satisfy Hawkins, who continued to rage and curse. But this could occupy only part of his attention. A few native warriors, driven crazy by bloodlust, attempted to attack even their erstwhile allies, so Hawkins ordered the firing of an arquebus or two to remind them where their loyalties lay. All around, fires raged, and a great pall of smoke hung over the scene, depositing a coating of ash upon the ground and on the heads and shoulders of the Englishmen.

Hawkins was right, as Tom Stannard knew full well as he looked around at the horrors before him. All thought of prisoners seemed to have been abandoned by the rampaging warriors, and if the victorious armies wiped out the entire population of Conga, there might yet be next to no slaves for the English to take to the Indies. Hawkins had sent Cabral to the two kings to implore them to restrain their troops, but as yet, there was no sign of his return. What was more, King Sheri's son had fallen during the assault on the landward rampart, so that monarch was unlikely to be in any mood for mercy.

Far from it. There was a great commotion over toward the far side of the town, principally the pitiful screams of many hundreds of men, women and children.

'Yonder, lads!' cried Hawkins. 'Let's be brisk!'

Keeping a tight formation, the English swept forward as a phalanx, presenting a formidable sight that deterred even the largest groups of battle-crazed warriors. By chance, Tom again found himself alongside Francis Drake, whose face was a mask of revulsion.

'Did you ever see the like, Tom Stannard? Did you ever dream such things happened?'

'Not I.'

'If we go to Hell, can it be worse than this?'

Tom made no reply before the movement of the men around them pushed them apart again.

Finally, the little English army reached the remains of the rampart, and looked out over a hellish scene. On that side of the town, a swamp lay between the rampart and the river. Into this, the victorious armies were driving hundreds of men, women and children from the defeated garrison of Conga. Wailing infants clung to their mothers as they tried desperately to keep their heads above the dark slime of the swamp waters. Men fought each other frantic-ally for a handhold on a mangrove root. Others trampled women and children beneath them as they tried to reach the river. Many heads struggled to stay above the dark slime of the swamp waters, then lost the battle and slipped beneath it. A few of the toughest young men managed it, but even those who could swim struggled against the strong current. A few reached the English boats, in the middle of the stream, and were hauled aboard. Fewer still reached the far bank and freedom. And all the while, regiments of the two victorious kings stood at the edge of the swamp, singing, dancing, and waving their spears.

'Where the hell is Cabral?' said Hawkins. 'This needs to stop. Christ's nails, haven't these savages had enough of blood?'

There remained no sign of Bruno Cabral, but it was also increasingly evident that the rampage had run its course. The English returned within the ramparts, and although unburned huts were being looted, the indiscriminate slaughter had ceased. Instead, prisoners were being herded together and marched toward the centre of the town. Tom saw Hawkins smiling with satisfaction and recognised the cause easily enough: the expedition's balance sheet now looked a lot healthier.

The Englishmen made their way back through the town to their original landing place and helped their boats to moor. A rudimentary camp was erected, and a swift roll call was taken. Four men dead, four likely to be so by the morning, and forty or so with slight wounds from the defenders' feeble arrows. There was also still no sign of Bruno Cabral.

One of the four dying men was from the *Jennet*, and Tom sat down by him. Ned Bultflower was a fellow of his own age, and Tom had known him since childhood. He was a jovial, well-liked man who had a wife and four children in a cottage just by St James hospital. But as Tom watched the blood ooze through the bandage that covered the terrible spear wound in Bultflower's side, he knew that his wife would need to adorn herself in widow's weeds.

'God be with you, Ned,' he said, as cheerily as he could manage.

'And with you and yours, Tom. It's over, then?'

'It is.'

'And this winning. Has it been worth it?'

'Admiral Hawkins seems to think so.'

Bultflower grimaced with pain. 'Good. Aye, good that I'll die for a cause that was worth it.'

Tom looked away, and tried to muster what words he could, no matter how feeble.

'You'll not die, Ned Bultflower.'

'That I will. Don't you feel the cold, Tom Stannard? 'Tis January, after all, and colder than a Dunwich cliff in a blizzard.'

Tom was still sweating from the oppressive heat of the evening.

'Aye, Ned, 'tis cold.'

'And you'll tell my Jane of my end, and see that she and the babes are cared for?'

'I swear it, Ned.'

'And can you hear the waves, Tom Stannard, and the church bells beneath them?'

'I hear them, Ned.'

Ned Bultflower coughed blood, and died.

Tom placed Ned's jerkin over his face, then stood and murmured the Lord's Prayer. No doubt his father would have intoned the requiem in Latin; Ned might have preferred that, for he, too, had largely adhered to the old ways. But Tom Stannard no longer remembered the words of the requiem further than its first line.

Tom needed distraction. Seeing that Hawkins was forming a party of men to go to the victorious kings' encampment in the town to fetch victuals, he volunteered to command it. The sun was all but down, fires were lit, and the songs of victory and celebration reached his ears almost as soon as he and his men were through the remains of the rampart. As they approached the centre of Conga, they had to push and shove their way through increasingly tightly packed throngs of native warriors, all of whom were exultant. There was a smell of cooking, too, a delicious aroma that Tom took to be pork. Perhaps there would be meat for the Englishmen's supper.

Tom and his men emerged into the centre of the kings' encampment. Sheri and Yhoma sat upon their thrones, watching contentedly as their warriors danced around the pyres over which their meal was being cooked. It took Tom a few moments to realise what he was seeing. The carcasses were human torsos. King Yhoma was feasting on what was all too apparently a roasted human arm.

On one of the pyres, the head was still attached to the torso, and the face was still relatively unburned.

Tom retched.

It was the face of Bruno Santos Cabral.

Seventeen

The house stood on Aldersgate, north of St Paul's. It was very large, for it also incorporated the owner's printing works, and the servant who admitted a shivering Meg into the hallway was liveried. She knew that this man now owned other properties in London, as well as landed estates in Suffolk, and that he had a colossal brood of children, none of whom seemed to be present. He had come a very long way from his origins, she reflected. But then, she had come a long way to remind him precisely of those origins.

The servant led her up the stairs, then knocked upon a door that was already open. An inaudible remark from the man within saw Meg's admittance. She stepped into a large, high chamber, with windows that stretched very nearly from the floor to the ceiling, giving a fine view over the thick snow through which she had trudged. The sheer amount of glass, and the opulence of the tapestries covering most of the oak-panelled walls, provided further testimony to the wealth of the occupant. A fire in the far wall cast a welcome heat.

The house's owner rose from a large chair, closing the book he had been reading. It was one of only two books in the room. The other, upon a stand set slightly back from the windows, was by far the largest that Meg had ever seen, and was elaborately bound in finely tooled leather.

She had seen a smaller, cheaper copy of it in the rectory of St Peter's at Dunwich. Whatever its size, and whatever its cost, it was the source of the prosperity of the man standing before her. She hated this book with a passion that went almost beyond reason.

'Margaret de Andrade, formerly Stannard,' said the man, punctiliously. 'You have grown far beyond the child I remember from Dunwich. Welcome, in the name of all that binds us.'

John Day was a little younger than her father, but looked far older, for he had chosen to sport the sort of very long beard, falling to below his breastbone, that was generally favoured by very senior bishops. His sumptuous gown, too, would not have been inappropriate garb for a prelate.

'Master Day,' she said. 'It is good of you to receive me.'

'Remembrance of times past deserves no less,' he said. 'You sailed here, then? An unpredictable voyage, especially at this time of year. Not many women would consider such an undertaking.'

He gestured towards two chairs by the vast book, and they sat, facing each other awkwardly.

'It was an uneventful voyage, Master Day. Cold and very slow, but uneventful. Still faster than any journey by road between Dunwich and London could be, conditions being what they are.'

Cold it certainly had been; there were even sheets of ice floating in the sea off the Essex shore. The towers of Greenwich Palace had been crusted with ice and topped with snow.

'Indeed,' said John Day. 'And how fares my home town?'

'Poorly, sir. The harbour becomes more silted by the year, so more and more families move away. Maison Dieu and St James hospital are both all but ruins. The market is now barely worthy of the name.'

The vast beard shook. 'I had heard as much, and regret it. I have not been back for years, as you know. No Days left in Dunwich now, and our house sold. But the market square, when your father and I were boys – the smells, the people, the bustle!'

There was a trace of a smile upon John Day's face, and Meg knew she had to seize the moment.

'I crave your pardon for taking up your time, Master Day, but if you have a place in your heart that loves Dunwich still, then perhaps you will spare some minutes to listen to the tale I have to tell.'

He nodded.

'Master Day, have you heard the name of Stephen Raker?'

'It is known to me,' said Day, 'as the name of Lucifer was known unto Christ.'

She told him of Raker's scheme to buy the Blackfriars, not sparing her stepmother's name. She omitted only the detail that Raker was, in truth, her father's brother, and – in Meg's opinion, at any rate – still intent on bringing down Dunwich to avenge the circumstances of his parent-hood.

'Troubling indeed,' said John Day, when she had finished. 'But I do not see how you think I can help.'

'My father says you are a rich and famous man.'

He laughed at that. 'Rich, perhaps. But famous? Publishers are not famous, Margaret. The authors whose works they print are famous.' He pointed at the vast volume upon its stand. 'John Foxe is famous. I merely put his words upon the page, bound the pages together, and sold the books.'

She had tried to avoid looking at the book, but now glanced toward it.

> *Actes and Monuments of these Latter and Perillous Dayes, touching matters of the Church, wherein are comprehended and described the great persecutions, horrible troubles, that have bene wrought and practised by the Romishe prelates, speciallye in this Realme of England and Scotlande, from the yeare of our Lorde, a thousande, unto the tyme nowe present.*

A mouthful. Instead, every man, woman and comprehending child in England knew it as Foxe's *Book of Martyrs*.

The book that Foxe and Day had produced between them was now so famous and so influential that even many of those who had actually attended the events described in it, and were thus eyewitnesses, now swore instead by the often lurid versions peddled within the pages. Naturally, Meg had read the section describing the rightful execution – or, as Foxe had it, the martyrdom – of William Flower, and found that it bore little resemblance to her recollection of events. But in the new England of Elizabeth, the bastard of Boleyn, it was not possible to say such things out loud. She knew people who had cheered wildly at burnings of heretics in Mary's time, but who now dressed soberly, prayed fervently in English in Peter's church on each and every Sunday, and could recite whole passages of this book by heart.

'Master Day,' she said, 'is it not true that this book can open doors for you that are closed to me, or even to my father? You can ask questions that I, a mere woman, cannot ask, and you can ask them of men in every position in the land – at court, in the law, in the Church. You can discover things that I could never even become aware of.'

John Day's face was expressionless. Perhaps he was flattered at being credited with so much influence; but there was something else in his face, too, something that troubled Meg.

'I remember you,' he said, at last. 'I remember you, when I came back to Dunwich and saw you in old John's church, reverently dressing the statues of the saints in the times when such affronts to scripture were permitted. And I remember the talks I had with your father about matters of faith. Over the years, those talks became more strained.'

Meg had feared this. She felt her mouth dry up and tightened her grip on the arms of her chair.

'I… I am loyal to the Church, and the queen,' she said.

'You go to church on Sunday only to avoid the recusancy fines,' he said sharply. 'Tell me something, Margaret. Have you read Foxe's book, there? Foxe's, and mine?'

'I have read passages… I mean, I do not own a copy, but—'

'And do you like what you have read?'

She knew now that her coming here had been a dreadful mistake. Between them, John Foxe and John Day had created a new history for England, and it was a history that Meg and the very many like her could never be a part of. No, worse: the *Book of Martyrs* made Meg and all the good, sober, religious people who wanted to worship God quietly and in the old way into the acolytes of Satan.

Meg could not give John Day an answer, for she knew herself well enough to know that her true answer was already written upon her face.

The silence between them seemed to become interminable. Through the windows, she could see daylight beginning to fail. Another heavy snow shower was blowing in on the west wind. At length, John Day summoned his servant, and ordered candles to be lit. After the man had left, Day stared intently at Meg.

'You are not of the true, reformed faith, Margaret Stannard, for I will not call you by your papist name.' He spoke now in a cold, matter-of-fact way. 'I strongly suspect that you and your father still hold to the Bishop of Rome, and all his sins and falsehoods. I have reason to believe, from what some in Dunwich told me years ago, that you know where the Doom painting is – that great idolatry from John's church that helped keep the people of our town in the depths of ignorance for so very long. I should have you thrown into the street, goodwife. I should leave you to make your way home, back to that godforsaken village, crumbling upon its cliff.'

Meg could feel her guts churning. But John Day sighed, steepled his hands, and then spoke more softly and kindly.

'But I am a man of Dunwich. It bore me, and it raised me. Whatever its fate may be is in God's hands, but I will not see it brought under the heel of Southwold and Stephen Raker. Moreover, your father was once a good friend to me, when we played down on the quays and mudflats of Dunwich harbour. He saved my life – did you know that? – when a hawser snapped on a Lubecker at the Dain quay. I know, too, that in her short life, my dear, dead sister, whom I loved beyond measure, was a good friend to you. God commands us to honour the place of our birth, and the friendships once treasured. He certainly commands us to repay the debts we owe. So yes, Meg Stannard, I will help you.'

Eighteen

The English ships were ten days out from the coast of Sierra Leone. With the additional vessels acquired by one means or another from the Portuguese or Frenchmen, the fleet was now ten strong, and a fine sight under full sail. The weather was calm and propitious, hot but less oppressive than it had been upon that terrible shore. The trade wind filled the *Jennet*'s sails, carrying her easily onto the great arc that swept south-westerly before, God willing, it would blow her north into the very heart of the Indies.

Tom Stannard stood at the starboard rail upon the quarterdeck, looking out over the limitless ocean. Bruno Cabral had told him of this seemingly strange course that ships had to take for the easiest passage to the Americas, and explained why it was harder to sail there directly. He had patiently demonstrated the navigation of the great ocean to Tom upon his portolans and rutters. Those charts now lay upon the table in the cabin beneath Tom's feet, but he could barely bring himself to look at them. They brought back the sight of Cabral's head upon the fire at Conga. Only in the last two nights had he been able to sleep without being woken time and again by the recurring nightmare of that sight. In it, Cabral's eyes were open, and he was attempting to speak, but Tom could not hear his words.

His father had been standing double watches, and Tom finally felt able to relieve him properly. Even so, he could still think of little else, and he was not alone in this. The men of the *Jennet*, usually ebullient, stood around listlessly, or else whispered to each other. For a foreigner, Cabral had been liked and respected. Ned Bultflower, too, was mourned. It was one thing for men of Dunwich to perish at sea; that was the fate they all expected. But to die in the hellhole of Conga, and, in Cabral's case...

Tom turned and walked to the larboard side.

It had taken the best part of a day of questions and halting mistranslations to establish what must have happened to Bruno Santos Cabral. John Hawkins had dispatched him to Kings Sheri and Yhoma to demand an end to the massacre of the inhabitants of Conga, but he must have been waylaid by a group of desperate defenders, killed and stripped, European clothes being highly regarded among the native people. Naked, he would have been indistinguishable from any of the countless dead natives, so it was pure chance that his remains were made a part of the grotesque feast of celebration for the victory of the two kings.

Hawkins had accepted the story, along with the profuse apologies of the two kings and their promise of several dozen more slaves by way of compensation. But Tom had his doubts, and expressed them to his father as soon as he returned to the *Jennet*. Cabral's body would not have been oiled, as that of every warrior on both sides was, so it should have been recognisable as not belonging to a native. True, European clothes were much treasured among the native people, but the only ones actually to wear them were kings; it was a curious reflection of England's long-neglected and much-mocked sumptuary laws, where clothes of certain kinds and materials were meant to be worn only by those of a certain rank. And King Sheri, Tom told his father, was roughly the same height and build as Bruno Cabral.

Jack had listened patiently, as he always did.

'Well, Tom, mayhap it happened as you think it did, or mayhap it happened as we were told it did. But it matters not a jot now. We will be off this coast in the morning, and even if we weren't, no man would ever be brought to justice for the killing of Bruno Cabral. Nothing can bring him back, and nothing can undo what happened to him. All we can do now, son, is give succour to his immortal soul. I'll say the requiem for him, and if and when we come to a proper church in the Indies, I'll pay a priest to say Masses. So when we're away from the shore, and from the eyes of Drake and his friends, will you join me in the requiem? If not for me, then for him.'

'Aye, Father, I will. But I'll add one thing more. When I next write to Meg, I'll ask her to light candles in Dunwich, and to find a priest to say a requiem for his soul.'

The English had left the coast of Africa in haste, not even taking time to careen. Thus it was a foul, slow fleet that made its way out into the great sea passage known as the Middle Crossing. But as he had explained to his captains, Hawkins had two reasons for such a rapid departure. One was to ensure that they were across the Atlantic before the worst of the ferocious tropical storms struck; the other was that every additional hour spent upon the sickly coast of Guinea increased the risk of men falling victim to disease.

Jack Stannard concurred, but still felt a strong sense of trepidation. Cabral, who should have been his pilot for the ocean crossing and the waters within the Indies, was dead, and although he and Tom had Cabral's charts, and could fix their position as well as any man in the fleet, these were still wholly unknown waters, further away and broader than any either of the Stannards had sailed before. But Hawkins and many of his men had been this way in the past, so the *Jennet* fell in astern of the *Jesus*, endeavouring to keep the huge flagship – and, at night, its telltale stern lantern – in sight at all costs.

That was how the voyage went, day after day, week after endless week. Watches changed, positions were established by compass, cross-staff and trailing board, men occupied themselves with the thousand little tasks and repairs that a ship always required, and parties worked the pumps or scrubbed the decks. They ate food that was increasingly tough or stale, the fruits they had taken aboard in Africa giving way to the old diet of poor john, salted mutton and hard cheese, with half-measure on Fridays. They drank water that was sometimes foul, or else rot-gut beer, which was worse. They went to the heads. All the while, they looked out at nothing but the infinite sea, the only variety coming from its myriad changes of colour from green to blue to grey. Without exception, every man aboard the *Jennet* had only ever sailed in waters where their ship was out of sight of land for no more than a few days. Now, for the first time, they all came to know the seemingly endless extent of the great ocean, and found themselves in awe of it.

Fortunately, although it was unconscionably slow, the passage was benign. There were no storms such as that which had struck them during the voyage to Tenerife.

To the contrary: now it was calms that impeded their progress. Many a day, the winds dropped to little or nothing, and a thick blanket of weed closed around the hulls of the ships. They would barely move for hours, sometimes days, on end, merely drifting forward almost imperceptibly on the ocean current. The air was heavy and cloying. Then the wind would pick up again, sails would be set, and men would gulp in fresh air as though it were the nectar of the gods.

Once a week, one or both of the Stannards were invited to dine with John Hawkins and some of his other officers and gentleman volunteers, a courtesy he extended to his other captains on the other days. Hawkins kept considerable state in his cabin aboard the *Jesus*, evidently reckoning that it befitted the Queen of England's admiral – or at least, a man who considered himself as such – to do so. Hence the silver plate from which his guests ate, the fine glasses from which they drank, the liveried pages who served them, and, most remarkable of all, the band of musicians that played during the meal.

Hawkins held forth upon one subject after another, his opinions always couched as though they were facts, with no man willing to contradict him. He spoke much of what King Philip was like, of the state of affairs in France and Flanders, of the evils of the Pope, even of such matters as the state of the roads in England. Jack listened dutifully, half an ear alert to anything that could be construed as worthy of reporting to Francis Walsingham, but it was notable that the one matter Hawkins always avoided was what they might find, and what they might do, in the Indies. The success of the voyage – perhaps, indeed, their very survival – depended on how the Spaniards responded to the arrival of this alien, heretical, interloping fleet in what they considered their own private lake; yet the matter was never even mentioned. After the second or third such meal, Jack came to a conclusion. Either John Hawkins thought their task would be so easy that it was unworthy of discussion, or it was a prospect that even he found too awful to contemplate.

–

One day, after they had been at sea for two or three weeks, Tom went down into the part of the hold where the slaves were being held. The *Jennet* was not a large ship by the standards of some of the others in the fleet, and Hawkins had allotted only thirty to her, placing most of the others in the much more commodious hulls of the *Jesus*, the *Minion*, the *Swallow*, and his own *William and John*.

As he entered their space, Tom was at once over-whelmed by both the stench of human waste and the pairs of eyes that suddenly fixed on him. He looked around. The *Jennet*'s allocation consisted of seventeen men, six women and seven children, but one of the men had died when they were barely six days out from Sierra Leone, and his body had been unceremoniously slung over the side, he being deemed not worthy of Christian burial. Two of the children were weak, and he could not see them surviving the voyage; but then, they would hardly fetch any great price. A strong chain, secured to bulkheads at either end, fastened the captives to each other at the ankles, and also to the ship. They were taken up on deck for an hour a day, both to exercise themselves and to give a work party the opportunity to clean the space where they were held, a task that had at once become the most hated on the ship. The men of the *Jennet* looked on them with various expressions in their eyes: contempt from some, fear from others, greed from those who were calculating their likely profit at the voyage's end, lust from some who spent that hour gazing longingly upon the naked breasts of the women or, in a few cases, on the bodies of the men or boys. In the eyes of some, there might even have been a hint of pity.

Tom Stannard was not sure which of these feelings reigned in his own heart and mind, so his going below decks to consider the slaves more closely was, in that sense, an attempt to know himself better. He looked into the eyes of several of the slaves, trying to deduce what they thought of him, of their condition, of what they believed their eventual fate might be. He saw no hatred there, and no curiosity, either. None of them attempted to throw themselves forward to beg for their freedom. None attempted to speak to him – not that he would have understood a word. One of the children, a boy, clung more tightly to his mother and began to weep softly.

Did they think as he did? Cabral had said they did not, and his terrible fate suggested that, at the very least, these people believed in very different things. Perhaps not, though. Tom remembered, many years before, walking unsteadily from a Westminster alehouse to see the final stages of the burning of a martyr, and observing his sister's response. England burned men too, the differences being that it supposedly did so in the name of God, and the spectators did not eat the victim.

Did they hate as he did? Oh, most certainly, Tom thought. Witness the fate of the people of Conga, so despised by their enemies that they were slaughtered, handed over to the English or herded into the river. That was a hatred that every man in England could understand. There were still oldsters around Dunwich who spoke of how many men their grandfathers or great-uncles had slaughtered in the wars between York and Lancaster, while even in his own time – perhaps even at that very moment, for all he knew – both the French and the Flemings were witnessing bloody massacres very much like that which had taken place at Conga.

Did they love as he did? The mother's tenderness towards her child, stroking his hair to calm him, reminded him of Catherine and their sons. But as for other loves, the loves that he felt…

One fellow seemed to be staring at him more intently than the others, and Tom averted his eyes. He made a show of testing the chain, then turned, left the chamber, and went above to breathe some fresh air and stare at the distant horizon.

–

Within a week, Tom Stannard obtained conclusive proof that the slaves also sickened and died just as Englishmen did. The first man to succumb was Rob Garwood, one of the brothers who had survived the great storm on the outward voyage. He failed to appear for his watch and was found in the heads, moaning feebly as the bloody flux poured from him. Within two days, he was dead. Half a dozen more of the crew fell ill, together with the same number of slaves. Tom tended them as best he could, using what little knowledge he had gleaned from his aunt and sister; he even had the unfamiliar experience of wishing that Meg was there in that moment, aboard the ship, for she would undoubtedly have had a better idea of what to do. As it was, his treatment consisted of little more than isolating each case as it developed, no easy matter in a relatively small ship; applying damp cloths to their foreheads; and giving them as much as they asked for of water, beer or wine, according to their choice.

The sickness was not confined to the *Jennet* alone. Word came across of cases in all the ships, including the flagship, and in the fifth week, the Stannards learned of the passing of Edward Dudley, the bluff old soldier.

'Perhaps it would have been more merciful if Hawkins had fired his weapon that day at Tenerife,' said Jack, as father and son stood on deck.

'Dudley was a good man,' said Tom. 'A brave soldier, too, and true to his word – mark how loyally he served Hawkins after he was spared.'

The first sign of discontent came from the men's eyes. Dunwich men were always confident, even with those who were supposedly their betters, but more and more of them looked away, or down to the deck, whenever Tom or Jack Stannard passed. Around the same time, men who were engaged in conversation fell silent when a Stannard came near, and responses to orders became more sullen, the orders themselves being carried out more slowly. Singing in the fo'c'sle at dusk-tide ceased, along with the sound of Tom Bateman's fiddle. Men became irritable with each other, taking offence at words that would usually have been passed over without remark. Fists were raised, parentages challenged. The Stannards said nothing of it to each other; they knew their crew, and knew that sooner or later, one of them would come forward to present their grievances.

It was Hal Ashby, of all men, who presented himself before Tom Stannard. A gaggle of men stood in the ship's waist, whispering to each other but clearly willing Ashby onwards. Jack, for his part, leaned upon the starboard rail, determined not to give any impression of undermining his son's authority.

'Beg pardon, T— that is, Cap'n Stannard.' Ashby's speech was hesitant.

'Out with it, Hal.'

'We – that is, the crew – well, truth is, I need to speak frank, like. To putter, if ye'll permit it.'

To putter: to raise a complaint. Tom smiled. He had not heard the expression since the old times in Dunwich.

'Hal, you and I have known each other since we were children, searching for bones from the old graves of John's churchyard at the foot of Dunwich cliff. You've always spoken frankly to me, and I don't expect you to stop because of where we are, or what we do.'

'Well. So, then. Cap'n, we never expected the voyage to be like this. We've always sailed in the seas around England – aye, down to Finisterre or Tenerife mayhap, but never anything like this. When you told us of this voyage, truth be told, we were all blinded by the prospect of coin. The wages we'd earn would be more than we'd get on ten voyages over to Antwerp or Bremen, and then there was all the talk of our share of profits from the cargo once it was sold. They, Cap'n. Once *they* are sold.'

'All true enough, Hal – and God willing, all of that will still come to pass.'

'But that's the thing. We're so very far from Dunwich, we've been away so very long, and we're still nowhere near these Indies men talk of. And what profit will there be if them below decks are all dead before we get there? What use our wages if we're all dead too?'

'God willing, Hal, the sickness is abating.'

'But might start again, from them in the hold.'

'So what is it the men want?'

Hal Ashby swallowed hard. 'To throw 'em all over the side, Cap'n. To cut our losses and set course directly for England. To return home to Dunwich, Tom Stannard.'

The audacity and callousness of it stunned Tom, who could think of no response. Instead, it was his father who stepped forward.

'Two things, Hal Ashby.' Jack spoke loudly, so that the men in the waist could hear. 'One. You say we should set course directly for England. And how do you propose to do that?'

Ashby looked around to his confederates for support, but saw only shrugs.

'You – you and Goodman Tom, here – can navigate the ship.'

'Aye, we can, unlike you. You're a good enough navigator in coastal waters, Hal Ashby, when you have seamarks to fix on, and even for crossing the German Ocean. But you'll never master Cabral's charts, nor the cross-staff, the trailing board, and all the rest. Do you know the stars? Can you tell Orion's Belt, or the Crab, or the Great and Little Bear?'

'But I wouldn't be navigating if you—'

'Two. If you throw the prisoners over the side, you'd best throw us over, too, for the only way you'll do that to them is by fighting your way past us. And if we're food for the fishes, Hal Ashby, then who's going to steer you back to England, eh?'

Ashby's jaw was wide open, and he was shaking.

'Master Stannard—'

'My ship, Hal Ashby, don't you forget that,' said Jack, his voice clipped and angry. 'So even if by some miracle you do get her back to England, you'll hang as pirates and murderers, the whole set of you. You know my daughter – and you know she'll make certain of it.'

Behind Ashby, men were slowly beginning to break away from the huddle by the mainmast. Ashby desperately turned one way and then the other, but saw no succour anywhere.

'F-forgive me, Master Stannard.'

Jack nodded. 'Done, Hal Ashby. For one thing, you're too good a hand for us to hang, or to have your back flogged raw. Too good a boatswain, at that. For another, I say this. Listen, you men there! We're on the fastest course to England – trust me in this. The winds and great current that carry us now sweep us all the way to the Indies, where they turn and sweep back across the ocean. Aye, we could try to beat due north, but it would take us far longer. So to get home, we must go via the Indies – and if we have to do that anyway, which we do, we may as well try to unburden ourselves of the slaves when we get there.'

Men were looking at each other, and whispering quietly amongst themselves, but it was clear that no counter-argument would be presented. The hands drifted away, and Hal Ashby, shamefaced, joined them.

Tom turned to his father. 'You were serious? About dying to stop them throwing the slaves overboard?'

'Of course, although I know I took your name in vain, Tom.'

'Aye, well, not as much as you took Meg's.'

Jack smiled. 'Did I, though? If she had any inkling that Hal Ashby and the rest of 'em had done for us, I'll wager she'd not bother with judge, jury and hangman. She'd slice off their cocks herself, stuff them in their mouths, then slit their throats.'

Tom laughed. 'Aye, Father, that she would.'

Nineteen

If Jack Stannard had been disappointed by his first sight of Africa, the same could not be said of his first glimpse of the Indies. The fleet made its landfall at the island of Dominica. Jack and Tom stood at the rail of the *Jennet*, looking upon mountains cloaked in lush trees, golden beaches, and towering rock formations. Steam seemed to be rising like a great cloud from the abundant vegetation, and waterfalls appeared to cut into every slope they could see. For a fleet running desperately low on fresh water, and with disease raging through both the crews and the slaves, it was a blessed sight.

But like Eden itself, Dominica was deceptive.

As soon as the fleet dropped anchor, Hawkins issued orders that only minimal shore parties were to be sent out, no more than one boat per ship, and that the men dispatched to refill the water casks were to be accompanied by a strong guard. There would be no general shore leave; bitter news for men who had been trapped within a stinking, leaking wooden hull crossing the great ocean for nearly eight weeks. Tom went across to the flagship to protest, but returned a little while later with a dire message from the admiral. Dominica was inhabited by one of the most ferocious native tribes in the entire Indies. Just before Hawkins' last voyage to the area, three years earlier, the tribes of the island had killed and eaten the entire crew of a wrecked Spanish man-of-war. As he recounted the tale to his father, Jack could see that Tom's face was white; doubtless he was thinking of the fate of Bruno Santos Cabral.

Over the next day and a half, the water casks were refilled. That done, the fleet sailed southward, sighting the hilly mainland of America two days later and making landfall at Margarita, the largest of three small, mountainous islands off the coast, and the only one that remained inhabited. Hawkins had told his captains that these islands had once been made rich by the abundant pearls to be gleaned from the oyster beds around them. But the beds had been farmed too vigorously, while the divers, drawn from captured native tribesmen, had been used so harshly that they died in their droves. The admiral had been here before, during his previous voyage, and hoped that the local officials would be as keen as they were then to buy some slaves.

However, in the evening when the English fleet came into the port at the south-east corner of the island, there was a collection of mean huts that served the island's principal town some miles inland, and it was swiftly evident that the entire place was deserted. The small fort under construction at the side of the harbour was empty. Hawkins sent a party ashore with a message to the governor, whose men were found hiding in the woods behind the town. The next day, following a formal welcome for the English admiral and his captains in the town square, the reason for the local Spaniards' trepidation became apparent: a French fleet had raided the area some months earlier, devastating the entire island. Within the hearing of the two Stannards, Hawkins expressed his sympathies to the island's governor and assured him that as a loyal former servant of his most glorious majesty the Catholic King Philip the Second, he, and his men, were of vastly superior conduct to the brutish French.

A week of peaceful trading followed. The ships restocked with fresh meat, and the crews dined on beef and mutton every day, marking the contrast with the endless days of salt fish, bread and biscuit during the ocean crossing. The local colonists proved eager to buy the iron, linen and bales of cloth carried in some of the other ships, and Jack cursed the fact that the *Jennet* had sailed from Plymouth with nothing more than a poor cargo of Devon stuff, rather than good Suffolk cloth, which would have sold for a substantial profit.

He and Tom were taking turns going ashore, and one morning, Jack found himself almost alone in the town square. It was the hottest day since their arrival, and Englishmen and colonists alike were resting wherever they could find shade. Hawkins and his immediate retinue had gone off for yet another formal meal with the governor in the fort that overlooked the harbour. Jack looked around one last time, then made his way into the church, a roughly built affair at one side of the square. He did not notice the one pair of English eyes fixed on him from a shaded alley in the far corner.

Within, it was blessedly dark and cool. Jack genuflected towards the altar, looked around at the candles, the statues of the Virgin and the saints, the crucifixes, and the brightly coloured stained glass in the windows, then knelt down, took out his paternoster and began to pray. As he prayed, he wept. Here, in this strange place, he was safe; in this little island of the true faith, the faith that Dunwich and England had lost. So he prayed for his family, for his town, for his dead Alice, for the immortal soul of Bruno Santos Cabral.

Eventually, he looked up, and realised a priest was eyeing him curiously. The fellow was tall, lean and bald, his vestment rougher than any Jack had ever seen on a cleric.

The priest said something in rapid Spanish, and Jack struggled to form a response. He began in English, but then tried '*Da veniam me, Patris*', hoping that his memories from long ago had translated 'Pardon me, Father' correctly.

The priest smiled. 'You're English?' he said, in Jack's own tongue.

Jack looked at him with astonishment. 'F–forgive me, Father.'

'You didn't expect to encounter a priest who speaks your language, in this of all places? But I was a Franciscan once, and during the reign of your late Queen Mary and my King Philip, I was one of those sent to England to restore the Greyfriars at Greenwich. God willed that we should endure only for four years, and since then, there have been many strange turns in my life to bring me to this place. I am Father Vicente Soriano.'

'And I am John Stannard, of Dunwich.'

'Dunwich… that name is known to me.'

'It, too, had a house of the Greyfriars. One of those within it, a man long since departed, was once a good friend to me.'

'And you hold to the true faith, John Stannard of Dunwich, despite all that has happened in your country?'

'I do.'

Father Soriano nodded. 'When did you last take any of the holy sacraments, my son?'

'It has been many months, Father. Even then, the communion I took was that enjoined by the queen we have now, so in English. As for confession… it has been several years.'

Soriano laid his hand on Jack's shoulder.

'Well then, John Stannard of Dunwich, we will correct that. I will hear your confession, then we will celebrate Mass, you and I. Afterwards, you will tell me of your old friend, my brother in Christ, may he rest in peace and light perpetual shine upon him.'

Jack's heart sprang within his chest, and he began to weep again.

—

From the isle of Margarita, the English fleet sailed west along the coast of the mainland, its men awed by the great mountains that reared up behind the shoreline. The ships anchored again inshore of a chain of small islands, in an inlet called Borboruta, where Hawkins hoped to careen his ships. As he admitted privately to Jack, Tom and his other captains, he also hoped to be able to surreptitiously sell some of the slaves, even though the governor of this area was known to be ferociously opposed to such activity. The attitude of the local bishop, according to Hawkins, was exactly the opposite, unlikely as it might seem for a prelate of the Church of Rome to welcome a fleet full of heretics. With the governor somewhere far upcountry, the English took full advantage of the situation. The *Jennet* was one of the first ships to be lightened of her cargo, then hauled up onto the beach and pulled over onto her larboard side by ropes. With the bottom of the other side of the hull exposed, the crew could get to work.

'Doubt if a Stannard ship's ever been so foul,' said Tom.

He and his father looked at the many months of filth that had accumulated on the bottom of the *Jennet*; the river mouths of Africa had been thick with vegetation and barnacles, so the ships of the fleet were already utterly foul before they sailed for the Indies. But Jack's attention was distracted by the sight of the slaves, exercising themselves on the beach while their floating prison was made good. A few merchants had already come down from the nearby towns and were sizing up what they saw. Perhaps sales might be arranged quietly and privately before the governor of New Andalucia, as this land was called, even heard about them, let alone issued a prohibition. Jack hoped so; the sooner the human cargo was off his ship, the happier he would be. But there was another consideration now that they had finally arrived in the Indies. It was time to act upon his commission from Francis Walsingham.

Father Soriano had given Jack much information about the governor, and he had no doubt that if Hawkins strained his patience too far, the Spaniard would respond with force. That evening, Jack learned that Hawkins intended to dispatch a strongly armed party overland to Valencia, seat of the amenable bishop, to persuade the local merchants of the merits of trading with the English down at Borboruta. At once, he went out to the *Jesus* in one of the *Jennet*'s boats and sought an audience with the admiral.

John Hawkins was deep in a copy of Foxe's *Book of Martyrs*.

'Cousin,' he said, looking up. He appeared tired and distracted.

'Admiral.'

'You seem troubled, my friend.' He did not signal for Jack to sit down.

'It is this expedition to Valencia under Barrett.' Jack had rehearsed the words he would say, but now it was time to speak them, they sounded like the lies a child would tell its parents when caught stealing from a market stall. 'Are you sure it is the right course to steer? Will it not be likely to cause a breach with the governor?'

Hawkins set down the book upon his chart table and stared at Jack as though he was seeing him for the first time, then spoke with uncharacteristic coldness.

'I am admiral here, Jack Stannard. You – what are you, exactly? Captain of the *Jennet*, or a supernumerary aboard her, under your son?'

Jack was not prepared for such a hostile response.

'Admiral, I meant merely—'

'Have you seen plays, John Stannard?'

'Plays?'

'Plays. Actors.'

'I saw the mystery plays when I was a boy – and more recently, at Orford, before they were banned.'

'So, then, that is what we have here. You act your part. You tell me I should not send Barrett to Valencia. I listen, I nod, I concur with you. That is your play, John Stannard, but it is not mine. And yours is no mystery.'

Jack felt a sudden sense of dread, but if he was truly playing a part, then he would play it to the end.

'I don't know what you mean, Admiral.'

Hawkins shook his head and rubbed his eyes. In that moment, he looked at least twice his age. 'God's blood, John Stannard,' he said, 'have you really spent all these months believing that I had no idea why you were on this voyage?'

'I say again, I cannot think what you mean, friend Hawkins.' But all the confidence had ebbed from Jack's voice.

'Really? Really, Jack? Do you imagine that the investors in this voyage are a joyous and united band, who love each other heartily? I think I know the court better than you, my friend, and it is a bear pit. Every man seeks to tear out the throat of his neighbour if it will bring him just one inch nearer to this place of honour, or that lucrative property, or that baron's coronet. So what any two or three men scheme privately to undertake is swiftly known to their rivals, who will do all in their power to undermine them.'

'I still do not follow,' said Jack, although in truth, he did, all too well.

Hawkins sighed. With that, too, he relented, and beckoned for Jack to sit. He even took up the jug of wine upon the table and poured two glasses, pushing one towards Jack.

'You know my good-father Gonson, of course. He is a godly man, a man who works prodigiously for the interest of England and our queen. But you know what, cousin Stannard? I may be married to his daughter, but I wouldn't trust him to hold my gloves. And there are others behind him whom I'd trust even less, all the way up to Secretary Cecil. So when Master Benjamin Gonson, allegedly on behalf of nameless others among our investors, informs me that he wishes your ship to join the expedition – well, I am put on my guard, and so I make enquiries within the bear pit. Hence, I know that you are a sort of spy, Jack Stannard.'

Jack stared at Hawkins, but could think of no response. To deny the charge would be to perjure himself, for although 'spy' was a foul word, that, in essence, was what Francis Walsingham had made him.

Hawkins steepled his hands and smiled. 'I feel for you, cousin. You've been sent on a fool's errand, you see. No man needs to restrain me from confrontation with the Spaniards – no man more than myself. Why do you think I'm so punctilious in sending letters to each and every jumped-up minor official of these colonies, flattering them to the heights and explaining exactly what I've just done, what I'm doing now, and what I intend to do next? Why do you think I keep a detailed record of everything that has happened during our voyage, as well as copies of every piece of correspondence I send and receive? I told you before, Jack Stannard. King Philip was my old master, and I'm the last man in England who'd want a war with Spain. Would that the same could be said of others.'

Jack finally reached forward for the wine, but took no more than a sip.

'What others?'

'At bottom, cousin Stannard, you and I are simple merchants. For us, it's all about the balance sheet, the profit and the loss. We bring a cargo across the sea – wine, wool, men, whatever it might be – and we sell it, so we should be content, and our investors should be happy. Ah, but it is not as simple as that. The place where we will make the greatest profit says we may no longer trade with it. Our investors know this, the queen most of all. They throw up their hands and say, "At all costs, John Hawkins, you must not have a war with Spain!" But in the same breath, they also say, "At all costs, John Hawkins, you must make us a fortune!" By demanding the latter, of course, they risk the former, but they somehow expect me – us – to prevent it from happening. Which is why I ensure that every single thing I do, and this fleet does, is chronicled in precise detail.

'And that is where we are, Jack Stannard. All of them, from the queen downward, want to avoid a war with Spain, but at exactly the same time, they all want to make themselves richer by means of trading where Spain does not want us to trade. Indeed, to make themselves richer by whatever means, which is why even the queen raised no objection to my alternative scheme after the Portingal cheats vanished, taking their lies of African gold mines with them. And all of them – *all of them*, Jack, the queen included – secretly dream the most forbidden dream of all, that I might somehow capture the King of Spain's bullion. Irreconcilable fantasies. You know that, and I know it. For now, perhaps, they can have both. But one day, as God is my judge, they will not.'

Jack took another sip of his wine. 'You want me to leave the fleet?' he asked, resignedly. 'God willing, using Cabral's charts, we can make our own way home.'

Hawkins seemed to consider the proposition, but his response, when it came, was unequivocal. 'What, and weaken my force by one strong ship, and part with men who have shown themselves sturdy warriors for England? An admiral who did that would be cutting his own throat. No, I trust we understand each other now, Jack Stannard, just as Dudley and I did after he attacked me. But mind yourself with my cousin Drake, for he is less forgiving than I when it comes to matters like this. He already suspects you of being a papist, which you are, of course.' He said it in such an offhand way that Jack almost missed the significance of the comment.

'I… I am true—'

'Oh, spare me, Jack Stannard. I couldn't care whether you worship my God, the Pope's God, Mahomet, or whatever deity those savages pray to – much good theirs have done them. There are followers of the old faith everywhere in this fleet, and I have no issue with that, though Frank Drake does, of course, as you heard upon Christmas Day. He's voiced suspicions of you to me, and if I confirmed them, he'd closet you with him for twelve hours a day so he could convert you. Be thankful, then, that it was one of my men, not one of his, that saw you go into the church on Margarita. Sees himself as a great missionary, does Frank. He's already converted a Welshman, and fancies saving the souls of others.'

Hawkins reached forward and refilled Jack's glass, even though he had drunk very little. 'For my part,' he said, 'I have to bear in mind that which some men might call treason. The law certainly might.'

'Your meaning?'

'Here we are, Jack, upon the Spanish Main, five thousand miles from England, months from home. The queen's blessed majesty has but one life, and one heart beating within her breast. What happens if, when we return, she no longer sits upon the throne, but Mary the Second does, by the grace of God? What if the dispensation in matters of faith is a new one – or rather, the old one? Your dispensation, Jack Stannard?'

Jack shifted uncomfortably upon his chair. 'Men should not talk upon such matters, John Hawkins.'

'True, but every man *thinks* upon them constantly, as you well know. Frank Drake is young, and fervent in his faith, and cannot even conceive of the clock being turned back again. But you and I were there in that room in Westminster, Jack – aye, as was my late father, God rest his soul – when your friend Halliday revealed the identity of the Duke of Alba. So we older men know how things can change in the blink of an eye, for we have lived through such things before. That being so, we should never discount the possibility that we will return to find Queen Mary on the throne and her uncle, the Cardinal Guise, warming his feet in the palace of Whitehall.'

We older men. Jack stifled a smile, for Hawkins could be no more than thirty-five or so. He was not much older than either Tom or Francis Drake.

He was right, though. Jack remembered the alarm in the autumn of the year sixty-two, when Queen Elizabeth fell ill with smallpox and seemed likely to die. Half the kingdom prayed for her recovery, half for her death, the latter half dividing into those who would see the Lady Catherine Grey upon the throne, her sister having already occupied it for nine days; those who advocated the claim of the Countess of Lennox; and the much larger faction who favoured the Queen of Scots. Of course, Elizabeth recovered, but for some days, William James, the vehemently reformist rector of St Peter's at Dunwich, and those who thought like him, had gone about their business very quietly indeed. Never was the word of scripture more true: *media vita in morte sumus* – in the midst of life we are in death.

Hawkins stood, picked up a rolled chart, and spread it out upon the table.

'So now that we understand each other, Jack Stannard, I have a proposition that I wish to put to you. It could be an order, but your willing concurrence is the better path. We are here at Borboruta' – he jabbed at the chart – 'and Valencia, where I still intend to send Barrett, is here. Regardless of what happens with that expedition, I mean next to sail for Rio de la Hacha, here. The official there, one Castellanos by name, was accommodating during my last voyage to these parts. God willing, we shall sell all the slaves and the rest of our cargoes, then we can sail for home. But I need to judge the state of affairs there first, and to sound Castellanos' temper – he was reprimanded and fined for dealing with me. So I propose to send two of the smaller, faster ships. I think one of them should be your *Jennet*. What say you?'

Jack smiled. 'I thought you didn't know who captains the *Jennet*, Admiral.'

'You can resolve that with your son,' said Hawkins. 'For the other ship, I propose to send the *Judith*. I have just moved a new captain into her, and he needs to gain experience of this sort of expedition – the need for diplomacy, and the like. If I send you with him, you can ensure that he does nothing rash.'

Jack understood the deliberate irony of Hawkins' remark.

'Who is this new captain, Admiral?'

'Why, my kinsman Frank Drake. Do you have any issue with that, Captain Stannard?'

Twenty

'Mistress! Mistress!'

Francis Birkes flew into Meg's cottage upon the heath without any pretence at decorum. It was fortunate that Meg was at her table, mixing potions; had she been upon her close-stool, or flannelling her naked breasts, there might have been cause for reprimand. Instead, her response was merely amused.

'Well now, Francis, what is so important that you have to break into a widow's cottage unannounced? And for God's sake, lad, take a few breaths before you speak.'

The boy did so, but when he began to talk, his words still came in gasps.

''Tis the Queen of Scots, mistress!'

'What of her, Francis?'

'News come to town this very hour! She escaped from her prison in a lake – she raised an army in a week, that she did – but the army was beaten, so she fled—'

Meg raised a hand. 'Wait, lad! She *escaped*?'

'Aye, they say her gaolers fell in love with her. They say all men do, mistress.'

'And this battle? What happened?'

'That they don't say, mistress, only that she lost. So she fled.'

'Where, Francis? Where did she flee to?'

'South, mistress. To the coast of Solway, they said, wherever that may be. Then she took ship, and she landed in England.'

'*England?*' Meg collected herself and tried to breathe calmly. 'So Queen Mary is in England?'

'That's what they say, mistress.'

'Where? Free, or a captive?'

'Don't know, mistress. Somewhere in the north. Furthest north I've ever been is Yarmouth. Don't know what's beyond there, mistress.'

Meg thanked the boy, gave him a cup of beer, and sent him to feed her chickens. She needed time to think.

Mary, the true queen, was free, and in England. Even if the usurper Elizabeth locked her up again, the important thing was that at long last, she was within reach of all those loyal Englishmen and women who prayed for the day when she sat upon her rightful throne. Moreover, even if Englishmen alone could not bring about that glorious triumph, the Duke of Alba and his army still remained in Flanders, doing God's work by rooting out the Dutch rebels and heretics. Surely Alba would come the few short miles across the sea, and put all to rights?

Truly, it was a great day, a propitious day.

Meg believed in omens; who in Dunwich did not? There could hardly be any clearer omen than this, telling her that now was the hour when she finally had to summon up her courage and undertake the task she had been putting off for days, even though she was confident that she had finally assembled all the information, and all the safeguards, that she needed.

The moment when she would finally confront her stepmother over her dealings with Stephen Raker.

It still seemed an obscenity to Meg that Jennet Stannard should sit like an empress within the house where she, Meg, had grown up. Spread across the entire settle where Meg had sat so often with her father, stroking their dog Tiberius, Jennet did, indeed, resemble some vast oriental potentate.

The contrast with the girl at her side was marked.

Mary Stannard, Meg's half-sister and youngest half-sibling, was now nearly fifteen. Tall and slim, sharing with her mother only unsettlingly brilliant white teeth, she already turned the head of every young man in Dunwich, and many of those of the older, married sort, too. Meg had been compelled to spend much time looking after the infant Mary, and always found her a distant, fractious child. The expression that she now bestowed on her half-sister was detached, aloof, and something else that Meg could not place.

'Well, Margaret,' said her stepmother, 'a fine pass it is when you summon your elders like tap boys. A fine show of respect for your father's wife, I say.'

Meg took a breath, and silently offered up a prayer to the Virgin. There was little point in prevaricating, even less in dissembling. Best to get straight to it, and allow the storm to break, then pass.

'I know what scheme you and Stephen Raker have been about,' she said.

Jennet bridled, but she could not stop herself blushing. 'Raker? A scheme with Raker?' she blustered. 'You are become a madwoman, Margaret Stannard.'

'He told me himself, when I encountered him at Blackfriars. And I saw you with him at Bungay fair, step-mother. Since then, I have asked questions. I have got to the bottom of your scheme, and when he returns from sea, my father will know of it.'

'If he returns,' said Mary, sharply.

The remark was so sudden, so cold and so vehement that Meg was taken aback. She looked at Mary anew, but saw only the same steady, assessing expression. Even Jennet, the girl's mother, was open-mouthed.

In that moment, Meg knew for certain what, until then, she had only half suspected. For all that she bore the Stannard name, Mary hated her father, her half-sister, and their entire family. She hated Dunwich, too. From her childhood, she had often spoken approvingly of London, its supposed delights, the many entertainments it provided, the grandeur of her Barne relatives who lived there, and the number of wealthy young men who thronged its streets. In the same breath, though, she disparaged the small, decayed town where circumstance of birth had placed her.

It was clear to Meg now, so blindingly clear.

Jennet Stannard, old, tired and hardly mobile, had not instigated the plot with Stephen Raker. Mary had. Her mother indulged her youngest child beyond measure, even to the degree of risking the wrath of her husband when Jack finally returned from sea. And none would suspect such a young, slim, pretty slip of a girl of such a deeply laid scheme. Meg, who should have done, had not, and inwardly cursed herself. But she did know one thing. She would never, ever underestimate Mary Stannard again.

As it was, she recovered her composure in short order.

'As I say, your scheme with Stephen Raker. You easing his path to buy the Blackfriars, thereby making him a freeman of Dunwich, if the palms of enough common councilmen are crossed. An easy step from there to ensure he is a common councilman himself, if not an alderman or even bailiff, by the time a parliament is next summoned.' Jennet looked uncomfortable now, but Mary remained utterly impassive. 'Raker has ambitions. He's been buying up farms, breweries, and houses all around the Sandlings – and he's been cultivating great men, none more so than Earl Sussex, the lord lieutenant. Wendon the archdeacon, too. Several others.'

Finally, Mary Stannard spoke. 'How do you know all this?'

'Sister, dear, you are not the only Stannard woman with a brain in her head. 'Tis no matter how I came to know all this, and yet more, as you'll find. So, then, our friend Raker. Our *uncle* Raker, Mary. There is a limit upon his ambitions, and it's a galling one for him. No matter how prosperous Southwold might become, it isn't a parliamentary borough, and has no prospect of becoming one – but no matter how decayed it might be, Dunwich is. So if Stephen Raker seeks election to the next parliament, he must do so for Dunwich.'

'This is fantasy,' said Mary. But Meg noticed that the girl was now the one talking, and that her mother was silent.

'Not so,' said Meg. 'Raker is hated in Dunwich, but coin is not. Stannard influence, and Stannard coin, thrown behind Stephen Raker, or at least not deployed to block his path, was one part of the bargain you made with him. I can imagine that the Cuddons and the rest of those on the common council who have no love for the Stannards will be only too willing to be bought for that cause. But no matter how much I thought upon it, I couldn't fathom what the other part might be. He had to give you something in return, and what could he possibly have to give? Aye, peace between Southwold and Dunwich, but in truth, the harbour channel has moved so far over to their shore that all the old quarrels have abated. There's no point in offering peace when there's no prospect of there ever being another war.'

'You are unnatural,' said Jennet, finally shifting her position upon the settle. 'One brief marriage to that Spanish boy—'

'A papist,' said Mary, interrupting her mother, 'and worse, perchance – God knows what you conjure there upon the heath—'

Meg raised her hand. 'What I am is not at issue here,' she said. 'The issue is what you have done, or attempted to do. It took enquiries on my behalf at court, and among the London lawyers, to discover the truth. Raker buys Blackfriars, exerts influence upon the other electors, and so brings into the next parliament both himself and his chosen candidate as Dunwich's second member. And that, as you well know, dearest Mary, would be our brother George.'

When John Day first told her this information, she could barely take it in. George, whose birth she remembered as though it were yesterday, whose arse she had wiped when he was a baby, whose grazes she had mended as he grew, whose guiles and stratagems she had come to be wary of. But George was now of age, and a lawyer. He was said to be well regarded by Sir William Cecil, the principal secretary. He would count as a local candidate, the name of Stannard being a mighty weapon in his arsenal, and would thus counterbalance Stephen Raker, whom many of the electors – the bailiffs, aldermen and common councilmen – would undoubtedly baulk at.

At last, Mary Stannard smiled. 'Well, sister, you have been thorough indeed. Who would have thought it, eh? But aye, then, brother George. Why not? What greater triumph could there be for the Stannards than for one of our own to be a member of the next parliament? You've known our father longer than Mother and I have,' the girl said, evenly, 'so don't you think he would forgive anything, even the arrangement with Raker, to place such a feather in the family's cap?'

Yes, perhaps he would, thought Meg. But he would be wrong, just as the two people before her in the so-familiar room were wrong. George might prove to be no worse than any of the other craven, self-serving mediocrities who crowded the benches of the House of Commons, but Stephen Raker was a different matter. Would he really be content to use Dunwich as a stepping-stone into Parliament, or would he use his new status to destroy the town from within?

But neither case would happen. Meg summoned up a thought of Mary, the true queen, finally come into her true kingdom, and pressed home her attack.

'All wishful thinking,' she said.

'I think not,' replied Mary, sharply.

'Oh, it is, sister, for it is all founded upon Stephen Raker buying Blackfriars. And in that, he was outbid in the augmentations office of the Exchequer. Blackfriars is sold, but not to him.'

Jennet's mouth fell open, and for the first time, Mary Stannard seemed agitated, almost angry. She had evidently expected everything except this.

'Sold? To who?'

'To a true son of Dunwich, a man the council will delight to have of their number. A man renowned among all those of the reformed religion, dear sister, so you should rejoice that the bearer of such an illustrious name owns land in the town once again.'

Mary was confused now, but Jennet nodded bitterly. 'John Day,' she said. 'John Day has bought Blackfriars.'

Finally, Mary's face, draining of colour, displayed a hint of emotion. The supremely confident young woman was gone, but there was still a defiance, a trait that Meg recognised in herself. So the half-sisters did have something in common, despite all.

'You'll pay, sister,' Mary vowed in a low, broken, barely audible voice. 'God be my judge, you'll suffer for what you've done.'

With that, and a parting stare that could have frozen the flames of Hell itself, Mary Stannard turned and made for her room, slamming the door behind her. Meg stood for a moment, looking with contempt upon the impotent figure of her stepmother, then let herself out. She knew the way well enough.

Twenty-One

The *Judith* and the *Jennet* made an easy voyage north and then west from Borboruta, the beaches and low hills of the mainland to larboard, the large isles of Curaçao and Aruba to starboard. Apart from a few fishing craft inshore and the distant sails of small vessels trading between the islands, they had the sea to themselves. The final leg of the voyage took them along a long, straight coast of broad golden beaches until at last they edged into the open roadstead of Rio de la Hacha, where the blue waters of the sea became a muddy brown thanks to the river from which the little town took its name. From the deck of the *Jennet*, Tom Stannard surveyed the prospect before them. The town was a miserable place; as at La Asunción on Margarita, the so-called houses, perhaps sixty of them, were no more than mud huts, and only two buildings were of stone – the church, and what must be the house of the Spanish administrator, Castellanos. Like Margarita, the place was meant to be the source of prodigious quantities of pearls. If that was so, Tom reflected, the Spaniards were clearly not investing the proceeds in the town itself.

He watched a boat pull away from the *Judith*. Drake was sending a message ashore, no doubt the usual courteous request to a local official to permit visiting ships to take on fresh water. They were very close to the shore now, and were a source of considerable curiosity for the mongrel collection of roughly dressed Europeans and nearly naked tribesmen and slaves who populated this poor excuse for a town.

So far, all was well.

Jack came up on deck at the precise moment that the first shot came from the shore. An arquebus ball struck the larboard wale of the *Jennet*, sending up a large splinter that narrowly missed his eye. The concealed Spanish troops ashore began a ragged fire, soon followed by the crack of three small cannon. Drake's *Judith*, further inshore, was the principal target, but the *Jennet* was also well within range.

'So Master Castellanos has decided not to chance another reprimand from King Philip,' said Jack.

'Aye, so be it,' said Tom. 'Let him have one from Queen Elizabeth instead, then! Jennets, to your guns, my lads!' With that, he took up his own arquebus, placed it upon a rest, and fired in the general direction of the town.

Given the shape of the anchorage and the state of the tide, the *Jennet*, like the *Judith*, could only bring one of her larger guns to bear. Tom went to it, checked the bearing and elevation, and then gave the order to the gun crew.

'Give fire!'

The range was not much beyond point blank, and there was a ragged cheer from the men as their shot struck the wall of Castellanos' house and loosed a shower of masonry.

The slaves below decks screamed and wailed at the sounds of battle immediately above their heads, perhaps bringing back memories of the battle for Conga.

'Well done, lads!' cried Tom. 'Let's show 'em more of what Englishmen can do, shall we?'

In truth, the exchange of fire between the two English ships and the small Spanish garrison was brief and ineffective on both sides. The Spanish weapons were too small to do any serious damage, while the English could bring too few guns to bear to destroy the town. As the sun began to sink and the shadows lengthened, Drake gave the signal for the ships to move further out, beyond the range of the Spanish guns. There they dropped anchor and waited for Hawkins and the rest of the fleet to complete their leisurely passage from Borboruta.

Hawkins and the main body of the fleet arrived in the outer anchorage of Rio de la Hacha five days later. The following morning Tom Stannard found himself standing in the bow of the *Jennet's* pinnace, one part of a small flotilla of English craft making for the shore to the west of the town, well out of the range of the Spanish cannon. Hawkins was confident that he could get Castellanos to back down by making a show of force, and the small army that formed up on the beach amply fitted the bill. Two hundred heavily armed men, sailors, gentlemen volunteers and the remnants of the late Edward Dudley's old troop assembled together in as military a manner as they could manage under a large flag bearing St George's cross, for they knew Spanish scouts were watching them from a little way inland, somewhere within the short, thick trees and cacti that covered the sandy terrain. Then, with Hawkins, Tom, Drake, Barrett and several of the other officers at their head, they set off to march towards the town.

They had not gone far before Tom saw, dead ahead, a makeshift rampart of sand, rocks and old carts, from which flew the red and yellow banner of Spain. The number of heads bobbing above the palisade, and the number of weapons from which the bright sun glinted, indicated that Castellanos had deployed his entire force, equal to or slightly larger than their own.

Hawkins called a halt. He turned to his officers, smiled, then nodded to one of the young boys from the *Jesus*, who at once held high a tall flagstaff and began to wave it, unfurling the large plain blue flag that it bore.

–

Jack Stannard, aboard the *Jennet* a little way offshore, saw the flag. He turned, noted that all the ships near him had seen it too, and nodded with satisfaction.

'Well, then, lads,' he cried to the gun crews along the starboard side of the ship, 'time to give King Philip a warm kiss from Dunwich!'

The men cheered, Jack checked the bearing and the situation ashore one final time, then gave the command.

'Give fire!'

The guns of the *Jennet* spat flame and roared, followed at once by those of Drake's *Judith* and the Hawkins-owned *William and John*. But even this barrage was overshadowed moments later as the batteries of the royal warships the *Jesus* and the *Minion*, anchored slightly further out, opened up. Smoke rolled over the entire English fleet, but the men of the *Jennet* had already reloaded their guns and were ready to fire once again.

–

Tom and the rest of the English force watched as the vicious thunderstorm of cannonballs poured down onto the Spanish defences. Several balls landed in the water, sending up great spouts, which showered spray over the men on the beach, but then the gunners on the ships got their range and balls began to strike unremittingly against the rampart itself. Shattered timber, sand, stones and human limbs exploded into the air. Wounded men screamed, and King Philip's flag was ripped in half.

Hawkins watched impassively for several minutes. Then he signalled to the same boy to wave his blue flag once again, and the fleet ceased fire.

Hawkins drew his sword, pointed it toward the shattered rampart, and yelled, 'God and the queen!'

The cry was echoed throughout the little army as it advanced. The arquebusiers and crossbowmen were in the van, firing at will into the broken and confused ranks of the Spaniards. Tom waited for the signal from the admiral, then moved forward with the pikemen and halberdiers, his sword drawn and ready. The response from the remains of the Spanish rampart was feeble, barely more than two or three arquebus shots. Some of the defenders were already fleeing back towards the town. Then Hawkins turned and shouted the order.

'Charge!'

Tom broke into a run. The sand was hot beneath his feet, the sun relentless upon his back, but strangely, he felt cold, intent only upon the enemy ahead. He had a curious thought of his half-brother Harry; so proud, as was his mother, of being one of the queen's soldiers, yet even before this day, he had seen much less action than Tom. The elder brother hoped he lived to tell the story, and to see the envy on his sibling's face.

Tom and Hawkins reached the rampart almost simul-taneously, with Drake and Barrett just a step or two behind. A Spanish pikeman attempted a thrust at Tom's chest, but it was an easy matter to deflect it, leaving the man defenceless. He wore a breastplate, so Tom thrust his sword at the man's groin, and a dreadful scream told him that he had struck home. Next, there was a man with a sword but wearing no armour, just behind and to the right of the pikeman. Tom swung at him, but the Spaniard deflected the thrust and attempted a counterattack of his own. Tom took a formal guard, a position taught him by his father, who had learned it in turn from the erstwhile friar Thomas Ryman. The Spaniard must have realised he faced a trained swordsman in the same moment that he saw the half-dozen Dunwich men from the *Jennet*, five armed with half-pikes and one with an upended arquebus that he was wielding as a club, charging across the remains of the rampart to come to their captain's assistance. The fellow turned and ran, with the Suffolk men screaming contempt after him.

Tom paused to take a breath, and looked around. The English already commanded the rampart, and the Spanish were in full flight.

'After them, my lads!' shouted Hawkins. 'On to the town!'

There was no attempt to regroup and take up a proper formation. The Englishmen ran forward like a mob pursuing a football from one village to another, howling obscenities as they did so. Ahead of them, the retreating Spaniards did not try to man the defensive palisade around the town, nor even to shut the gates. Instead, they simply ran straight through the town and out the other side, fleeing into the countryside beyond.

The English reached the town square, where Hawkins gave the signal to halt. The men gathered in the shade under the walls of the church and Castellanos' own house. Some slumped to the ground, some joked and laughed with friends, and some refreshed themselves from the fountain in the middle of the square. Tom took a few mouthfuls of water, then lay down on the dirt of Rio de la Hacha and fell asleep at once.

He was wakened by the sound of Hawkins' voice. The admiral was standing on the steps of the church, addressing a crowd of several dozen Spaniards, presumably the merchants and ordinary residents of the town, using Robert Barrett as his interpreter.

'My friends,' he said in a mild tone and with a smile on his face, 'I want nothing more than to trade with you in peace. Aboard my ships, we have many things that you lack – wool, cloth, ivory, slaves, spices, cutlery. We are argosies, my friends, and we want nothing more than to provide you with the things you crave. The things Spain does not send out to you.

'Now, I have sent messages back and forth to Treasurer Castellanos, who skulks out there beyond your rampart. He stands upon the letter of the law, saying that even if I set the entire Indies on fire, he would not grant me a licence to trade here.' When Barrett's translation reached those words, Tom saw many of the Spaniards shake their heads and murmur discontentedly to each other. 'My friends, we all know there are good laws and there are bad laws, and I say that this is a bad law. Is Spain aware of your needs, here in this place, when it sends so few ships to you? Do those in Spain really know anything about you, here in this town?' More murmuring. 'My friends, I was a servant of your noble King Philip. No man respects His Majesty more than I do. So think upon what I have said, and if you then think as I do, tell Treasurer Castellanos that you wish to trade with the English. We have your interests at heart, my friends—'

Hawkins' peroration was interrupted by a sudden cry of '*Fuego!*'

Tom turned, and saw smoke rising from the other side of the town.

Rio de la Hacha was ablaze.

-

The cause of the fire was apparent at once. A small group of a dozen or so exceptionally drunken Devon men staggered into the town square and prostrated themselves before Hawkins, then began to accuse each other of knocking over the candle that had started the blaze. As the town's residents rushed to try and save their properties, Hawkins flew into a temper.

'How, pray, did a candle come to be knocked over, when I gave strict orders that no man was to enter any building in this place? Fuckwits. Captain Drake, take their names. We'll deal with them once this is over. All hands to suppressing the fire!'

Tom got to his feet. 'Jennets, to me!' he cried.

The Suffolk men gathered around him, and together they began to run through the streets toward the heart of the blaze.

It was not a great inferno; Rio de la Hacha was too small for any such thing. But the houses were simple structures, with baked mud walls and straw roofs, kept deliberately rudimentary because of the endless cycles of tropical storms, earthquakes and French raids that forced the townspeople to rebuild every few years, sometimes even after a few months.

As he organised one of the lines of men relaying buckets of water from the harbour, Tom realised that the actual damage to the town was not what mattered to Hawkins, who was striding about barking orders like a man possessed; it was all about the message. Castellanos had suggested Hawkins sought to fire the entire Indies, and now Rio de la Hacha burned. Hawkins was rightly furious that all his hard work to convince the townspeople to overturn Castellanos' ban on trade might be undone by a few clumsy sailors searching buildings for wine.

Taking their cue from the furious admiral, the Englishmen worked like demons to put out the fire. Officers and men took their places in the human chains bringing water to the blaze, with Tom himself battling to save one house, truly no more than a hut, with the same determination as if it was his own home. As he and two other men of the *Jennet* dampened down the last flames, he turned and saw three tiny figures standing at the door, staring at him with great round eyes. For one fleeting moment, as he breathed hard and wiped the sweat from his eyes, he thought that two of them were his Adam and Peter; but if that was so, who was the third? Then he could see properly again, but just as he beckoned to the children to come to him, their mother ran forward, scowled at Tom, and shepherded them away.

When the English reassembled in the town square, perhaps one third of Rio de la Hacha lay in ruins. Hawkins called his officers together for a conference upon the steps of the church, but just as Tom joined them, a delegation of prominent citizens of the town appeared, bearing a message from Castellanos in which he claimed that he was pleased the English had burned the town, for King Philip would rebuild it and he, Castellanos, had plans in hand that would lead to the destruction of the English heretics. Hawkins made a great play of reading this with a stern expression on his face, then climbed a couple of steps and assumed a stance reminiscent of the famous pose of Harry the Eighth of famous memory, his arms akimbo. Tom smiled, for he had seen his wife's kinsman do this many times. Hawkins should have been an actor in one of the old mystery plays in the time before they were banned.

'My friends,' he began in familiar fashion. 'My fellow loyal subjects of His Majesty King Philip.'

Barrett translated, but Tom heard Hawkins' sharp aside to his interpreter: 'Name of God, Rob, put a smile on your face. We want these people to believe they really are our friends.'

Barrett complied, and Hawkins continued, berating Castellanos for expressing pleasure at the destruction of so many houses, suggesting that the reconstruction would merely be an opportunity for the treasurer to line his own pockets, and promising the rather more immediate prospect of compensation from Hawkins himself, here and now. All the English wanted was a licence to trade, which was also surely what the good citizens of Rio de la Hacha wished for.

Tom could see several of the Spaniards turning to each other and nodding; Hawkins was winning the argument. The admiral pressed home his case by going down into the body of the Spaniards, shaking hands, bestowing gifts, and escorting them back to the gate. But it remained to be seen whether friendly persuasion would be enough, and whether the citizens of the town would now be able to persuade Castellanos to back down.

–

In the end, it took a stroke of good fortune to resolve the matter once and for all. Jack and Tom were dining together aboard the *Jennet* when news came that one of Castellanos' personal slaves had deserted and presented himself before Hawkins, claiming to know where the treasurer had concealed the town's store of gold. A strongly armed expedition was sent into the forest that night and found the treasure exactly where the slave said it was. The next day, the Stannards watched from *Jennet* as the large wooden chests were hauled aboard the *Jesus*.

Jack observed the scene with mixed feelings. God willing, it would resolve the deadlock between Hawkins and Castellanos; and so it proved, with the treasurer of Rio de la Hacha accepting with unalloyed bad grace the English admiral's proposal that the gold would be handed back in return for a licence to trade, which led in the days that followed to the sale of a substantial number of slaves, many of them, strange to say, to Treasurer Castellanos himself.

But Jack could remember Thomas Ryman teaching him the notion of a pyrrhic victory, and as he heard the cheers from the *Jesus* as the gold was hauled aboard, he could not help but feel that this was one such. For one thing, once the English fleet sailed away, Castellanos was bound to rewrite the history of what had happened at Rio de la Hacha, recasting it to his own advantage. And when the news finally reached him, King Philip would hardly be indifferent to what would be portrayed as the deliberate burning of his town, and the subsequent capture of his gold, by men he undoubtedly regarded as English pirates. Jack recalled Francis Walsingham's words about how little it might take to trigger a war between England and Spain, then offered up a silent prayer to the Virgin.

Twenty-Two

Jennet *in the bay of Cartagena upon the coast of*
New Andaluce
This twentieth day of August

My sweet, my Catherine, my love,

    I write this with no present prospect of sending
it. There are no ships here sailing for England, and
we intend for that blessed shore ourselves, so it may
be that this letter will return with me. If God so
wills it, though, then perhaps it will return instead
of me.

    We have continued to sail along the coast,
calling at ports where Hawkins believes he might
sell the remainder of the slaves. He says that time is
short. The season of the great winds called hurrica-
noes will soon be upon us, while a Spanish fleet
may arrive in these seas at any time. Thus we
have put in to a roadstead called Santa Marta, a
small and miserable place backed by great mountains that the local people call the Sierra Nevadas.
Here I went ashore with our little army of one and
a half hundred men, our advance bringing about
the immediate surrender of the town. But it was
all a sham, the governor having agreed privately
with Hawkins that he would give the pretence

of surrendering to overwhelming odds and then granting a licence to trade under duress. Our next port of call, Cartagena, where we lie now, is much bigger, with stronger defences and a large garrison. We have eschewed the inner harbour and so lie far out, well beyond the range of the Spaniards' guns. The governor refuses to entertain us, even denying us the simple right to take on fresh water. We have sent out scouting parties, though, and have found undefended wells in the midst of dense forest on an island south of the town. From these we have replenished our casks, so that, at least, is a blessed relief.

You will be gladdened to know that we eat well. The beef of these parts is abundant beyond all measure, and at least the equal of the meat that we eat in England. I have also tried some of the foods native to these lands. The fruits and vegetables of the Indies are strange beyond measure, but some refresh the throat better than anything I have ever tasted. I bring you one of them for curiosity's sake. I expect it will be rotten within by the time we return to England, but at least you will be able to see its singular appearance. For some reason, God alone knows why, it is named a pineapple, although it looks like no apple that I have ever seen.

We have sold all but a handful of our living cargo. I thank God for it – both that we have finally made a profit to make the entire enterprise worthwhile, and that these creatures may now have some sort of lives ashore, rather than being herded below decks. As the last of them left the ship, I recalled Cabral's words, that he was not the same as these people. His dire fate, which I recall every night in my dreams, suggests otherwise. At any rate, those who killed him so horribly thought he was the same as them, or rather worse, and I do not doubt that they would have done likewise to me if events had gone differently. These are not thoughts to dwell upon, my love. My father could unburden himself of such painful imaginings in a confessional, should the governor of Cartagena relent and he be able to find a church ashore, but for us good Protestants, there is only prayer and the burden of our own thoughts. Amen.

I beseech you, dear wife, don't let Adam spend all his time looking at the images in Foxe's book. They are too terrible for a boy of his years, and children should be running and laughing before the cares of this world crowd in upon them. I have no doubt that his brother Peter will be doing that in full measure. I know you will have done your best to curb the lad's impudence, but do not spare the rod in that regard.

I pray for you and the boys many times each day. I pray that I will return soon, and I vow never to go upon another voyage such as this. These new worlds are not what fools in England claim them to be, with great cities paved with gold and rivers of silver. They are desperate places for desperate men, and in that I count those in our fleet who revel in being here, Frank Drake foremost among them. I am also minded to retire from the sea and manage affairs from on shore, as Hawkins' brother does. I have not said this to my father, for he would find it *unaccountable. He will continue to go to sea until his dying day, for it is in his blood as it is not in mine. I worry for him, though. He has seemed much older of late, and I pray he is not weakening.*

Orders are newly come from the flagship for us to make ready to sail. Our course will be northerly, and set for the westernmost point of the great island called Cuba. Then we will endeavour to beat our way through what is called the Florida channel, thence into the open ocean beyond. Once there, God willing, fair winds will take us safe home to Plymouth, and bring me to your arms.

God guard and keep you, my sweet Catherine. Be well and be good until we meet again, in this world or the next.

God save Queen Elizabeth.

With all love from your husband, faithful unto you and to God,

T. Stannard

Only prayer and the burden of our own thoughts... Faithful unto you, and to God.

The words were not quite lies, but they were not quite the whole truth either; and the fact that Tom felt impelled to sit and write what would almost certainly be an unnecessary, perhaps even unsent, letter to his wife, an act that concentrated his mind on her and their children to the exclusion of all else, spoke of an uneasy conscience. It also spoke of one considerable omission from his account of what had transpired at Cartagena.

We have sent out scouting parties, though, and have found undefended wells in the midst of dense forest on an island south of the town.

Not quite the whole truth.

—

The first inkling Tom had of the trouble to come was when he saw the *Jennet*'s pinnace returning unexpectedly early from the heavily wooded island of Bomba, a half-mile or so across a broad channel from the port of Cartagena. It contained no water casks, which it should have done if its task was complete. Instead, it held only its crew: a grim-faced Hal Ashby, and two men who seemed to be under restraint. It was young Matthew Bradlow and an old hand from Blythburgh named Anthony Sargeant. Jack Stannard was asleep in the *Jennet*'s stern cabin, and some instinct told Tom it would be best not to wake him.

'Well?' he demanded of Hal, as the boatswain of the *Jennet* stepped onto the deck.

'A word, Cap'n', said Ashby, taking Tom to one side and speaking quietly.

'What is it, Hal?'

'Buggery, Tom. No way to dress it up. I noticed they were missing from the work party at the second well, so I went into the woods. Saw Bradlow taking Sargeant over a fallen tree trunk, clear as I'm seeing you now.'

'Bradlow taking Sargeant? Not—'

'No, it was Bradlow. He's confessed it, too, and half a dozen of the men who came with me saw it.'

Tom felt the blood drain from his face. Such unequivocal evidence, with so many witnesses, should mean only one thing. But *Bradlow*...

'Bring him to me.'

Ashby beckoned to the youth, who was brought over by Mark Ferris. Bradlow, a scrawny lad with a round face, had been weeping, and the other men on the deck were staring at him with a range of expressions: some disgust, certainly, but also a fair measure of pity. Word travelled fast, and there were no secrets aboard such a small ship as the *Jennet*. Tom hoped against hope, though, that perhaps there was still one secret left.

'Well, then, Will Bradlow,' he said, 'you know what the bosun here says?'

'Aye, Captain Stannard,' the lad replied, in little more than a whisper.

'So what say you?'

'Nothing to say, Cap'n.'

'You don't deny it?'

'Can't deny it, Cap'n, not with all the witnesses.'

Say he forced you, boy. But the overwhelming evidence, and Bradlow's own admission, contradicted that.

Just then, Jack came up on deck, having been woken from a light slumber by the strange conversation taking place among the men standing on the deck directly above where he lay. He looked over to Tom, caught his son's eye, but merely nodded, then joined the ranks of the curious onlookers.

'You know that the penalty prescribed by law for buggery is death,' said Tom, trying to keep his voice steady. 'If it went to the admiral for his judgement, I don't doubt that he'd say the same, and impose the same sentence as any judge and jury in England.'

All around the deck of the *Jennet*, men were glancing at each other and nodding. Tom knew that Bradlow, who came from a popular family in Dunwich, was well liked; had the much older, sullen, and frequently drunken Sargeant, an outsider to boot, been the instigator, their attitude might have been very different.

He had to make a decision, and he had to make it as a ship's captain, not as anything else. He knew men's eyes were on him, but he felt an utter fraud. He deliberately looked away from where his father stood, offered up a silent prayer, and then began to speak.

'There is the law of England,' he said, 'but we are very far from England. Then there is the law of the sea. Sometimes that is more forgiving than the law of the land, sometimes it is harsher. We face greater dangers than those on land' – a growl of agreement from the crew – 'and thus we do things differently, by custom handed down to us from all those who have sailed the seas before us, since time immemorial.' Another growl. 'What's more, we are a ship of Dunwich, and we all know that Dunwich has always had special privileges, special rights, also since time immemorial. Dunwich was the seat of emperors and ancient bishops, and they gave us laws all our own.' The growl turned into loud and cheers and shouts of 'Aye!' 'So I say this. Matthew Bradlow here shall have fifty lashes, Anthony Sargeant there twenty. The matter is then to be closed and never spoken of again, with any man who does so to be subject to twelve lashes. This sentence to be carried out when the *Jennet* is not in company and not overlooked by other ships in the fleet, as we are now. Does any man dispute this?'

Heads shook vigorously. Tom was gambling that no true-born Suffolk man would want the Devonian Hawkins to sit in judgement on one of their own, with the certainty that a man so desperate to maintain the favour of the queen and some of her ministers and courtiers would impose the full rigour of the law of the land; this despite the fact that his own mercy towards Edward Dudley, a man who had attempted to murder him and perhaps committed a form of treason against the Queen of England's admiral, was arguably even more egregious. But all that being so, no one from the *Jennet*'s crew would want two floggings carried out in full sight of the other ships of the fleet, all of them manned primarily by Devon men, when questions would inevitably be raised about the cause of the punishments. There was, of course, the unspoken possibility that the *Jennet* might never be on her own during the rest of what every man in the fleet hoped would be their voyage home.

Tom would deal with that eventuality if it arose. As it was, he ordered the release of Bradlow and Sargeant, then turned to see that his father had come to his side.

'Well done,' said Jack. 'I don't know if I'd have had the courage, or the foolhardiness, to go against both the statute book of the realm and our admiral.'

'Foolhardiness, I think,' said Tom, although in his heart he knew that other sentiments had also driven him. 'If word of this should ever reach Hawkins, or lawyers back in England – my brother George, or your Master Walsingham...'

'It won't. We know all these men, Tom, and they trust us. No man on the *Jennet* would betray you. As for George and Walsingham... I'm the only man on this ship who would be likely to tell either of them. But you're my firstborn son, Tom. I still recall the day you were born – how happy I was, how happy your poor mother was. How unhappy your sister was.' They both smiled at that. 'So rest easy, lad. One thing more, though, for conscience demands I say it.'

'Father?'

'I know how hard this was for you, and why.' Jack smiled. 'As I say, you're my firstborn son, Tom Stannard.

I've always known. You'll not want to hear it, but one advantage of the old faith – my faith, your mother's faith – is that it looks upon such things a little differently to the hellfire-and-damnation sermonising of your friend Drake and his ilk.'

Tom stood speechless upon the deck of the *Jennet* as his father turned and went off to the pinnace, intending to go ashore with Hal Ashby to complete the filling of the water casks.

–

As he looked out at the distant ramparts and towers of Cartagena, Tom's thoughts raced. His father's words came to him time and again, battling against his own doubts about the verdict he had given. What would Hawkins do if he found out that the captain of the *Jennet* had excused an undoubted sodomite from the full rigour of English law?

But there was an even more insidious thought than that, and it began to torment Tom Stannard.

What sentence would he have handed down if the roles had been reversed? What if the ugly and unpopular Anthony Sargeant had been the instigator, rather than the young, lean and supple Matt Bradlow, with his winning smile?

Tom went below, took the cork from a flask of wine, drank directly and deeply from it, then sat down to pen a letter to his wife.

Twenty-Three

As she walked back to Dunwich through the ancient forest of Westwood, Meg de Andrade sang a merry tune to herself. Her patient, a house carpenter of Blythburgh, looked set to live, against the odds. Letters had come from her father and brother. True, they were more than six months old, sent at Christmas from some infernal place called Sierra Leone and miraculously reaching Dunwich after, it seemed, a shipwreck and a particularly circuitous overland journey through Spain and France. But as she turned the letters over and over in her hands, Meg had a powerful sense that both of those dear to her still lived. Even so, her father's concern for the Raker affair seemed like ancient history now, for she had resolved that matter herself, trumping her stepmother and sister in the process. Moreover, she had seen much more of Philip Grimes during the course of the summer, and increasingly liked what she saw. Mayhap she would finally accept his offer and become a respectable goodwife again, rather than the strange, solitary woman who lived upon the heath. The only matter of discontent for Meg was the Queen of Scots, who remained firmly under lock and key in one northern castle after another, the usurper Elizabeth evidently fearful of the manifest rightness of her cousin's claim. But if God so willed, perhaps that matter would be resolved satisfactorily, too.

She came into Dunwich, and at once saw her half-brother Ned standing by the old lazar hospital of St James. The expression on his face was pained, and just for a fleeting, impossibly glorious moment, she wondered if he was about to convey the news that Jennet Stannard was dead.

'Sister,' he said, 'I have been looking all over for you. You must come with me.'

'Must, Ned? What is this "must"? Why "must" I do anything at your behest?'

'It is by command of the bailiffs and the Reverend James.'

'And since when have I paid heed to any of them?'

Ned swallowed hard, and for a moment, Meg felt a fleeting sympathy for him. His mother and sister would have compelled him to do this; Edward Stannard had not an ounce of initiative in his body, and precious little more of courage.

'It is better if you come, sister.'

Curiosity got the better of her, and she fell in beside him, increasing his discomfort by making no attempt at all to engage him in conversation. They turned north to follow the course of the ancient Palesdyke, then walked along Maison Dieu Lane, past the ruinous hospital of that name and the Stannard house where Meg had grown up. A left turn took them down to the harbour, under the lee of Cock Hill, and then toward Hen Hill, passing the remains of St Francis's chapel.

Meg could now see a substantial crowd assembled on the low summit of Hen Hill, in truth no more than an ancient, grass-covered sand dune barely deserving its name, and suddenly had an inkling of what was about to happen.

They climbed up the well-worn path. Perhaps two score of curious townspeople stood around, murmuring to each other as Meg approached. She knew almost all of them well, and knew with almost complete accuracy which ones would send sympathetic glances her way and which would shun her; or at least, would shun her until they or their children needed a cure, at which time they would crawl back to her, making out that this day had never happened. There, too, stood Thomas Cowper and John Bradley, bailiffs of Dunwich for the year, and next to them, William James, the stooped, hawk-nosed reforming rector of St Peter's, attired in austere black and white vestments.

Meg had no cause to fear these men. She had recently cured Cowper's son of a sweating sickness, Bradley was a mere cipher, and while James might chide her for her backsliding on those Sundays when she deigned to attend St Peter's to avoid falling foul of recusancy fines, she knew full well that his superior, Archdeacon Wendon, sympathised with the old ways. But then she saw the other party, standing in the shadow of the ruinous windmill that had stood upon Hen Hill since time immemorial. It consisted of her stepmother Jennet, her half-sister Mary, and Hugh Ebbes.

Mary, grinning broadly, tried desperately to catch Meg's eye, but instead, she fixed her gaze upon Ebbes. He looked at the ground, shuffling his feet like a small boy caught in an orchard.

Finally, she looked upon the small pyre that had been erected on the summit of Hen Hill. It reminded her of the one that had consumed the heretic William Flower at Westminster. But whereas that, perhaps, had been God's will, the opposite was true of the travesty that was about to be played out that afternoon in Dunwich. For placed on top of the pyre was a large panel, or rather set of conjoined panels. Some of the whitewash had been cleaned off, revealing the familiar face of the Devil of the Doom.

'You are not here to face trial, Margaret de Andrade, sometime Stannard,' said the Reverend James, clearly revelling in his moment. Thwarted ambition seeped out of every pore of this man, who considered himself worthy of being an archdeacon at the very least.

'Then why, precisely, am I here, sir?'

'To witness holy work done in God's name. God's, and that of her blessed majesty Elizabeth, our queen.'

'I doubt if Queen Elizabeth concerns herself overmuch with what happens on Hen Hill in Dunwich, sir.'

'Careful, Meg,' said Bailiff Cowper, as representative of the secular arm of the queen's authority. In normal circumstances, he was a friend, cousin to the forthright widow who had been the Stannards' servant when Meg was a child.

'This,' said William James, pointing to the pyre and turning upon his heel so he could emphasise the point to every man, woman and child on the hill, 'is the so-called Doom of Dunwich, a monstrous piece of popish idolatry that once held the people of these parts in its superstitious thrall. Do you deny, Margaret de Andrade, that since the destruction of St John's church, where it was housed, you have hidden this vile, beastly and ungodly relic, contrary to all the injunctions issued by the Queen's majesty and her bishops?'

'And if I have,' said Meg defiantly, 'what crime is it?'

'It is a crime against God's holy law, and against His will,' said James, looking around his makeshift congregation for approval. To his obvious annoyance, there was very little, other than from Jennet and Mary Stannard.

'But what crime is it against the law of the land, Master James?'

'No law has been broken,' said William Cowper. 'It has been enjoined by Parliament and convocation alike that those concealing holy relics – that is, superstitious and proscribed items – should surrender them. But the concealment in itself is no crime, and there are no penalties under the law.'

'It is a crime against God's law!' insisted James. 'As for the penalty, Margaret de Andrade, that will be the damnation of your immortal soul! You will burn in hell, woman!'

'Mayhap one of us will burn, sir. Shall we toss a coin for it?'

James's face was puce. 'You are impudent, woman!' he yelled. 'It is not fitting from one of your sex!'

'Father,' said Cowper, 'remember why we are here.'

William James recovered himself and made to speak again, but Meg pre-empted him.

'I have observed, Master James,' she said, 'that "impudence" is a word often used to describe the truths that some folk do not wish to hear. Well then, let me be a little more impudent, and say this. The Doom painting was venerated and loved in this town for centuries. The old faith was followed in Dunwich for countless centuries more. My life has not been long, but Lord, haven't we seen more change in my time than in all those times previous? Who, then, is to say that things will not change again, and that folk will venerate the likes of Doom paintings once more?'

'Treason!' screamed a young woman's voice. Meg felt a stab of pain and anger when she realised it was her half-sister Mary. 'She envisions the death of the queen! That is treason!'

James nodded vigorously, but Cowper raised a hand. 'The widow de Andrade has made no mention of the queen's blessed majesty,' he said. 'Does any other here believe that such was the import of what she said?'

Men and women looked at each other, but with the exceptions of William James and Meg's own family, none nodded.

'Was it your intent, Meg?' asked Cowper.

'Sir,' said Meg, bowing her head, 'I would never demean, nor even dream of speaking treason against our lawful sovereign, the queen's most excellent majesty.'

Her hands were behind her back, concealed by her kirtle, so none saw that her fingers were crossed; nor did any know which queen she had in her thoughts.

'Well, then,' said Cowper reluctantly, 'let's get this done with.'

Meg went over to the huddle of serpents that was nominally her family, now joined by Ned, who clearly wished to be somewhere else. But she ignored them, particularly Mary's furious gaze, and instead stood before Hugh Ebbes.

'Oh, Hugh,' she said, simply.

He continued to stare at his feet.

'He's no better than me,' he mumbled.

His words struck Meg like an arrow to the heart. Poor, faithful Hugh had not betrayed her and the Doom for money, nor for the favour of Jennet, Mary or Ned Stannard. He had betrayed her out of jealousy of Philip Grimes.

She turned away and saw that Cowper had commanded a lad to bring a blazing torch to light the pyre. Fate decreed that it should be Francis Birkes, who stared at Meg with an expression of utter misery on his face.

William James raised his hands and looked heavenward.

'Genesis Chapter Nineteen tells us that the Lord rained fire and brimstone upon Sodom and Gomorrah,' he declaimed. 'Today, we bring fire here to cleanse this relic of ungodliness and superstition from Dunwich, for as the Book of Hebrews tells us, our God is a consuming fire. No more shall the people here fear or venerate this graven image, this unholy abomination that offends our Lord and all His righteous believers. Let this be an end to the Doom of Dunwich!'

He signalled to Francis Birkes, who handed him the burning brand. James stared exultantly at Meg, then thrust the flame into the pyre. It had been a dry week, the wind was fresh and south-easterly, and the fire caught at once.

The sight of flames starting to lick at the face of the Devil of the Doom brought a strange response from Meg. Her defiance evaporated. She could sense her stepmother and half-sister willing her to break down, to wail and weep and scream, perhaps even, in what they might have thought the best case, to fling herself onto the pyre to perish with the image that had meant so much to her. She knew that Mary would be exulting in this revenge for the affair of the Blackfriars, even if it was a petty triumph in comparison. But Meg would not give her sister the satisfaction of tears. Instead, she sank to her knees and began to pray.

Neither the Reverend James, nor the bailiffs, nor the Stannards, nor almost anyone else standing upon Hen Hill could hear her prayers, for she said them in her quietest murmur, and the crackling of the blaze before her ensured that her words did not carry beyond Francis Birkes, who was too young and too much a child of the new dispensation to know what she was saying. The Reverend James undoubtedly and rightly suspected that her prayers were in Latin, but they were not the ones he might have expected her to recite; say, the act of contrition, or the litanies of the Virgin Mary.

Instead, as the pyre bearing the Doom painting burned, sending a pall of smoke out over Dunwich river towards Southwold, Margaret de Andrade thought of her father and her brother, of Luis and Philip Grimes.

As she did so, she smiled to herself and quietly murmured the *Te Deum*, the great hymn of victory.

Twenty-Four

Jack Stannard could see the dead.

They were there in front of him, on the storm-lashed deck of the *Jennet* as yet another vicious wave smashed into her stern. There were his father and mother, there his dead brother Adam, there Thomas Ryman, and there, at the head of them all, his dear Alice.

'Come to us,' they were saying. 'Join us.'

He wanted nothing more. It was the depth of the night, he was secured to the mizzenmast by a lifeline, and he was sodden through with rain and sweat. The ship was pitching and rolling like a shot horse in its death throes. Jack had not slept at all in three days, and not properly for three weeks.

'Come to us. Join us.'

He rubbed his eyes, and the vision disappeared. It was replaced by the very real presence of Tom, who came on deck, waited a moment to adjust to the pitch of the hull, then staggered his way over to where his father stood.

'My watch,' he said.

'Not time,' said Jack, shaking his head. 'Near a full glass to go.'

Tom grinned. 'Ship's captain's the only judge of when the watch changes. It was you who told me that, long ago. And it's you who tells me I'm the ship's captain now.'

Jack wanted to argue the case, but he was too exhausted.

'Aye, aye, then, Cap'n Stannard. You have the ship.'

'I have the ship.'

With that, Jack untied himself from his lifeline, went below, and fell onto his sea-bed. He was asleep in an instant. It was not the sleep of dreams, but in that briefest moment before his head struck the canvas sack that served for a pillow, Jack saw and heard the dead again.

'Come to us. Join us.'

—

Cape St Anthony, a low promontory that constituted the westernmost point of Cuba, was in sight when the first storms struck the English fleet. The winds suddenly blew hard from the south-east, whipping up turbulent seas that hammered against the hulls. The accompanying rain was warm, but vicious and unremitting. The Stannards, like all the other captains in the fleet, knew from their charts that the lee shore of Florida was somewhere away to the north, so they had no choice but to beat up against the wind for as long as the storm lasted, praying for a change in the weather that would allow them to finally proceed through the Florida channel and then out into the open ocean.

Under minimal sail, most of the canvas having been reefed, the *Jennet* tacked continually into the wind, that being the only course of action that would keep the ship roughly in position. All the while, the timbers groaned like the cries of a great sea creature, the shrouds and sails made strange discordant music, and water sought out every tiny crack and hole that would allow it to enter the body of the ship. Below decks, men sat or lay braced against knee timbers, barrels and guns, awaiting their turn to go above and adjust sail at the next tack, or take their shift at the pumps, which worked constantly. As the hours of the storm stretched into days, and men were unable to go to the heads to relieve themselves, the stench within the lower decks grew ever more foul.

From time to time, a brief break in the driving rain permitted a glimpse of one or more of the other ships of the fleet. Somehow, Hawkins and his crew were keeping the vast and ancient *Jesus* afloat. The Stannards and the more experienced men in their crew wondered at this, for they knew that if things were bad aboard the *Jennet*, they would be far worse aboard the great royal man-of-war; they had all heard the tales of how terribly the huge ship had coped with the storm they had encountered on the outward voyage. Seams that had been patched up after that onslaught of the elements would have come apart again, and God knew how hard the men of the *Jesus* were having to work her pumps.

The answer, albeit an indirect one, came at dusk, when the flagship signalled for the fleet to bear up. Tom was on watch, and ordered up men from below to take the ship through the change of course. The *Jennet* turned away and now ran before the wind, her lookouts struggling to keep in sight the stern lantern of the *Jesus*. Dawn was another leaden grey affair, revealing nothing but the loss in the night of one ship, Hawkins' own *William and John*. Jack and Tom debated her disappearance. The sea was bad, but not bad enough to overwhelm a ship; if any vessel in the fleet was to be lost that way, it would surely be the lumbering *Jesus*, not one of the more nimble hulls like the *William and John*. She could hardly have run onto the Florida coast, for if one ship did so, then all the rest would follow. Perhaps some great rock had done for her, Tom suggested. Perhaps, his father agreed; but he thought it more likely that the lookouts had simply failed to see the signal from the flagship, so the *William and John* was probably still where the fleet had been until the previous evening, still trying to hold position against the wind off the coast of Cuba. Whether she would ever make it home was now in the hands of her captain, her crew, and God.

'By the mark, eight!'

The leadsman's cry gave the Stannards their first indication that they were almost upon the feared lee shore of Florida. Not long afterwards, young Battlebridge, up in the crow's nest on the mainmast, yelled, 'Land ho!' and within a half-glass or so, the Stannards themselves could see the low, featureless shore.

For two days, the bedraggled fleet edged along the alien coast, ever watchful for hidden reefs, hoping against hope that they would stumble across some deep, commodious, and unguarded anchorage where the ships could be repaired, and stock could be taken of their situation. Above all, if the sun or stars finally deigned to appear in the skies above them, they might even finally be able to establish where they were. But when the skies did lighten a little, presaging a change in the weather, the hopes of the Englishmen were swiftly disabused. Within the space of a few hours, the wind swung around from south-east to north-east, and although the air was fresher, it was also markedly colder.

'We must furl sails and batten down again,' said Jack.

'Why, in God's name?' said Tom. 'Look yonder, Father, the clouds are breaking. And we've barely had time to air the ship – it still stinks below decks.'

'Hawkins told me of this weather. It's what he feared most, Tom – we have tarried too long in the Carib after all. A day or two less at Cartagena… but it is no matter now. When the wind comes into this quarter, and the great clouds of birds fly south across the sea, then a hurricano is coming. Naught we can then do, Tom, but to run before it.'

'A hurricano, though, Father? A winter storm? God in heaven, it's only just past the first week of September.'

'And God in heaven has decreed against us, son. Best make the ship ready.'

Once again, the sails were reefed and furled, the hatches battened down, the casks and all other large movable items lashed securely. Thus when the frightful new storm struck, the *Jennet* was ready for it. This time, there was no need for tacking, nor, indeed, for much manoeuvring at all. The ships of the English fleet could only run before the bitterly cold, howling north wind and pray that it flung them out into the broad, open waters of the Carib Sea, and not onto the shore of Cuba.

For three more days, the men largely huddled below decks, trying to keep warm and dry in the intervals between the back-breaking shifts on the pumps and the whipstaff, or assisting the carpenter to plug the leaks that sprang open everywhere. Jack or Tom went through the entire ship every hour or two, trying to keep spirits up and sometimes praying with the downhearted. Jack even led the men through the entire repertoire of favourite songs from the Dunwich alehouses, his soaring tenor voice a strange counterpoint to the endless wailing of the wind and the roar of the waves as they smashed against the hull. Only a few joined in the choruses of the old songs about Robin Hood and Chevy Chase, and their voices were feeble alongside Jack's, but at least some of the men who were too cold or disheartened to sing smiled at the familiar old tunes.

However lustily he sang, though, and however hard he tried to cheer the men, Jack knew full well that every single one of them understood the desperate truth. They were no longer on course for the ocean, and then home to dear England. Instead, they were being blown in the exact opposite direction, far into the Carib Sea, towards unknown shores where not even John Hawkins had ever sailed before. One thing was certain, though: those shores, wherever they were, would be ruled by the Spanish, and hostile.

—

All storms finally blow themselves out, and towards the end of the third day, the northerly tempest that had driven the English fleet far into the Gulf of Mexico finally subsided. There was no land in sight, only an extensive series of reefs over which the waves broke relentlessly, and not one man in the fleet, not even John Hawkins, had the faintest idea where they were. But the fleet hove to, and as the stars came up, both Jack and Tom took out their cross-staffs, made their fixes, and then consulted the charts left them by Bruno Cabral. Finally, Jack looked at Tom, willing him to give the right answer.

'Nineteen degrees of latitude by observation,' said the younger Stannard.

'I concur,' said Jack. 'And we know from our dead reckoning that we can't have gone back through the channel between Cuba and the mainland, not with the current running at near three knots, so we must be west of the Yucatan.'

Tom studied the chart laid out before them. There was the great peninsula, sticking up from Mexico like a giant thumb. There lay the coast of Mexico itself, sweeping all the way around to Florida, which had been so tantalisingly close just a few days before. This was an unknown sea. Few ships, let alone English ones, ever came into these waters. Yet somehow, the fleet had to find a port. Even assuming that the weather held for a few precious days, it would be impossible for the *Jennet* and the others simply to turn and head for England once again. The ships cried out for repair – God alone knew what state the *Jesus* was in by now – while the water casks had to be replenished and the men needed rest.

The answer to their prayers came the next day in the shape of two local merchantmen, sailing downwind away from Yucatan. Hawkins sent Drake off to intercept them, and although one put on sail and got away, the slower vessel proved easy prey. Soon afterwards, Tom and the other captains of the fleet received a summons to attend the admiral aboard the *Jesus*.

As he went aboard her, Tom saw that the great ship was in a dire state indeed. He exchanged greetings with the once fastidiously elegant gentleman volunteer George Fitzwilliam, Edward Dudley's old foe from Tenerife, now as hirsute, bronzed, pungent and cynical as the hardiest foretopman. Fitzwilliam told him that during the latest storms, the gaps between the great ship's planks grew so wide that fish came in through them and thrashed out the last of their lives in the bilges.

Hawkins was in his usual place, behind his table in the great cabin. Tom had not seen him since Cartagena, but thought he seemed to have aged in that short time. If this was indeed so, then the cause of his worries was obvious:

Hawkins knew, as did every man in the room, that they had almost no options left. The only positive, determined face in that company belonged to Francis Drake, still seeming supremely confident that the Protestant God of Elizabeth's England would ultimately smile upon them once again. There was no indication that the admiral and his acolyte had heard of the affair with young Bradlow at Cartagena; nor, come to that, had Tom and his father spoken of it again.

The captured Spanish captain was a glum-faced fellow of about Hawkins' age. The cause of his anxieties was equally obvious: he would undoubtedly be convinced that his cargo of wine from the Carib islands, and probably his ship, too, was about to be stolen from him by these perfidious English pirates.

Gradually, though, Robert Barrett, acting as always as Hawkins' interpreter, coaxed more and more information out of the fellow, who swiftly became markedly garrulous.

'He says that all the ports of the gulf to westward, bar one, are small – too small for a fleet such as this, at any rate. There's a good port to windward, Campeche on Yucatán, whence he himself has just sailed, but...'

Barrett had no need to say any more in a company of seamen. After their travails in recent weeks, the last thing the Englishmen needed was to have to beat back against the wind, constantly tacking as they did so and further draining the bodies and wills of shattered men who were already in the blackest pits of exhaustion.

'And the "bar one" to westward?' said Hawkins, irritably.

Barrett asked the Spaniard another question, and the fellow launched into a lengthy and animated speech. Tom, who had picked up a few words of Spanish from his erstwhile brother-in-law Luis de Andrade, as well as visits over the years to several Iberian harbours, could make out a little of what he was saying, and noted the frequency of two words that he certainly knew: *armada* and *flota*. Thus when Barrett finally translated, he already had a fair sense of what he would say.

'There is one good harbour, and only one,' said Barrett. 'San Juan de Ulúa, the port for the city of Veracruz. It has all we need – ample space and facilities for repair, all the provisions we could wish for, and it is only four days' sail from here.'

The captains, Tom included, looked at each other with satisfaction. Tom smiled broadly, but Hawkins raised a hand.

'Wait,' he said. 'I have heard of this place. It is the principal port on the entire gulf, is it not? The chief port of Mexico? If that is so, how heavily defended is it?'

'That is what he went on to say, Admiral,' said Barrett. 'It is not a strong place. True, there are new fortifications, and a garrison, but this fellow reckons none of that will be able to offer us much resistance. But sometime this month, the incoming *flota* will arrive there. If it has had favourable winds across the ocean, it might already be there, for all he knows. And it will be even more formidable than usual, for he says it is bringing over the new viceroy of New Spain.'

Even Francis Drake was taken aback by this news. The defences of San Juan were one thing, but the entire *flota* was another. The great fleets were legendary throughout Europe. Once a year, huge galleons sailed from Spain, taking out whatever Mexico needed – and, in this case, bringing over its new ruler. But far more important than what it took out was what it took back. All the gold and silver from the mines of the Americas was loaded aboard this one fleet, then shipped back to Old Spain. The treasure of the annual *flota* was a byword throughout Europe. It made King Philip by far the richest monarch in the world, able to set out vast armies and fleets simultaneously across the globe. The Duke of Alba's army in the Netherlands was funded by the bullion from the *flota*, as were fortresses and garrisons far to the west and south of where the English fleet lay, all the way to the borders with the Ottoman Turks. Some even said that treasure from the *flota* secretly subsidised those in England who wished to overthrow Queen Elizabeth and set up a second papist Queen Mary in her place.

Tom had a sudden thought of his sister Meg.

Mariners of England, France, and every other nation that wished Spain ill dreamed of somehow capturing an entire homeward-bound *flota*, and laying those untold riches before their own sovereign – naturally, after they had secured their own entirely justified percentage of the proceeds. More immediately, though, the problem facing Hawkins and his captains was not how to capture the *flota*, but how to avoid it.

'I say we have no choice,' said England's admiral. 'If we are fortunate, the authorities at San Juan will allow us to repair and replenish there, and if we are even more fortunate, we can sail for England before the *flota* arrives. I say that is what we do. Does any man here disagree?'

No man did, but every one of them, Tom included, knew the colossal risk John Hawkins had just committed them to. The guns of San Juan would be one thing; if necessary, the English could probably find some way of dealing with them, as they had at Santa Cruz de Tenerife and Cartagena. But the guns of the *flota*, King Philip's strongest war fleet, his mightiest armada, were another matter entirely.

Twenty-Five

Captain Antonio Delgadillo stood upon the rampart of San Juan de Ulúa, the red and yellow flag of King Philip flapping briskly above his head, and felt more nervous than he had ever done in the twenty-five years of his life. The *flota* was in sight and approaching the harbour. Some of his men were scurrying to ready the great guns for the formal salute, while others were mustering in their ranks, ready to come to attention when Delgadillo gave the order. He had long dreamed of gaining glory in battle as part of one of Castile's invincible *tercios*, perhaps under the command and even the eye of the mighty Duke of Alba himself. With the solitary saving grace of the young widow Isabella Bergara across the bay in her little house in Veracruz, the reality of his posting to this barren, humid, pestilential place was very different indeed, but today might go some way toward compensating for that. He had the opportunity to salute, and even to present himself before, the new viceroy of New Spain, and if he carried out his ceremonial duties punctiliously, perhaps the viceroy would notice and suitably reward the young garrison commander.

The approaching ships were very close now. Only two of them were large men-of-war, but the rest had probably been scattered by the recent storms, and would doubtless make their own way to the harbour in due course.

Delgadillo looked around the anchorage. In truth, it was a poor place when compared with the likes of Sevilla and Cadiz. The harbour was formed by reefs, on the largest of which stood the newly built fort where Delgadillo waited. Ships could secure to large mooring rings set into the wall of this, for deep water came right up to the edge of the reef. An ancient hulk provided the main port facilities; otherwise, the flat, windswept island of San Juan, never more than three feet above sea level, offered nothing but a roughly built chapel and the huts that housed slaves and soldiers alike. To the west, across the north channel, a few buildings were scattered along the shore of the mainland. Yes, a poor place; but through it passed the treasure that sustained Spain's great empire, and that thought, in turn, sustained Antonio Delgadillo's ambitions.

The *flota* came on, the great flagship at its head leading the way through the Gallega channel. Delgadillo unsheathed his sword, brought it up before his face, and shouted the order for the general salute. The honour guard came to attention and the guns of the battery fired five blank rounds to welcome the new viceroy to his realm.

As the smoke cleared from the ramparts, Delgadillo realised that something was very wrong. The gunports of the incoming men-of-war were all open, and, he now realised, had been open even as they approached the reefs. Moreover, although the flags flying from the mastheads of the fleet were torn and dirty, Delgadillo could not see any of the familiar colours and symbols of Spain. His disquiet was momentarily eased by the return of salute from the flagship, which immediately altered course to come in directly to one of the mooring rings. But the orders being shouted on the great ship sounded unfamiliar. With a mounting sense of horror, Delgadillo realised that they were in a language other than Castilian; to be precise, in a language that was not spoken in any of the constituent kingdoms of King Philip's empire.

The first shout came from somewhere down by the moorings.

'Lutherans! Heretics! *Madre de dios*, spare us!'

Delgadillo lowered his sword. 'Hold fast, men!' he shouted to the honour guard. But they were already breaking and running, joining the headlong flight of slaves and whores toward the small boats drawn up along the shoreline of the island, their means of escaping to the mainland and, they hoped, to safety. Meanwhile, the invaders were swarming ashore, securing the cannon that had so recently been under Delgadillo's command.

The young captain turned and saw that only eight men had eschewed flight and remained steadfast. He swallowed hard, his pleasant dreams of recognition by the viceroy, glory in one of Spain's elite regiments, and marriage to Isabella Bergara all evaporating before his worried eyes. He sheathed his sword, uttered a prayer to the Virgin, and prepared to seek out the commander of the English fleet.

–

By nightfall, the *Jennet*, secured by hawsers to one of the fort's mooring rings, was as ready for war as she could be. Jack and Tom Stannard paced her deck, checking the sakers and the small arms, exchanging greetings and ribaldries with the men. From time to time, one or other of them looked across to the fort, where the Spanish colours still flew; Captain Delgadillo's conference with Hawkins had been conducted with perfect civility, the young officer being assured that he remained in command of the island and that the English fleet's intentions were entirely peaceful, its admiral's only wish being to refit as quickly as possible and then to be gone.

'Ten days, Hawkins says,' said Jack. 'That's all we need, he says. Well, if he can get that old wreck the *Jesus* fit for an ocean crossing in ten days, he's a better man than me.'

'Perhaps he'll abandon her,' said Tom. 'Distribute everything across the other ships.'

'Aye, that's what I'd do. But remember, Tom, the *Jesus* is the queen's ship. I reckon our admiral doesn't fancy having to explain to Her Majesty why he hasn't brought home one of her biggest men-of-war, not to mention the queen being a notorious miser, or so it's said. She'll begrudge every penny lost with that hull, no matter what state it's in.'

They passed along the deck, Tom falling into conversation with Hal Ashby, and Jack made his way to the stern to check that the *Jennet*'s kedge anchor was properly secure. Then he went up and stood at the highest point of the deck, looking out across the anchorage toward the setting sun, away behind the distant mountains of Mexico. He thought of Francis Walsingham's injunction to him. What folly it seemed now, after all they had already done to offend King Philip; but surely now they had put paid to any lingering hopes that peace could be kept between Spain and England. No matter how polite Hawkins and the Spanish captain were to each other, the undoubted truth was that an English fleet had sailed into a Spanish port and secured it by force of arms. Hawkins could write all the letters of explanation he liked to the authorities of Mexico, and perhaps even to his 'old master' King Philip himself for all Jack knew, but there was surely no doubt what the Spaniards would think. What the upshot of it all would be, God alone knew.

That thought was still on Jack's mind when he retired to bed and fell into a deep, dreamless sleep. He was wakened what seemed no more than a moment later by Tom, who shook him vigorously.

'Well?' said Jack as he got to his feet.

'Hawkins hasn't got his ten days,' said Tom. 'He's barely had ten hours. The Spanish fleet's in sight.'

–

As he was rowed out to the *capitana*, the flagship of the *flota*, Antonio Delgadillo's stomach was tight and his hands were shaking. He saw the vast personal standard of the viceroy flying from the mainmast of the great galleon, and prayed that this moment would not mark the end of his career – or, indeed, his life. He had spent much of the last day playing over the circumstances of the English fleet's arrival, trying to think of justifications for his actions; rather, for his inaction, in not realising that it was an enemy fleet and not resisting its takeover of the island. No matter how hard he tried, he could come up with no response that convinced him. If he could not do that, he reasoned, then he would hardly convince the viceroy. So, as the boat came under the towering side of the flagship, Captain Delgadillo fingered his rosary beads ever more desperately.

He was led below, to the vast, opulently decorated cabin at the stern. This contained a half-dozen standing men, who by their look and garb could only be the captains of the fleet. One wore an admiral's whistle of command. These standing men were gathered around a large chair, upon which sat a tall, thin man of sixty or thereabouts with piercing eyes, sunken cheekbones and a wispy grey-brown beard. He wore plain black with a high ruff. Delgadillo bowed low.

'Captain,' said Don Martín Enríquez de Almanza, distant kinsman of King Philip and the new Viceroy of New Spain. 'There appear to be heretics infesting your harbour. Perhaps you would be so good as to explain to us how they come to be there?'

Delgadillo embarked upon the speech he had rehearsed over and over again, playing down as much as he could his failure to identify and resist the enemy fleet. To his relief, the viceroy seemed uninterested in this, although Delgadillo could tell from his ferocious expression that the admiral, standing by Don Martín's side, was less forgiving. The viceroy was keener to learn of the numbers, weapons and dispositions of the English, and of the nature of his adversary, the infamous pirate Juan Aquines.

'He claims to have served King Philip?' said the viceroy. 'How curious. But you say he has proposed terms, Captain. I am intrigued to discover what these might be, for the notion of a heretic pirate dictating terms to a viceroy of Spain is even more curious.'

Delgadillo swallowed hard and took a deep breath. 'Excellency, he proposes that the two fleets share the anchorage peaceably, that peace to be secured by an exchange of hostages. For as long as it takes them to refit their ships, the English will retain control of the island and the fort. Then they will leave, again in peace. Those are his terms.'

A heavy silence pervaded the cabin. Several of the captains looked at each other, their expressions incredulous. Don Martín seemed to be contemplating a previously unnoticed defect in one of his fingernails. Then, finally, the viceroy of New Spain spoke.

'Audacious, I'll grant him that. Impertinent beyond measure, of course. And, need I say it, unthinkable. Now, I am naught but a soldier, and know nothing of the ways of sailors. Even so, I say that once all our ships have rejoined us, we simply attack and destroy these heretical scum without a moment's delay. You, Captain Delgadillo, have told us that their largest ship is little better than a wreck, and most of the others are too small to worry us. We have the numbers, we have the righteous cause of God and King Philip on our side, and none shall stand against us.'

Several of the captains nodded, but it was clear that the admiral was deeply troubled.

'Excellency,' he said, 'with respect, to do what you propose would lead to wholesale slaughter.'

'Of course it would, Admiral Luxan. The slaughter of worthless deluded heretics, whose lives do not count. If any survive, they can become slaves in the galleys—'

'No, my lord, I meant the slaughter of good Catholic Spaniards. Our men.'

Don Martín turned and looked at his fleet commander with astonishment writ large upon his long, thin face. 'How so? Are the English ships not as weak as the captain here has described?'

'The ships alone are, Excellency. But remember they now control the guns in the fort too, and have arranged the batteries on their ships to cover all other lines of fire. There are only two channels through the reefs that are deep enough and broad enough to admit ships of our size, and even then, we can only pass through one at a time. If we try to do that, Excellency, the English will destroy the entire *flota*.' There was a gasp from some of the other captains, but the more senior ones were nodding. 'If they do that, then they may very well decide to march on Veracruz. The garrison there was decimated by the summer's plague and will be in no condition to resist them, so there will be nothing to stop them seizing the storehouses and securing all of the king's bullion.'

Delgadillo blanched. He knew from Isabella just how much lay within the storehouses, waiting to be brought down to San Juan for loading aboard the *flota*; the size of the treasure of Veracruz was a matter of pride and endless fascination for every inhabitant of that city.

'There is another consideration too, my lord.'

'Namely?' said Don Martín, irritably.

'The fleet has to go into harbour soon, Excellency – preferably immediately. The northerly storms will become worse and more frequent. If one blows up while we lie here, offshore and exposed, we will be blown far to the south, perhaps down to the very bottom of the gulf. Not only will we stand little chance of beating back up to San Juan de Ulúa, even if we can do so in the teeth of the English guns, but we will have no other harbour at all available to us. There is nothing south of here, Excellency – nothing whatsoever.'

Don Martín shifted uncomfortably upon his temporary throne. 'Admiral, you are seriously telling me that I must accept this Lutheran pirate's terms?'

'I am, my lord. If I may speak frankly, I am astonished that a commander in such a strong position as his is willing to offer us terms at all. I certainly would not, were I in his situation. So I say that we get safe into harbour, trusting that the exchange of hostages will persuade the English to keep their word. What happens after we are safely at anchor, of course…'

At last, the austere Don Martín smiled. 'I take your point, Admiral. Oh, I take your point indeed.'

—

It took three more days before the *flota* came into the harbour of San Juan de Ulúa. All that time, a strong offshore wind blew, keeping the formidable Spanish ships out at sea. The Stannards, like every man in the English fleet, prayed that this presaged another of the northerly storms, such as that which had driven them back from the Florida channel. But it did not, and the wind finally dropped sufficiently to allow the Spanish vessels to begin to slip through the Gallega channel, south of where the English ships lay and well within range of their guns. The banners and ensigns of Spain flew proudly from staffs and mastheads.

Jack and Tom watched the spectacle from the stern of the *Jennet*, still moored fast to the wall of the fort; they, in turn, along with the rest of their countrymen, were being watched by Antonio Delgadillo, standing on the tower roof within the fort that he still nominally commanded in the name of King Philip.

'Hawkins is a fool,' said Tom. 'We should have defied the Spaniards and refused them entry. He's letting the fox into the chicken coop, that he is.'

'Hawkins thinks himself a man of honour,' said Jack. 'What's more, he really feels the sense of loyalty to King Philip that he brags about. It's a Spanish harbour, and England isn't at war with Spain, so how could he deny the viceroy entry into his own port? Besides, Hawkins is a great man for what he calls the fellowship of the seas. He says that in all conscience, he can't expose fellow sailors to the perils of the sort of storm we came through. He also says that if the Spanish fleet is wrecked in such a storm, then how will Queen Elizabeth explain that to King Philip?'

Tom shook his head.

'A man of honour? A fellowship of the seas? God spare us, Father, 'tis madness. And ten hostages on each side? He really thinks that's enough to keep the peace?'

Jack made no reply. He was intent on watching the principal Spanish ships warp into their agreed positions at the berths on the south-west side of the island, physically separated from the English, who were moored together in the south-east, closer to the potential escape route through the reefs. The *Minion*, the westernmost ship of the English fleet, marked the demarcation line between the two fleets, close to the inert hull of the old hulk. The Spanish ships, like the English, were moored so tightly to the shore that their bowsprits overhung the land.

'Old Cesar de Andrade once told me something about Spanish noblemen,' said Jack. 'He said that your grandee is usually a mighty indolent fellow, and that he cares only about three things. One is the purity of his bloodline, to which end he'll obtain a papal dispensation to marry his sister if he has to. Well, his niece, at any rate. Witness the example of King Philip's family, the Habsburgs. The second thing he cares about is his stable, that his horses may be superior to those of his neighbour. And the third thing he cares about, above even the others, is his honour. If that honour is affronted, your idle nobleman will become a demon of activity, plotting and scheming until he has his revenge. I told that story to Hawkins, and he said aye, it was true, and that the viceroy's honour as a nobleman of Spain would ensure that the truce held. I drew a different conclusion, Tom, but forbore from telling it to our admiral, who'd not have welcomed it.'

'And your conclusion was?'

'We've already mightily affronted the viceroy's honour. Having to accept the terms offered by a man he'll certainly regard as a pirate and a heretic? I recall something else Cesar de Andrade once told me. As far as a Spaniard's concerned, any agreement struck with heretics, no matter how formal, no matter how legal, is utterly worthless. They look on you as the walking damned.' Jack said it with a smile, but Tom noted his father's switch from 'we' to 'you'. 'So you mark my words, over there on his flagship at this very moment, Don Martín is plotting his revenge on those he sees as upstart heretics.'

Twenty-Six

It was the strangest of days. The Spanish ships completed the process of coming to their berths and mooring, while the crews of the English ones began to undertake repairs and to prepare for careening. Ashore, Englishmen and Spaniards eyed each other suspiciously, although every once in a while, one or two of one nation approached one or two of the other, exchanged biscuits, bread or wine, and attempted a few tentative words of the other's language. By the middle of the afternoon, a few on each side were even kicking a ball around. But aboard the ships, the atmosphere was tense, with every gunport open and no man more than a yard or so from a weapon.

Aboard the *Jennet*, Jack and Tom heard that there seemed to be suspicious movement aboard the great hulk that lay between the *Minion* and the Spanish ships beyond it. Hawkins sent a messenger over to demand an end to any underhand activity, and the viceroy sent back respectful assurances that the Spaniards, for their part, had no such intent. As it was, the Stannards busied themselves in ensuring that the *Jennet* was ready for any eventuality. Like every ship in the fleet, axes stood next to the cables that secured the hull to the mooring ring, and by the capstan. The ship's entire armoury of small arms, arquebuses, pikes, swords, bills, and crossbows, together with ammunition, was massed on deck, carefully concealed behind canvas and wood screens in case any Spaniard in the fort should venture to look closely at the English ships. Piles of round shot and chain shot lay alongside each saker, along with tubs of water to cool the gun barrels after each firing. But all the while, men murmured among themselves at the admiral's folly in allowing the Spanish fleet into the harbour at all.

As the sun began to set, Jack Stannard received an invitation from Hawkins to sup with him aboard the *Jesus*.

'Supper?' said Tom incredulously. 'With the peril we're in?'

'Aye, supper,' said Jack. 'But I can't turn down our admiral, and may glean something of his intentions. Besides, he'll be thinking that the Spanish won't attack at night, and in that, I don't doubt he's right.'

Jack climbed down into the *Jennet*'s pinnace, which lay between the ship and the shore, forming a bridge between the two. As he did so, something made him turn to look at his son and wave, as he had always done when the little boy on the quay at Dunwich had stood weeping as his father set off on another voyage. He also called out the words he had always shouted from his ship as it moved away from its berth.

'*Dominus tecum*, Tom.'

Thomas Stannard seemed taken aback by being addressed thus, but replied nonetheless.

'And also with you, father.'

Then Jack turned and was gone from his son's sight.

-

The scene in the great cabin of the *Jesus* was unexpected. Hawkins, dressed in one of his finest outfits, had assembled a gathering of a dozen or so of his officers and gentlemen volunteers, of whom Robert Barrett was the only one that Jack knew well. The ten Spanish hostages, elegantly dressed but clearly nervous young men, stood together, reminding Jack of the huddle of their countrymen in the room in Westminster so many years before. Their counterparts who had gone to the Spanish flagship as surety for the truce included Edward Dudley's old adversary George Fitzwilliam. Hawkins' pages, among them his own nephew, Paul, and the black lad, Samuel, were serving wine into the admiral's finest Venetian glass, unused since the entertaining of the merchants of Tenerife. Strangest of all, the admiral had once again assembled his band of musicians, who were playing works that Jack recognised, and sometimes even hitting the right notes.

'Jack Stannard,' said Hawkins. 'Welcome, cousin. Here, take some wine. All's well aboard the *Jennet*?'

'Well indeed. We are as prepared as we can be, Admiral.'

'Good. And no doubt you're wondering why I should commit such folly as to entertain in my cabin, when the Spaniards may seek to slaughter us at any time?' Jack made no reply, but suspected that his face told its own story; in any case, Hawkins did not wait for an answer. 'Why, it's all one of the oldest games, Jack. They seek to reassure us that they have no warlike intent. Well, I don't believe them, and for all the viceroy's assurances, I suspect that they're secretly putting men into the hulk. But, in turn, we seek to reassure them that we have no such intent either, even though we are fully ready for battle, and what better way of doing that than for them to hear sounds of merriment coming from our flagship?'

Jack thought it a dubious line of reasoning, but Hawkins seemed to have entire faith in it, so he kept his peace.

Hawkins lowered his voice. 'But I know you've lied to me again, Jack Stannard.'

Jack felt a grip of ice around his heart.

'Lied? How, Admiral?' Hawkins knew of Jack's efforts at Walsingham's behest, and he knew he adhered to the old faith. What else could the admiral possibly construe as a lie?

'You know I love music,' said Hawkins, merrily. 'Hence my band, yonder, which many – Drake for one – consider a frippery and an indulgence. But I have heard it said, John Stannard of Dunwich, that you possess the finest singing voice in the fleet – that you once sang before Cardinal Wolsey himself. Now, is that true?'

'I can hold a note,' said Jack. 'And yes, our choir sang before the cardinal, just the once.'

'And you've concealed that truth from me this entire voyage, which I account a lie, cousin. I have no right to ask you here, in this place and in these circumstances, but I crave your indulgence, and hope you'll give us a song or two.'

It was madness. Jack knew that somewhere in the hereafter, his beloved Alice would be laughing uncontrollably, probably in company with the shade of Thomas Ryman. Yet a part of him was still the young boy who wanted nothing more than to perform before the great, and there in the harbour of San Juan de Ulúa, the Queen of England's admiral was asking him to sing. So he nodded, and went over to talk to Hawkins' musicians.

From the Spanish ships, just as from the English, Jack Stannard's voice could be heard clearly. The viceroy of

New Spain went up on deck to listen, and exchanged an astonished look with Admiral Luxan. High up in the tower of the fort, Captain Antonio Delgadillo shook his head: so it was true what they said, that the English were all madmen. Aboard *Jennet*, Tom Stannard heard the distant but unmistakable sound of his father's voice, and wept.

Jack sang on, giving his audience 'Greensleeves', 'John Barleycorn', 'I Shall No More to Sea', and four or five more. In his mind, he was no longer aboard a ship, thousands of miles from England; he was singing again to his Alice, as he had done to woo her in Dunwich, so many years before, and it seemed to him that he had never sung so well in his life.

'The sin of pride, Jack Stannard,' Alice would have said. The thought made him smile.

His performance was greeted by cheers and applause from all, including the Spaniards. The admiral and all the others present in the great cabin of the *Jesus* praised him to the heights and plied him continually with wine.

'The sin of drunkenness, Jack Stannard.' He could almost hear her voice creeping softly from the damp timbers of the *Jesus*.

When the evening finally ended, Hawkins insisted that it would be too hazardous for Jack to attempt to return to the *Jennet*, and that he should take a bed for the night aboard the flagship before going back to his own ship at dawn. If the Spaniards were going to attack, said the admiral, they would not do so before then.

Against his better judgement, Jack accepted the offer.

–

He was wakened at dawn by the unmistakable sounds of a ship's crew making ready for action. He made his way to the upper deck, and found armed men moving swiftly to man the sides of the huge old flagship. He went to the quarterdeck, where he found Hawkins, dressed in his armour, standing close by a number of his other officers. Of Robert Barrett, there was no sign. It seemed he had been sent to the viceroy to deliver a protest about the Spaniards' suspicious activity, but had not returned.

'Never trust a Spaniard,' said Hawkins. 'My fellow servants of King Philip, and this is how they respect a truce. I fear I have undone us all, cousin Stannard, but best to be certain.'

Jack looked around. There was clearly activity ashore, with the sounds of running men and the occasional glint of a blade or breastplate through an embrasure. Closer at hand, there was movement aboard the hulk, and it was this on which Hawkins was focused. With Jack and a half-dozen others at his side, he crossed over to the *Minion* to take a closer look, taking a crossbow from the hands of his nephew as he did so. Jack, meanwhile, took up a loaded arquebus from one of the stacks standing ready on the *Minion*'s deck.

There was clearly activity within the Spanish hull: the sounds of large numbers of men trying and failing to move about silently. In the bow, ropes were being loosened and adjusted to inch the hulk closer to the *Minion*. Suddenly, one man came into plain view on the upper deck, a senior officer by the looks of his elaborate armour and helmet. He glanced about, as though uncertain of where he was, then saw Hawkins standing upon the fo'c'sle of the *Minion*.

'It's the vice admiral,' said Hawkins. 'Ubilla. I think we need no further proof of what they're about, by God.'

There were more shouts ashore, within the fort; shouts in English, proclaiming an alarm. Hawkins shouted something at Ubilla, his Spanish so rough that even Jack could get a sense of it. England's admiral accused Spain's of deceit and ungentlemanly conduct, to which Ubilla replied in rapid Castilian that the two Englishmen found hard to follow. But they both caught Ubilla's final words: that he was a fighter.

'You are quite right!' cried Hawkins, then took aim and loosed his quarrel.

There were shouts aboard the hulk, and Spanish troops rushed forward to cover their vice admiral. Jack lifted his arquebus, took aim and fired, feeling the vicious kick of the gun into his shoulder. As the smoke cleared, he had the satisfaction of seeing one of the soldiers at Ubilla's side slump to the deck, clutching at his chest.

The shots from Hawkins and Jack were the signal for general battle to commence. A trumpet sounded aboard the viceroy's flagship, the *capitana*, and men emerged from cover to attack the English positions ashore. Guns fired, steel struck steel, but it was clear to the admiral and his party, crossing back to the *Jesus*, that the men at the shore batteries were hopelessly outnumbered and would be overwhelmed in short order.

Aboard the *Jesus*, just as aboard the *Minion* to larboard and the *Swallow* to starboard, men were hacking at the mooring cables and manning the guns without waiting for orders from their officers. Jack knew that Tom and the men of Dunwich would be doing the same aboard the *Jennet*. He wished he could return to his ship, and cursed himself for accepting the admiral's invitation to sing; but there was no time for that now. The only way he would get back to Tom, and the only way the English fleet would extricate itself from its desperate position, was by fighting for their lives.

The bows of the Spanish hulk came round, and struck the bows of the *Minion*. Screaming triumphantly, Spanish troops began to leap over onto the deck of the English ship. Most of the *Minion*'s men seemed to be below decks, no doubt readying her larboard battery, so very few came forward to resist the onslaught. Seeing this, Hawkins immediately barked out an order.

'God and St George, repel those treacherous villains! Rescue the *Minion*! Trust in God that the day will be ours!'

With a roar, men from the *Jesus* began to leap onto the lower deck of the adjacent *Minion* and charged to the defence of their countrymen. By now, though, both of the great English ships had severed their head ropes and were beginning to drift out from their berths, so there were no more than a few minutes before the hulk and the *Minion* were breaking apart, stranding the Spanish vanguard and preventing reinforcements from coming across from the hulk. Steadily, the advantage of numbers shifted in favour of the English, who pressed the Spaniards further and further back into the bows of the *Minion*. Seeing their colleagues in the front ranks perish on heretic pikes and swords, many of the others abandoned the fight and jumped into the waters of the anchorage.

The *Jesus* and the *Minion* were finally clear of their berths, and Hawkins ordered the helm of the flagship brought over. Men were sheeting sails home, but as yet the ship had little momentum. The Spaniards on the upper deck of the hulk were now opening up a furious fire with their arquebuses and crossbows, and the English ships responded in kind.

'Admiral!' cried Jack. 'Have you a weapon to spare?'

He had left the arquebus he had fired against the Spaniard on the hulk aboard the *Minion*.

'Of course,' said Hawkins, then turned to his nephew. 'Paul, supply an arquebus to Captain Stannard here, and keep him well supplied with powder and shot!'

The lad grinned. 'Aye, aye, uncle!'

He collected a weapon from the pile by the mizzen mast and handed it to Jack, who primed it in the manner that old Thomas Ryman had once taught him. As he did so, he looked around, assessing the state of the battle. The *Jesus* and the *Minion* were beginning to edge slowly westward, clearing the stern of the hulk. The greatest ships of the Spanish *flota* were still secured to their mooring rings, their crews making no attempt to bring them out to take on the English vessels.

'Why don't they unmoor?' shouted Jack, above the din upon the upper deck of the *Jesus*. 'The wind would favour them just as much as us.'

'Not their way of fighting,' said John Hawkins. 'The viceroy is a soldier – fought under Alba himself, they say. So he wants a land battle, which is why he put men into the hulk, hoping to surprise and board the *Minion*, then us. But it's not the way Englishmen fight, eh, cousin Stannard? Let's show them what is!'

First the *Minion*, then the *Jesus* had a clear line of fire against the first of the huge Spanish ships, the *almirante*, or vice admiral's flagship. Jack watched, impressed, as several great shots from the *Minion* struck their target. The *Jesus* was so close behind her fellow royal man-of-war that she would be able to fire well before the gun crews of the *Minion* had been able to reload. Hawkins and his master gunner bellowed encouragement to their own gun crews, manning the starboard battery. Then England's admiral judged his moment.

'Steady… steady… *Give fire!*'

The sakers on the upper deck of the *Jesus* opened fire, followed moments later by the culverins on the gun deck below. The range was point blank, and Jack Stannard witnessed the effect of a broadside from a great man-of-war. He had seen a sea fight before at the battle between the English and French fleets off Portsmouth in 1545 when the *Mary Rose* went down, taking his friend and mentor Thomas Ryman with it. But he had watched that from a distance, and in any case, there had only been a few desultory exchanges of fire, at the very limit of both fleet's ranges.

This was a very different affair. The firing of the guns made even the huge hull of the *Jesus* shudder, as though it was being torn apart. The noise outdid the loudest thunder Jack had ever known. Flame spat from the mouths of the sakers, then thick smoke that made him choke and cough rolled back over the deck. But the effect of the broadside was even more astonishing. The English shot wreaked devastation on the *almirante*, shattering the delicate stern gallery and windows of the great cabin, driving vast holes through the hull and sending huge splinters of wood inward or upward. The swivel guns on the fore- and aftercastles of the *Jesus* fired a barrage of chain shot, tearing through the standing rigging and decapitating at least a half dozen Spaniards who were trying to reinforce the quarterdeck. Jack fired his own arquebus, but had no particular target; if any men were left alive on the upper deck of the *almirante*, they were keeping their heads down.

The guns of the *Jesus* were hauled inboard for reloading. The ship was still barely moving, so by the time the starboard battery was ready to fire again, the relative positions of the two vessels had changed little. The master gunner went from gun to gun, judging the best moment to fire. Once again, the English guns roared out, but now they were often firing into the holes they had already made, so their shot had to be penetrating into the very depths of the Spanish ship.

There was only a moment's warning of what was about to happen. What seemed to be a deep rumbling, far inside the hull, burst into a great explosion that drowned out even the noise of the English cannon. The central part of the upper deck of the *almirante* seemed to lift bodily upwards in a column of flame and thick black smoke, then shatter into a thousand shards of wood. Simultaneously, the blast burst out of both sides of the hull. Jack staggered to keep his footing, and that action saved him from the huge splinter that flew through the place where he had been standing just a moment before.

The men of the *Jesus* began to cheer wildly, but Hawkins and his officers immediately went about the deck, ordering them to resume their stations. The *almirante* might be destroyed, but the English ships were now edging toward the admiral's ship, the *capitana*. Its mainmast continued to fly the standard of the viceroy of New Spain, so it was likely that Don Martín was still aboard.

Jack caught the eye of John Hawkins. The admiral nodded grimly, but Jack could see the triumph in his expression.

Against all the odds, perhaps England would, after all, taste victory this day.

Twenty-Seven

Away to the east, the *Jennet*, her mooring hawsers cut, edged away from her berth, and Tom Stannard prepared to give the orders to bring her around, to make sail, and to join the larger ships in the battle taking place beyond the hulk. But although he and his men cheered when they saw the *almirante* blow up, Tom could see something his father and Hawkins could not, and it chilled him to the very heart.

Outside the fort, the English had thrown up temporary gun batteries to complement the cannon within the fort itself. Guns had been taken out of the larboard batteries of the larger ships, and they were trained on the Spanish vessels. But from the *Jennet*, Tom was able to see the huge force the Spanish had sent ashore at dawn. These troops fanned out from the fort, overwhelming the men Hawkins had deployed to defend the fortifications. Worse, they were now shifting the positions of the guns in the makeshift batteries, training them to fire on the English fleet instead of the Spanish. Tom did not doubt that within the fort, exactly the same would be happening. That being so—

The first of the shore guns opened up, those now trained towards the *Jesus* and the *Minion*. Tom watched as the Spaniards found their range, and more and more shot hit the two great ships, especially Hawkins' flagship.

He prayed for his father, but never reached the amen. Two great shots struck the water no more than a few feet from the bow of the *Jennet*, sending up huge spouts that soaked those on deck. The next salvo was bound to hit, and the *Jennet*, warping out of her berth and still virtually bow-on to the mooring, could not bring any guns to bear in reply.

When the Spanish guns fired again, they wreaked havoc. One destroyed the bowsprit, then shattered the starboard side of the fo'c'sle. The other smashed into the larboard beam, shaking the entire hull and smashing a great hole through the timbers. Tom could hear a scream below decks, but had no time to go in search of the casualty.

'Hal Ashby! Get four more men on the capstan! The rest of you, take a weapon, then forward with me!'

As more men went to join Ashby, who was in charge of the warping effort, Tom and a dozen men of Suffolk ran forward, found a position at the rail with a field of fire, and opened up with arquebuses or crossbows. If only they could force the gunners ashore to keep their heads down until the ship was clear of the berth…

The next two shots hit the *Jennet*. One, a lucky effort, struck the mainmast itself, and Tom saw with horror that the great timber was toppling. He barely had time to register this before a ball struck the hull close to him, ripping loose great splinters and sending them into the very heart of his crew. Knocked back as he was by the impact, it took him a moment to recover and look around. He saw at least a dozen corpses, or parts of corpses. One of them belonged to Hal Ashby, a splinter three feet long protruding from his breast and another, smaller, from his forehead. The deck was a pond of blood, and dying men were screaming for mercy. The mainmast tilted at a crazy angle, held up only by some of the standing rigging.

The *Jennet* was lost, as was the *Swallow*, close by her. Ashore, Spanish troops were rushing forward to man boats. Away to the west, the wreck of the Spanish *almirante* still burned, while the flagship, the *capitana* itself, was settling lower and lower in the water. But the *Jesus* and the *Minion* were under increasingly heavy and sustained gunfire from the largest guns in the fort and elsewhere on the island; guns that until barely an hour earlier had been in English hands.

To the east, though, Drake had got the *Judith* clear of its mooring, and was unfurling its sails. Hawkins had placed no batteries that far from the Spanish fleet, their intended target, and as the outermost of the English ships, the *Judith* was able to manoeuvre as she willed, free from hostile fire. Drake was conning the ship's head toward the south-east, into open water and away from the battle, but Tom could not fault him in that; the *Judith* was a small ship, like the *Jennet*, and could do nothing to affect the outcome, which was now surely obvious. But God willing, some Englishmen might yet escape with their lives from the disaster at San Juan.

'All hands!' cried Tom. 'With me, to the pinnace! We're abandoning ship!'

—

The *Jesus* was taking shot after shot, and her own return fire was weakening. She was the largest ship in the English fleet and still flew the tattered rag that had been the royal standard of England, so she was naturally the principal target for the Spanish gunners ashore. The great old hull, already weakened by the storms encountered during the voyage, was taking on water and listing. Jack heard the ship's carpenter report to Hawkins that the mainmast had been struck by several shots, saw the admiral nod, and observed the confident expression he put on to face the men, even sending his page Samuel to fetch him a tankard of beer. But he also turned momentarily toward Jack, and raised his eyes to the heavens in a gesture of utter despair.

The page brought the admiral a silver goblet, and even as Spanish shot continued to hammer the hull and rigging of the *Jesus*, and sweep her decks, Hawkins raised it to the men within earshot.

'God bless you, boys! And with His blessing, the day will still be ours! Fire again as your guns bear, then again, and then yet again! God save the queen!'

Hawkins put down the cup, but even before the echoing shout of 'God save the queen!' had died away, a cannonball struck it and drove it clean off the ship. A second earlier and it would have done the same to the body of John Hawkins. As it was, England's admiral saw the horrified expressions of all those around him, Jack included, and put on a broad smile.

'Have no fear, men,' he cried, 'for God, who has saved me from this shot, will also deliver us from these traitors and villains!'

He had hardly finished before another Spanish salvo struck the ship: chain shot, now, and aimed high. There was a sickening cracking sound, and Jack looked up to see the foremast torn in two, the upper part dangling precariously amidst the rigging. The fallen foremast and weakened mainmast meant that the huge old ship would never be able to bear sail again, certainly not that day in the harbour of San Juan de Ulúa. In that moment, it was clear to Jack Stannard that the flagship was doomed.

Hawkins had been silent for some moments, staring at the scene around him. Jack wondered if he was blaming himself for letting the Spaniards into the harbour, for trusting them to keep the truce, for ignoring the possibility that they might overwhelm and take control of the very gun batteries he had ordered to be erected.

At last, the admiral seemed to come to a decision, and Jack heard the order he barked at John Sanders, boatswain of the *Jesus* and her acting master in the absence of Robert Barrett.

'Signal to *Minion* and *Judith* to come alongside – our lee will protect them from enemy fire. We'll move as much as we can into them, then try to get out of the harbour.'

No order to *Jennet*. Jack could not see what was happening out to the east, where the view was obscured by the Spanish hulk, now empty and swinging from the few ropes that continued to secure it to the fort, and the wreck of the *Swallow* beyond it. But Hawkins' lookout, still at his station in the crow's nest high up on the shattered mainmast, would be able to see, and would have communicated that knowledge to the admiral. It meant only one thing: the *Jennet*, Jack's ship, built to his specifications and named for his second wife, was lost. Whether his son was lost with her – whether he would ever know Tom's fate at all – was in God's hands. The thought was too dreadful, and Jack dared not even pray, for he knew if he did, he might lose the tight grip he was keeping on his tormented feelings. Instead, he raised his arquebus and fired in the general direction of the fort, although he knew it was well beyond his range.

During the next half-turn of the glass, the two great English ships edged together, the smaller and nimbler *Judith* responding to the signal to abandon its safe station near the eastern channel, coming alongside the *Jesus* rather more swiftly than the *Minion*. The Spanish continued to concentrate their fire on the flagship, leaving the other vessels, protected by the towering sides of the *Jesus*, relatively undamaged. The *Judith*, in turn, came in under the lee of the *Minion*. The ship's officers of the *Jesus* organised parties of men to move anything valuable into them, ready for transfer to the other two ships. On the other side of the ship, men continued to fire the great guns, albeit raggedly, and some of what had once been Edward Dudley's company of soldiers were still firing arquebuses. Their salvos would have no effect on the fort or the other Spanish batteries, but they might at least deter the viceroy and his officers from sending troops in boats to try and board the English ships.

All available hands were engaged in bringing up essentials and valuables from below decks on the *Jesus*, then throwing or hauling them over to the slightly lower upper deck of the *Minion*, where men lined the rail to receive them. Barrels of food and water came up with bags and boxes of gold, weapons with the officers' navigational instruments. It was frantic work, all of it conducted to the accompaniment of gunfire from the *Jesus* and its enemies, but Jack played his part, going below decks to search for anything portable that might be worth saving. At the very least, it took his mind off what might be happening with Tom and the other men of the *Jennet* – if, that was, they still lived.

He was making his way through the gloomy and nearly empty gun deck of the *Jesus* when he heard a pitiful wailing from the hold below, together with other shouts in a language he recognised but did not understand. He knew the source of the cries at once: the forty or so slaves that remained unsold, along with the ten Spanish hostages. He saw Boatswain Sanders at the other end of the deck, overseeing a party of men bringing up swords from the armoury, and hailed him.

'Sanders! Those below – are we freeing them?'

'Just more mouths to feed, the admiral says. The Spaniards can do what they like with them when they take the ship.'

'But what if the ship sinks?'

The boatswain shrugged and made no answer. Jack thought to say more, but both their heads turned upward as a first scream, then a second, came from the upper deck, above their heads. Both bore just one word.

'Fireship!'

Twenty-Eight

For two hours or more, the *Jennet*'s pinnace had held its position off the eastern end of the island. The Spaniards showed no sign of wishing to pursue it, massing all their troops further west at the fort and the batteries. But unless Tom steered a course far to the south, out of range of the Spanish guns, it would be impossible for him to reach the remaining English ships, even if his exhausted men were then able to beat back up into the teeth of a continually strengthening northerly breeze. No: if Hawkins hoped to escape, as he surely must, then Tom needed to hold the *Jennet*'s boat where it was and pray that one of the fleeing vessels picked up him and his men. And if none of the ships escaped the onslaught taking place to the west, then Tom Stannard had only one course of action left: beaching his boat and surrendering to the Spanish.

From their makeshift position, the survivors of the *Jennet* could see both the *Minion* and the *Judith* come under the lee of the flagship, and Tom guessed what must be happening; the shattered condition of the *Jesus*, especially of her masts, was clearly visible even from such a distance. At length, he saw the *Judith* unmoor from the flagship and set course eastward. The Spanish continued to concentrate their fire on the two large ships, so the *Judith* was able to proceed relatively unhindered, beam-on to the stiff northerly breeze. Her course would carry her directly to the pinnace, and Tom gave the command to turn the boat's helm to carry it westward to intercept her.

When the *Judith* was within range, Tom hailed her. Francis Drake's head appeared above the fo'c'sle rail.

'For mercy's sake, throw us a line!' cried Tom.

'Fend for yourself, Stannard! We're overladen as it is!'

Tom could not believe what he heard.

'Overladen? How?'

'Overladen, I say! Men and goods from the flagship! There's no room for you here!'

'Christ's nails, Drake! Mercy, man! We're all Englishmen – save us, for God's sake!'

Drake made no reply. Instead, he lifted an arquebus, levelled it at the *Jennet*'s pinnace, and signalled for a good dozen more of his men to do the same.

'Save yourselves, Stannard of Dunwich,' he cried angrily. 'I told you in Plymouth that it was only just beginning between us, but this is where it ends.'

Tom stared at the receding hull of the *Judith*, then raised two fingers toward Francis Drake before ordering his crew, with Mark Ferris at the helm, to bring the boat about and make for the far distant *Jesus* and *Minion* instead, even if it meant being sunk by a shot from one of the shore batteries. They were barely level with the shattered remains of the *Jennet*, over which Spanish troops swarmed, when he saw the fearful sight of the fireship emerge from behind the west rampart of the fort, its course set for the *Jesus* and the *Minion*.

–

The fireship was a terrifying spectacle, bearing down on the northerly wind toward the English ships. Dusk was now falling, and the twilight only added to the fearful effect. Flames spat and danced the length of its upper deck, up its masts and along its yards. It was shrouded in a vast pall of smoke, through which sparks blew out toward its targets. It was as though hell itself had been set afloat, and was bearing down directly to claim all their souls for Lucifer. Aboard both the *Jesus* and the *Minion*, men were screaming and praying – not a few, Jack noted, crossing themselves in the old way, even aboard the flagship of Protestant England's admiral.

'Damn fools,' said Hawkins. 'Nine times out of ten, fireships miss – no man aboard to steer them. The tenth time, a good crew simply pushes it aside with poles. But for that to happen, the good crew has to be stout-hearted.' He raised his voice to shout at both crews. 'Hold your nerve, men! Hold your nerve, and all be well! Be stout-hearted Englishmen, in God's name!'

But on the *Minion*, his injunction was falling on deaf ears. Although Captain Hampton and the ship's officers tried to prevent it, the men were taking matters into their own hands, cutting through the cables that secured the *Minion* to the *Jesus*. Slowly, a gap began to grow between the two ships.

'Thomas Hampton!' cried Hawkins. 'Damn it, Captain Hampton, control your men!'

Hampton looked across, a grief-stricken expression on his face, then raised his hands abjectly.

The first man jumped from the deck of the *Jesus* onto the slightly lower one of the *Minion*. Another half-dozen followed him at once, but others, already nervous about the width of the gap between the two ships, held back. All the while, the smoke from the fireship grew thicker, the heat from its blaze became more intense, and more sparks fell on the deck or onto men's clothing and hair.

'Jesu!' said Hawkins suddenly. 'Where's my nephew? Where's Paul?'

'I saw him a moment ago, Admiral!' cried Jack. 'He's up forward, afraid to jump!'

'Then go to him, Jack Stannard, for God's sake! Get him safe to the *Minion*! I'll see you both aboard her!'

'Aye, aye, Admiral!'

Jack ran forward. Paul Hawkins was standing at the ship's rail, holding a plate and goblet adorned with precious stones, no doubt part of the treasure from the admiral's cabin.

'Paul!' cried Jack. The lad looked at him, uncomprehending. 'Paul Hawkins! Your uncle orders you to jump to the *Minion*, lad! Can you do it?'

The boy looked at the gap, then back up at Jack. He nodded, dropped the valuable objects to the deck, and went to the rail. John Hawkins saw this from the quarterdeck, nodded and smiled. Then another thick pall of smoke from the fireship enveloped the deck, and the two parties lost sight of each other.

For a man standing close to Jack and Paul, this was the last straw. He climbed onto the rail and attempted to jump, but fell short and plunged into the sea between the two hulls. Jack murmured the *Ave Maria*, but Paul Hawkins watched in horror as the doomed man flailed and screamed before disappearing below the waves. The boy turned as if to run below decks, but Jack took his arm and led him back to the ship's side.

'You're young, Paul Hawkins,' he said. 'Would you think twice about jumping that distance over a stream in

Plymouth? No, you would not. Trust in God, lad, and you'll be safe.'

He did not add that although a youth could easily jump such a distance, a man of his own age probably could not.

The admiral's nephew readied himself, but just then the smoke from the fireship cleared briefly, and Jack and his young charge turned to see the admiral leap the few feet onto the starboard side of the *Minion*, landing heavily on its quarterdeck. Men scrambled to assist him. Paul shouted to try and attract his uncle's attention, but the admiral was too far away, the roar of the Spanish guns too loud, and just then a powder barrel on the fireship exploded, causing a chorus of screams from the men of the *Minion*. Jack looked around to see if another English boat was nearby, but there were none, and the *Minion* was pulling away rapidly. The gap was now too great for either of them to jump, even if they could pluck up the courage to attempt it.

Jack turned to look in the other direction. The fireship was very close now, its heat warming his face and that of the admiral's weeping nephew, but it was clear that the blazing hull was going to drift harmlessly past the stern of the *Jesus*. Perhaps the *Minion* would send a boat back for the many men who remained on the lost flagship, beseeching and howling oaths from the ship's side. But in his heart, Jack knew this was a forlorn hope. The only boats he could see through the gathering gloom were Spanish ones, pulling away from the hulk and the fort, intent on boarding the abandoned *Jesus*.

No, there was one more boat, just visible in the distance, seemingly steering directly for the *Minion* from the east. Even in such poor light, and at such a distance, Jack recognised it instantly as the *Jennet*'s pinnace. Why the men of Dunwich had not reached sanctuary aboard

Drake's *Judith*, which must have sailed straight past them, was a mystery; but, praise be, Jack saw a line being thrown from the *Minion*, and the boat – *his* boat – being drawn in.

All around him, men were weeping, praying or both. Young Paul Hawkins was still watching the departing *Minion*, perhaps yet hoping against hope that his uncle would somehow return and rescue him from the fate that otherwise awaited him. But the first of the Spanish boats was already coming alongside the hull of the *Jesus*.

It was over. Paul Hawkins looked up at Jack, his young eyes tearful and imploring. Jack made an effort to smile, and put a hand on the boy's shoulder.

'Whatever happens, lad,' he said, 'remember this. Always believe you will return home again. Believe that you'll go back to Plymouth one day, as I believe I will return to Dunwich. Aye, lad, believe that you will see England once more. But until that day dawns, you *are* England. It is in your heart. It is in your soul. Wherever you may be, England remains in the essence of you, and you in it.'

He had no idea where the words came from; perhaps they had been in a sermon he had once heard, or in something Thomas Ryman had said to him. They could not have been his own, that was for certain. After all, he was naught but a mere sailor of Dunwich.

The boy looked at him through wet eyes, and mouthed a silent thank you.

The Spaniards were very close now, but Drake and Hawkins had abandoned them to their fate.

Jack watched the *Minion* manoeuvre away from the carnage in the anchorage, praying that his Tom was somewhere aboard her despite all; praying that, against all the odds, his son was safe.

The few dozen desperate Englishmen left on the deck of the shattered flagship were still screaming vainly at the receding ship. A few looked to Jack for leadership, but he had none to give. None of them would see England again, he reckoned. For his part, he would never see another Dunwich dawn, nor the smile on the face of his daughter Meg, nor the grave of—

The first Spanish soldiers emerged onto the upper deck, their morion helmets and sword blades glistening in the brilliant sun.

Jack Stannard muttered the Lord's Prayer and prepared himself for death.

But in his heart, he knew that death was not the worst fate the Spaniards could inflict.

—

As the last of the day's sun sank in the western sky, Captain Antonio Delgadillo emerged onto the upper deck of the huge but broken English flagship. He saw the little huddle of men and boys over by the remnants of the fo'c'sle, but they were making no attempt to resist; how could they, when more and more Spanish troops were emerging from the hatches? Instead, Delgadillo signalled to a pair of trusty men he had briefed for this very mission. They strode to the ensign staff, pulled down the filthy remnants of the heretical flag, and hoisted in their place the pristine scarlet and gold banner of Castile and King Philip. Delgadillo's men cheered wildly, and the young captain himself raised his sword to salute the colours. God willing, the viceroy would have seen the deed through the twilight, and both promotion and Isabella Bergara might lie within reach once again.

One of the Lutherans started to walk towards Delgadillo. He was an old man, with leathery skin and wild hair, and he carried a sword. Several of Delgadillo's men had their guns trained on him, but there was no need for them to fire. The Englishman reversed his blade, presenting it hilt first to Delgadillo. A pity it was not Juan Aquines himself, but an English sword would still make a fine gift for the viceroy.

The Englishman spoke, and to Delgadillo's surprise, his words were in Latin, a tongue he had thought extinct in a realm of pestilential heretics.

'*Miserere, in nomine Dei*,' he said. Mercy, in God's name.

Delgadillo nodded, took the proffered sword handle, and accepted the surrender of John Stannard of Dunwich.

Epilogue

January 1569

The snow was sweeping in from the south-west as the *Minion* finally came into Plymouth Sound, over fifteen months after she had sailed from the same harbour. Tom Stannard stood on deck and reflected on all that had passed since the fateful battle at San Juan: how the men aboard the *Minion* had woken at dawn in the outer reaches of the harbour to find that Drake's *Judith* had mysteriously vanished in the night; how the *Minion* herself had escaped the anchorage in the teeth of a storm that threatened at every moment to wreck her upon the reefs; how quarrels and fights had broken out among an overlarge crew forced to eat rats and boiled hides; how half the men aboard preferred to abandon the ship and its apparently slender prospects of crossing the ocean in order to take their chances ashore further up the Mexican coast. Only then had the *Minion* finally set sail for England. Leaking, stinking and foul, she had wallowed her way across the Atlantic, each mile a very purgatory. Men died of disease, sometimes several of them in one day, so that by the time the ship reached the coast of Spain – ironically, the nearest landfall – only half of those who had sailed from Mexico's shore, in turn a quarter of those who had fled from San Juan, remained alive.

Tom Stannard looked out at the familiar landscape of Plymouth, now blanketed in white and glimpsed only occasionally through the snowstorm. God willing, Catherine and the boys were alive and well, and would be glad to see him. The men of the *Minion* had learned of the state of the kingdom while they were revictualling at Vigo, from English merchantmen in the harbour there; word of Hawkins' activities in the Indies had evidently not yet reached that remote corner of Spain, or else the *Minion* and the survivors aboard her would certainly have been arrested. So they learned that Queen Elizabeth was well but still unmarried, talks with the Archduke Charles of Austria, King Philip's cousin, having failed; Queen Mary, it was said, was also well, but in prison in the north. What his sister Meg would make of that, Tom could only imagine. He prayed that his sister's tongue, and her adherence to the old ways, had not led her into trouble.

As the battered, rotten and ancient hull of the *Minion* finally edged towards the Cattewater, Tom Stannard turned his thoughts once again to one of the two principal subjects that had consumed them during the long, hideous voyage across the ocean: Francis Drake, and how he could have revenge upon him.

—

At exactly the moment when the *Minion* was saluting the fort on St Nicholas Island, Meg de Andrade was entering the ruinous precinct of Dunwich Blackfriars. She could scarcely credit that it was almost a year to the day since she had encountered Stephen Raker in the very same place. So much had happened, and in a sense, it was even stranger to think that she now stood within the property of John

Day, bought with the profits from the most obnoxious, most untruthful book ever written in English.

In the ruins of the old chapel, where the good, honest friars had worshipped God for so many centuries, she genuflected instinctively towards the now non-existent altar at the east end, and said a prayer for her father and brothers. Her prayers were more perfunctory now. There had been no word from either of them since letters sent from the coast of Africa over a year before. She had received these just after the event upon Hen Hill, when the true colours of her half-sister Mary had finally been revealed. In her mind's eye, she still saw the flames, heard the crackling of the burning wood, and saw the flush of triumph and hatred upon Mary's cheeks as she sought ways to convince the assembly that her sister was guilty of treason.

Poor Mary, so utterly confident in her victory, so exultant that day at the summit of Hen Hill.

Meg walked over to the roofless wreck of the south transept, approached a stout door, and opened it with a key she took from her bag, gazing at the familiar sight of the flight of stairs leading down into the crypt. She took out a candle, struck a flint upon the wall, and lit the wick. Then she began to descend into what had once been the crypt of the Blackfriars.

It was dark and cold. A rat scurried across the floor, but Meg hardly flinched. Instead, she went directly to the large panel of whitewashed wood propped against the corner of the crypt, laid her hands upon it, and grinned like a little girl.

The Doom was safe, and she prayed that both her play-acting upon Hen Hill and John Day's indifference to demolishing the old Blackfriars would keep it so.

That, and her foresight when her half-brother Ned had begun to come more often to the harbour, as part of her stepmother's transparent scheme to replace Meg in the management of the Stannard affairs. She had known that it would only be a matter of time before he found the Doom, and he was sure to report it to his mother, who would take great delight in destroying the precious relic before Meg's eyes. So it needed to be moved to a place of greater safety, and as she thought upon this in her cottage upon the heath, Meg decided to add one simple refinement.

She wrote to Philip Grimes, persuaded him to come to Dunwich, and commissioned him to make a copy of the Doom.

Out of love both for her and for what the great painting represented, he concurred.

'There are ways of making a painting look older than it is,' he said when they met at an alehouse in Blythburgh to discuss the proposition, 'but anyone who knew it well will see through the disguise in an instant.'

'That's the beauty of it,' said Meg. 'My stepmother has never seen it. Aye, many are alive who remember it, but they only viewed it from a distance, from the floor of John's church when it was high up in the rood loft. Neither of the priests we have in Dunwich now has ever seen it. Better, there are only a handful who have seen it close to, or have touched it. I am one, my father is another. A third died on the *Mary Rose*. So if my stepmother or half-brother, or anyone else for that matter, should ever find your copy, Phil, I'm certain as God is my judge that they'll take it for the real Doom.'

So they had. The Doom painting dragged out of the Stannard boat shed and burned upon Hen Hill was Philip

Grimes's copy, little more than a few weeks old, while the original had been taken away in broad daylight at the bottom of a cart of timber and thatch, ostensibly going from the harbour to Meg's cottage to provide material for its repair. Hugh Ebbes knew none of this, for even though Meg was then unaware of his jealousy for Philip, she had seen how, more and more by the day, he looked at Mary Stannard.

She wanted so much to tell her stepmother and half-sister of the trick she had played on them, but it would remain her secret; she was, after all, the guardian of the Doom. It would have been Philip Grimes's secret, too, had he not died in November of a sudden bloody flux, which not even Meg's best and most desperate remedies could cure. Meg mourned him still, not least because she had resolved that, if her father and brother failed to return from the Indies, she would finally accept his offer of marriage.

As she prayed over the Doom of Dunwich, Meg regretted more than anything else that she had not been able to tell Philip of her decision before he died.

–

Tom Stannard's feelings about Francis Drake had changed during the course of the voyage home. In the immediate aftermath of the debacle at San Juan, he had thought of revenge, pure and simple, and in its most straightforward form. If Drake got back to England, and if the *Minion* returned home too, then Tom would seek him out and kill him. Perhaps he might dress it up as a duel, or perhaps he would just run a sword into his guts and have done with it.

Hawkins was more sanguine. Several times, he seemed to hint that Drake's apparent desertion was inexcusable, although he seemed unwilling to accept that his kinsman had deliberately refused fellow Englishmen sanctuary aboard his ship. But he always qualified such remarks immediately, talking of circumstances that might be unknown to him, reasons that might yet amply explain why Francis Drake did what he did. Tom gave such comments a hearing; he could do little else, for he was one of only a half-dozen of the Suffolk men of the *Jennet* who had survived the expedition, with every other man on the *Minion* being a follower of Hawkins, or Drake, or both.

Time, and the prospect of the endless ocean, helped to bring him to a different view of the matter. He was a man with responsibilities. Whether his father lived or not, Tom was now the head of the Stannard family, and he needed to return to Dunwich as soon as he reasonably could. No doubt Meg would have coped well enough, but ultimately, only a man's authority could keep all in order, and keep their stepmother in her place; a loathing of Jennet Stannard and her brood was one thing that Meg and Tom shared. Even more importantly, though, if Tom hanged for the murder of Francis Drake, as he surely would, what would become of Catherine and the boys?

So he thought of more subtle strategies, as he knew his father would want him to. He would go at once to London to speak to Will Halliday, and perhaps go through him to Master Benjamin Gonson, or even to the mysterious Master Walsingham of whom his father had spoken.

But more days passed, and even this stratagem crumbled in his mind. Assuming that the *Judith* had got safely across the ocean and made directly for England rather than following the easier course for Spain, Drake would have returned well before the *Minion*, and would have had plenty of time to assemble and present his case. Above all, whatever Tom's own private doubts about Francis Drake's conduct, John Hawkins was surely bound to lend the weight of his own word to that of his most favoured kinsman. Drake's would be the truth that the great men who had invested in the voyage would accept, and Tom doubted whether he had the abilities or the connections to undo that. This Walsingham and the rest of his kind would care about two things only: the amount of profit accruing to them from the voyage (a bitter disappointment, Tom reckoned), and the damage done to England's relations with Spain. There was no war as yet, and those with whom they had conversed at Vigo were convinced that capturing the bullion from the *flota* was the only act that would compel King Philip to declare war on England. Oh, he would rage and send letters of protest to his erstwhile sister-in-law Elizabeth, but the King of Spain had more important matters to contend with.

Despite the Duke of Alba's vicious persecution, the Dutch were still in armed rebellion against their monarch, with the rebels being aided by subsidies from Queen Elizabeth. Open warfare was raging in France once again, with Spain providing troops to the Catholic armies and England providing aid to the Huguenots, just as Jack and Tom Stannard had done. Most importantly, the Turks were advancing against Christendom once more, and King Philip, treasuring above all his title of the Catholic King, was leading the resistance to them. Three wars at once, and three powerful enemies; Philip certainly would not want to fight England as well, the men at Vigo reckoned. But Tom Stannard had now witnessed the power of Spain at first hand, and he knew that if ever King Philip was free of one or more of his conflicts, he might choose to punish England for its so-called heresy, for its assistance to his enemies, and for the depredations of men like John Hawkins and Francis Drake. He might even seek to take back the throne he had once occupied, and reign once again as Philip, King of England.

No, when all was said and done, Drake would have to wait, for both England and Tom Stannard had more important fish to fry. Revenge, Tom reflected, would be sweet enough whenever and however it came. Indeed, perhaps it already had for all he knew, and by a far greater hand than his. Mayhap the sea had claimed Drake and the *Judith*; after all, unlike Tom, the Devon man was utterly inexperienced as a navigator and ship handler. But deep down, Tom knew it would not be so. Whatever else he might be, Francis Drake was the sort of fellow who possessed the most outrageous good fortune.

Finally, as the *Minion* edged towards her berth in the Cattewater, Tom turned his thoughts once again to his father, as he had done during every hour of the voyage, praying that he still lived, and possessed of a curious certainty that he did.

During the whole course of the passage, most notably during this, the very last leg of it, the one thing he had not prayed for, nor even dreamed of, was the unexpected gift that Catherine presented to him during their tearful reunion: a lusty boy of some eight months in age, a new brother whom Adam Stannard clearly resented mightily. Peter, though, even livelier and more forthright than he had been before the fleet sailed, doted upon the baby, seemingly regarding him as his best friend in the world.

When the Stannards took the child to be christened, Catherine having delayed that ceremony until her husband returned or was known for certain to be dead, there was no doubt what name his parents would bestow upon him.

He was called John.

Historical Note

To address this book's not inconsiderable 'elephant in the room' at the very beginning: the Drake/Hawkins expedition of 1567–9, upon which much of this story is based, was primarily a slaving voyage. There is simply no way of glossing over this, nor of concealing the fact. Therefore, from the moment I conceived this trilogy and knew that these events would provide the backdrop for the second book, I wrestled with the question of how to address contemporary attitudes to slavery.

It was impossible to give the Stannards and the other characters twenty-first century 'woke' sensibilities about the subject; that would have been patently unhistorical, to say the least. In this sense, the past really is a foreign country, and people definitely do things very, very differently there. Having said that, it would be disingenuous to claim that all sixteenth-century people were indifferent to, or uncritically accepting of, the nature of slavery. Judging by some of his writings, John Hawkins probably was; he bracketed slaves indiscriminately with other 'merchandise' and said of 'the Negro' that in his 'nation is seldom or never found truth'. For him, slaves were simply one commodity among many in his cargoes, albeit a particularly lucrative one. On the other hand, one of his gunners aboard the *Jesus*, Job Hortop of Bourne in Lincolnshire, clearly considered the act of buying and selling human beings to be a somewhat strange notion, and one worthy of special comment. Francis Drake's attitude to black people was ambivalent. He accorded respect to those who were of use to him, but treated others with utter callousness, notably Maria, the black woman taken from a ship encountered during his voyage of circumnavigation, who was raped (quite possibly by Drake himself) and abandoned to die on an island when she was heavily pregnant.

More generally, slavery was simply not an issue in sixteenth-century England: as Miranda Kaufmann demonstrates in her excellent book *Black Tudors*, Hawkins' three slaving voyages to the Caribbean in the 1560s were not repeated by the English until the 1640s, so he was very far from being the instigator of the transatlantic slave trade (especially because the French and Portuguese had got there long before him, and on a far larger scale). There was a widespread assumption, supported to a degree in law, that slavery simply could not exist in the 'pure air' of England, and there was always a small but significant number of free black people in Tudor England, some of them in quite prominent positions. Thus not all Africans were slaves (my fictional Bruno Santos Cabral is by no means an impossible, nor even an unlikely, figure), not all African slaves were traded by white people, and certainly not by English people (as Hugh Bicheno points out, the Muslim slave trade from sub-Saharan Africa was always much larger than the transatlantic one), and not all slaves were African, a point well made in an excellent blog by Professor Adam Nichols at http://corsairsandcaptivesblog.com.

Now, I realise that some who read this book might be offended by my decision to take this line. But with all due respect to them, it seems to me that deciding to ignore aspects of the past simply because one finds them distasteful, or – far worse – seeking deliberately to conceal or distort elements of the historical record is a markedly dangerous course of action. Revolutionary France, Nazi Germany, the USSR, and pretty much every other totalitarian state in history obtained and retained power by, *inter alia*, omitting or distorting vast tracts of their national histories. So no matter how much one might want to, one simply cannot 'no-platform' the past, nor rewrite it to fit one's modern preconceptions and prejudices.

–

Historians have argued long and hard about just how quickly and deeply the English nation became Protestant. The interpretation that I have presented – namely, that very many people warmly welcomed the return of Catholicism under Mary, and that many continued to hold on to at least some aspects of the old faith for years under Elizabeth – will undoubtedly have the eminent authors of some of the books I read at school and university, and some of the great historians who taught me at the latter, spinning in their graves. If anyone doubts my take on the religious situation, though, I refer them to the series of superb and formidably researched books by Diarmaid MacCulloch. For those wedded to the legends of 'the Virgin Queen', 'Gloriana', and the 'Protestant wind' that scattered the Spanish Armada, it is a useful corrective to remember that Elizabeth nearly died of smallpox in October 1562, as Jack Stannard recalls in Chapter Nineteen, and if she had, then maybe Meg Stannard's dearest wish would have been granted after all

– and British history would undoubtedly have been very different indeed.

Another inconvenient truth that has often been written out of history books, and certainly out of popular consciousness, is that Philip II of Spain, the villain of the Spanish Armada (Hollywood movies, *passim*), once reigned as King of England, as joint (if uncrowned) sovereign with his wife Mary, but he did. Anyone who doubts this should google images of the coins of the reign, where the heads of husband and wife appear side by side. It is equally true that John Hawkins always referred to Philip as 'my old master', and traded shamelessly upon the relationship – undoubtedly exaggerating it furiously as he did so – in his dealings with local Spanish authorities, merchants and townspeople in the Americas.

I have (probably) played fast and loose with the historical record by having Hawkins' father alive in April 1555, when he had almost certainly been dead for at least two months by then. The burning of William Flower, though, took place at the time, in the place, and in the circumstances that I have described; and a number of monasteries, including Westminster Abbey and the Greyfriars at Greenwich, were indeed restored in Mary's reign, albeit only briefly. Of course, the prospects of a permanent restoration of Catholicism in England depended on Mary and Philip's heir being Catholic, and in the spring of 1555, there was a widespread belief that the queen was pregnant and approaching full term. Latin Church music was specially composed and prayers were offered up, but by the summer, it was clear that there was no pregnancy. Nevertheless, for a few short weeks, the Catholics of England were full of hope for the future, and it is in this period that I decided to set the Prologue.

Mary actually died childless in November 1558, and was succeeded by her Protestant half-sister Elizabeth, the daughter of Henry VIII and Anne Boleyn. Elizabeth proceeded cautiously, and her own public gestures of faith were initially ambiguous. Indeed, until events from the late 1560s onwards changed the situation and pressure grew from committed Protestant statesmen like Francis Walsingham (who was a relatively minor figure in 1568), Elizabeth's policy was best summed up by the famous sentence about not making windows into men's souls. As long as Catholics kept a low profile and attended their local parish churches, no particular pressure was placed on them, and, except in the case of a few individuals who chanced their arms rather too boldly, they were certainly not persecuted with any great rigour. The 'Elizabethan religious settlement', culminating in the Thirty-Nine Articles of 1563, was significantly more moderate than the changes carried out in Edward VI's reign, retaining some elements of the Catholic liturgy – which, in turn, infuriated the growing numbers of those who wished the Church of England to move towards simpler forms of worship, more in line with what they saw as the 'best practice' of European Protestantism. Many of these people were nicknamed 'Puritans' by their opponents. Francis Drake may or may not have been one of them, but he was certainly a staunch, arguably fanatical Protestant who personally converted men to that faith.

The years 1567–9 were remarkably tumultuous, even by the standards of sixteenth-century Europe. In France, tensions were rising during an uneasy peace between the Catholic majority, its figureheads being the young King

Charles IX and his mother Catherine de Medici, and the Huguenot (Protestant) minority, led by the Prince of Condé. This peace had endured, just, since the end of the so-called 'first war of religion' (1562–3). The fictional episode in Chapter One would have immediately preceded the outbreak of the so-called second war, following an attempt by Condé to seize the king at Meaux; a few months after my imaginary episode took place, a Huguenot coup in Antoine Mielle's La Rochelle turned the city into the stronghold and unofficial capital of French Protestantism. Meanwhile, there was widespread rioting and iconoclasm in the Netherlands, then ruled by Spain but containing a large number of Calvinists. To quell the discontent, Philip II dispatched a powerful army led by his most famous general, the Duke of Alba. For months, rumours about this army's destination ran like wildfire through Europe, but it ultimately reached Brussels, where Alba immediately began a brutal crackdown under the auspices of his newly instituted 'Council of Blood'. This, in turn, triggered the outbreak of a full-scale rebellion, known in Britain as 'the Dutch revolt', but in the Netherlands as the beginning of its eighty-year war of independence from Spain.

In Scotland, too, there was violent conflict between Catholics and Protestants. Rumours of Mary Queen of Scots' involvement in the death of her second husband, Lord Darnley, seemed to be given credence by her over-hasty marriage to Darnley's alleged murderer, the Earl of Bothwell, and led to her deposition by a party of Protestant lords. From then on, I have reported Mary's doings in 1567–8 essentially as they happened. Meg de Andrade, née Stannard, was certainly not the only English person who secretly believed that Mary was actually already the *de jure* Queen of England by virtue of Henry VIII's divorce from Catherine of Aragon being invalid, meaning that his marriage to Anne Boleyn was bigamous and that Elizabeth was therefore illegitimate. In 1569, not long after the events of this book take place, a rebellion arose in the north with the avowed intent of placing Mary on the English throne, and her very existence continued to pose a threat to Elizabeth until her eventual execution in 1587. Meg, and all of those who thought like her, are now usually written off in novels and films, and even in some 'proper' history books that should know better, as 'traitors': proof, as if one needed it, that history is always written by the winners.

All of this, then, was the backdrop against which Hawkins' voyage, his third to the Caribbean, took place. Originally proposed by two shady Portuguese adventurers called Luis and Homem, the original intention was to search for fabled gold mines in west Africa. This was a remarkably persistent trope in the early modern era; long before I conceived the idea of the Stannard trilogy, a story at once similarly true and similarly mythical, albeit set almost exactly one hundred years later, formed the basis of my second 'journal of Matthew Quinton', *The Mountain of Gold*. Hawkins, though, probably always intended to turn the expedition of 1567–9 into another slaving voyage to the West Indies, having made good profits for himself – and, more importantly, for his powerful backers at court and in the City of London, including the queen – during his two previous ventures.

For the purposes of this story, I needed to insert a Stannard ship into John Hawkins' squadron. To do so, I simply substituted the *Jennet* into the place actually occupied by the *Angel*, the smallest vessel on the voyage.

Such an action might outrage purists and sticklers for strict historical accuracy, but I make no apologies for so doing. Similarly, and again entirely for narrative reasons, I have sometimes compressed, omitted or modified certain events during the course of the voyage, which, after all, lasted for a total of some fifteen months. To give just one example, I have slightly altered some elements of the strange confrontation between Hawkins' ships and the Flemish squadron at Plymouth in August 1567. The Flemish admiral Wathen (or de Wachen), Lord of Campveer, did not leave his ship, but sent one of his officers – and that officer went to protest to the mayor of Plymouth before going to see Hawkins. However, Hawkins' actions and statements aboard the *Jesus* are drawn closely from the historical record.

Similarly, I have compressed and sometimes omitted some of the minor operations of, and incidents experienced by, Hawkins' fleet on the coasts of both west Africa and the Caribbean, although in most cases – including such 'stranger than fiction' incidents as the mock execution of Edward Dudley and the actions of even quite minor figures like Captain Antonio Delgadillo – I have adhered closely to the historical record. This is true even of the other 'stranger than fiction' elements in the story. For example, Hawkins really did take a personal orchestra on the voyage. I have probably underplayed those occasions when members of the expedition witnessed incontrovertible evidence of cannibalism among the African tribes they encountered, especially in the aftermath of the capture of Conga, while I apologise to Oliver Cromwell for 'borrowing' his famous remark about 'stubble to our swords' and placing it in the mouth of Robert Barrett.

For all these events, and, indeed, for the course of the real voyage that forms the backbone of this book, I have used a wide variety of sources. Rayner Unwin's *The Defeat of John Hawkins* blurs fact and fiction quite uncomfortably at times, but is the only stand-alone treatment of the voyage. There are several biographies of both Drake and Hawkins, going back to Sir Julian Corbett's venerable *Drake and the Tudor Navy* and J. A. Williamson's two gung-ho biographies of Hawkins. Among more modern works, John Sugden's biography of Drake is detailed, perceptive and balanced; on the other hand, Harry Kelsey's studies of both Hawkins and Drake are driven too much by the author's attempt to project modern attitudes toward slavery into the past. For a corrective, Hugh Bicheno's *Elizabeth's Sea Dogs* provides a perceptive, well-written overview, and places Hawkins and Drake firmly within the broader milieu that they inhabited.

Otherwise, I used a number of the original primary sources on which all of these books depend to a greater or lesser extent. These included Hawkins' own narrative, together with those of two other members of the expedition, Miles Phillips and Job Hortop. These were published in Richard Hakluyt's famous and hugely influential *The Principal Navigations, Voyages, Traffiques and Discoveries of the English Nation*. I also studied the manuscript account of the expedition in the British Library, Cotton MS Otho E.VIII, folios 17–41. Finally, Michael Turner's *In the Wake of Sir Francis Drake*, the upshot of half a lifetime's single-minded determination to visit and photograph every location Drake ever went to, no matter how much they might have changed and no matter how many times the author got beaten up or arrested, provided valuable insights into the geography of several of the places described in this book.

–

As in *Destiny's Tide*, the first book in this trilogy, most of the action on land takes place in Dunwich. It seemed to me that there was little point in writing an entirely new account of the town for this historical note, having covered this ground in the preceding title, so the section in italics that follows has been copied from that; those who have already read this can, therefore, skip the next paragraphs!

> *The story of Dunwich, 'England's Atlantis', is not really as well known as it should be. Indeed, it's possible that some will know the name solely from H. P. Lovecraft's famous and seminal tale of the supernatural, 'The Dunwich Horror'; this took only the place name from the village in Suffolk (and that probably unwittingly), otherwise setting the story in rural Massachusetts, but it has spawned two films and countless references in popular culture. As for the real Dunwich, almost certainly once the seat of the Bishops of East Anglia, as late as the thirteenth century it possessed the same geographical extent as London, was listed as one of the ten most important towns in England, and was regarded as the best harbour on the east coast. But a series of catastrophic storms, notably in 1286, 1287, 1328, 1347 and 1362, effectively blocked its harbour and swept away large areas*

of the town, which eventually declined to the tiny hamlet that remains today.

The story of this 'lost city', and its endless battle against the sea, was well told in Rowland Parker's famous book Men of Dunwich, *first published in 1978, which was an important source for this story; so, too, were Nicholas Comfort's* The Lost City of Dunwich, *Thomas Gardner's* An Historical Account of Dunwich *(first published in 1754), and many archaeological reports on the digs and surveys, including those underwater, carried out at Dunwich over many years. Thanks to these sources, many of the character names in this story are taken from real people who lived there at the right time. Indeed, some of them held the actual offices I have attributed to them.*

For instance, Thomas Cowper and John Bradley served as bailiffs of Dunwich in 1568, while William James was probably the rector of St Peter's church at this time. Similarly, Sir George Barne and Sir William Garrard were Lord Mayor of London in the years given, the Duke of Alba was indeed the head of Philip II's household when he was King of England, and so on. John Day, who was almost certainly born at Dunwich, published Foxe's *Book of Martyrs*, dominated the London book trade for years, and bought extensive country estates, somehow finding time to do all this in between fathering twenty-six children by his two wives. The inscription on his memorial at Little Bradley church, Suffolk, is a delightful window to the age (I have modernised the spelling):

Here lies the DAY that darkness could not blind

When popish fogs had over cast the sun
This DAY the cruel night did leave behind
To view and show what bloody Acts were done
He set a Fox to write how Martyrs run
By death to life Fox ventured pains & health
To give them light DAY spent in print his wealth
But God with gain returned his wealth again
And gave to him as he gave to the poor
Two wives he had partakers of his pain
Each wife twelve babes and each of them one more
Alice was the last increaser of his Store
Who mourning long for being left alone
Set up this tombe herself turned to a STONE.
obiit July 1584.

Otherwise, the characters of Philip Grimes and Stephen Raker are fictitious, and the Blackfriars of Dunwich was actually sold off relatively quickly after its dissolution, rather than remaining unsold for years.

—

Finally, I am aware that some readers might be surprised, if not shocked, by my presentation of Francis Drake as one of the 'bad guys' of this story. In my defence, I would point out that, at the time when the events of this book are set, Drake was still a relatively young man, probably no older than his mid-twenties. His great days and great voyages were all still ahead of him, and it is very likely that his character and attitudes were not yet fully formed; indeed, one of his biographers has suggested that the action at San Juan de Ulúa (the strictly correct Spanish spelling of the name) was the great turning point of his life, setting him on an anti-Spanish crusade that drove him until his dying day. Whether or not that is the case, it's certainly true that even some of Drake's most devoted enthusiasts describe him as 'ruthless, vainglorious, an attention seeker [who] tended to boast... too fond of his own ideas and uncollegial' (website of the Drake Exploration Society).

It is certainly true that I have attributed to Drake actions, statements and attitudes for which no evidence whatsoever exists, and his refusal to let Tom Stannard and his men board the *Judith* is, of course, wholly fictitious (although the ship's night-time departure from San Juan de Ulúa, which even Hawkins regarded as a betrayal, is not). Conversely, I don't believe that I've directly contradicted the evidence either; after all, this is a novel, not a work of history, and this is what novelists do. Besides, there's a part of me that is still the little boy who avidly watched the 1960s TV series *Sir Francis Drake*, starring Terence Morgan, so I'm certainly not interested in knocking Drake off any pedestals!

–

The Stannards will return in the final book of this trilogy, set against the backdrop of the Spanish Armada in 1588.

Acknowledgements

Thanks once again to my agent, Peter Buckman, and to Michael Bhaskar and Kit Nevile at my publishers, Canelo, for their ongoing support. Secondly, I reiterate the thanks I paid in *Destiny's Tide* to those in Dunwich and its environs who helped make this story a reality, notably Jane Hamilton, Tim Holt-Wilson, and above all, John Cary of Dunwich Museum. My thoughts on Sir Francis Drake, the less savoury aspects of his career, and the sixteenth-century maritime connections of Devon were given much sharper focus by the workshop that I attended in May 2019 at Buckland Abbey, the house that Drake purchased. My thanks to Julie Farguson, fellow of Wolfson College, Oxford, and the other organisers for setting up the day and inviting me to this excellent event, part of the 'Making Maritime Memories' collaboration between the National Trust and the University of Oxford. Thanks, too, to Hugh Bicheno, author of *Elizabeth's Sea Dogs*, who has been an assiduous reviewer of the first book and a thorough, forthright and perceptive 'beta reader' of this one. As ever, though, my principal 'thank you' is to Wendy, both for her direct input and for her moral support.

David Davies
Bedfordshire, September 2019